ALEX FINER

Deepwater

Hutchinson

London Melbourne Sydney Auckland Johannesburg

Hutchinson & Co. (Publishers) Ltd
An imprint of the Hutchinson Publishing Group
17–21 Conway Street, London W1P 6JD

Hutchinson Group (Australia) Pty Ltd
30–32 Cremorne Street, Richmond South, Victoria 3121
PO Box 151, Broadway, New South Wales 2007

Hutchinson Group (NZ) Ltd
32–34 View Road, PO Box 40–086, Glenfield, Auckland 10

Hutchinson Group (SA) Pty Ltd
PO Box 337, Bergvlei 2012, South Africa

First published 1983
© Interstellar 1983

Set in Linotron Baskerville by Input Typesetting Limited

Printed in Great Britain by The Anchor Press Ltd
and bound by Wm Brendon & Son Ltd,
both of Tiptree, Essex

British Library Cataloguing in Publication Data
Finer, Alex
  Deepwater.
  I. Title
  823'.914[F]   PR6056.I/

ISBN 0 09 153790 8

To Linda

1

Three miles below the surface of the ocean, the monster cut smoothly through the dark, cold water. It travelled a few feet above the seabed. A low throbbing echoed eerily from within. Turbulence disturbed the carpet of shells and sand. A plume of sediment swirled in its wake muddying the draught of water.

A powerful beam shone forwards from the unblinking eye on the metallic snout. But the corridor of light quickly grew cloudy and stretched only yards before it was swallowed by the darkness. Particles of underwater debris shimmered in the beam. They hung suspended in the water, glistening like tiny jewels – a kaleidoscope of glitter.

A black wall of water 3 miles thick separated the desert floor from the warm rays of the sun on the surface. The temperature was 2°C. Pressure was several hundred times that of the surface world. Yet this presented no impediment. The monster moved inexorably onwards, following the stunted beam of light at a sedate and steady pace.

And then it stopped.

A large outcrop of rock rose sharply from the seabed blocking the monster's passage. The eroded remains of a prehistoric volcano dwarfed the cigar-shaped cylinder which remained stationary, suddenly unsure of its way forward.

The eye of light played on the rockface. A second and then a third, fourth, fifth and sixth beam illuminated the scene. They emanated from raised patches around the snout. They bathed the rock in light and the dark underwater world revealed brief glimpses of life.

A crab-like crustacean was caught in the widening circle

of light and scurried away on spindly legs. It crossed the penumbra and was swallowed by a shroud of enveloping darkness. A worm as thick as a man's arm and twice as long shrank back into its protective tubular shell, half-buried in the seabed at the base of the rock. Only the swaying lilies seemed undisturbed.

The monster needed information. A dozen long antennae protruded from above the eyes of light. The low throbbing which had accompanied the cylinder's progress across the seabed changed frequency. The water around its bulky outline seemed to glow. Then the monster began to move gently backwards away from the rock. It stopped and came forward describing an arc around the obstacle.

The manoeuvre had been repeated many times. This alien invader was crossing an immense underwater plain, a submerged landscape of dramatic proportions, scarred with canyons and escarpments, ridges and jagged hills. Across the Pacific floor, the coast of California lay 3000 miles to the east. Two hundred miles ahead the seabed began to slip slowly downwards into an underwater valley that at its deepest was 6 miles below the sunlight and fresh air on the surface of the planet.

Hours later the monster found the first evidence of what it had come so far to find. A single beam of light was trained on the ocean floor. Halfway down the long valley incline the surface suddenly changed. Bathed in the light for just an instant was a track cut into the seabed. Then it was gone. Further spotlights snapped on and the cylinder veered sharply round to find further trace of the path.

With extra light brightening the gloom, the path loomed up. It was some 12 feet wide and stretched across the seabed in a straight line. On either side, the ocean floor was littered with sand and detritus. But the path itself was flat and even, just like a road running across open country. Something else had passed this way before.

The monster positioned itself above the path and, like an animal tracking its prey, set off in pursuit.

2

The sun was high in the cloudless sky. It cast a shadow of the helicopter on to the gentle rise and fall of the ocean 300 feet below. Weather conditions were perfect which suited the passenger who had never fully overcome his distrust of helicopters. From the ground, they looked vulnerable, almost frail. Inside, they were noisy and claustrophobic.

There were two other men on board. The pilot sat to the passenger's left, occasionally checking dials and a map clipped to the small table between them. The crewman sat in the helicopter cargo hold at the rear. He was a lanky, slow-moving Southerner. His job was to look after the crates and boxes being delivered by the helicopter.

The Scorpion was on its regular supply run to the *Voyager*. It was a long flight from the base in San Diego. Even at 230 knots, close to the helicopter's maximum speed, the flight time was sixteen hours and involved a refuelling stop on one of the US carriers.

The helicopter crew had been making the same trip every week for four months, delivering food, medical supplies, machinery, lab equipment and mail. On each trip, after dropping off its cargo, the helicopter was loaded with crated cargo from the *Voyager* which was carried back to the mainland after an overnight stop and further refuelling on a carrier.

A few weeks ago, the crewman had decided to satisfy his curiosity by looking inside one of the crates during the return flight. Prying off the lid as carefully as he could, he had found dozens of transparent plastic bags, each labelled with coordinates and numbers. The bags contained nothing but small black misshapen rocks.

In the cockpit, the passenger stretched wearily. Like the others he wore an all-in-one flying suit. He had been studying files and documents and looked forward to the end of a tedious journey. He put on the headset resting in his lap and wiggled the earphones until they were comfortable. He adjusted the microphone to his lips.

'How long will it take to get the freight unloaded and you boys turned round?' he asked.

'A half-hour, same again to load,' the pilot said. 'It might take longer. We're carrying more than usual – enough food to last months. God knows what they've got for us. The word back at base was that we're not coming back. Is that right?'

The passenger was irritated by the pilot's inquiry. 'I've already told you. Your job is to fly me. Just stick to that.'

'Yes-s-sir.'

The passenger spotted a glint of light on the horizon where the sun and sea blurred together. He pointed. 'That her?'

'No, sir.' The pilot consulted his charts. 'Probably a Japanese trawler. We passed the freezer mothership a while ago.'

'Foreigners swarming about all over the place.'

'Too right,' the pilot said, anxious to share the passenger's prejudice. 'There's a Norwegian running the mining operation on the *Voyager*. You'd think there were Americans qualified for the job.'

'I'm sure there are,' the passenger said. 'There's an Englishman on board too. Met him?'

'Peters? The guy in charge of the lab?'

'That's the one. What do you make of him?'

'He showed me round one time when we'd brought him out a special tank. He's fished up some odd creatures. A smart alec.'

'How do you mean?'

'Thinks he knows it all.'

The passenger drummed his fingers on his knee. An uneasy silence between the two men returned.

A few minutes later, the pilot announced that the *Voyager* was on the horizon. He checked the instrument panel, switched off the autopilot and eased back on the throttle. As the *Voyager* grew larger, he ran through the pre-landing checks.

The passenger leaned forward to see what he could of the ship.

'Strange looking tub, isn't she,' the pilot said.

The passenger ignored him. He was absorbed. He could already identify several features. The vessel looked half oil rig, half cargo vessel.

The strange end of the boat was the stern. Its main feature was the 120-foot drilling rig which seemed completely out of scale with the rest of the ship. The stern itself was open, forming a horseshoe harbour over which the rig towered. The rear deck was stacked with lengths of pipe. The passenger understood what they were for. When the ship was mining the seabed, the pipes were joined together to form one huge length of tubing that stretched from the *Voyager* right down to the bottom of the sea, several miles below. A mining head at the end travelled along the seabed, sucking up whatever lay there to the *Voyager*. There was a pump room below decks. It was, the passenger knew, nothing less than a gigantic vacuum cleaner.

A muddy plume spread out on the sea's surface behind the ship. The passenger could just make out its source – the waterfall of discarded slurry pouring into the sea from the stern. The colour of the plume changed from ocherous brown through a bright yellowish green, to a more subdued green that became less obvious with increasing distance from the ship.

The passenger recognized in mid-decks a yellow bathysphere, looking from the air like the iris in the eye of the ship.

The bow was conventional enough. In front of the bridge was an area marked off as the helicopter pad. The white paintwork on the hull was stained with streaks of rust. The passenger disapproved.

The helicopter was close enough now for him to pick out the faces of those craning up from the deck. He could also see someone in a tracksuit jogging around the deck. As he followed the figure, he realized it was a woman.

The passenger pulled a file from the open case beside him and found the page he wanted. He ran his finger down the list. There were two women among the crew. Two women among eighteen men. One of the women was the doctor, in her late forties; the other was much younger, twenty-six years old, and worked in the marine biology unit. The only navy on board were the lieutenant in command, the navigation officer and four enlisted men. He looked down at the jogger who had now stopped and was looking skywards at the helicopter. From her appearance, he realized it must be the younger Kipling woman. She and her husband worked for the Englishman.

The headset crackled as the pilot made contact with the bridge. 'Supply helicopter Echo Bravo Delta requesting permission to land. Over.'

A lazy voice, like that of a disc jockey, answered. 'This is *Voyager*. Good to see you. We're headed southwest at four knots. No breeze. You're cleared to land. In your own time. Over.'

The helicopter began its descent to the landing pad.

'There, that's him.' The pilot pointed at one of the reception committee gathered below on the foredeck. 'Peters is third from the right. Talking with Bell, the captain. Quite a line-up he's arranged. You must be important, sir.'

The passenger wasn't listening. He craned to see Peters, and Bell – the man whose command he'd come to take over. They had turned their backs to shield themselves from the downdraft. A loose canvas on a lifeboat flapped madly as the pilot brought the helicopter down on to the deck. As soon as the wheels had touched and the noise of the rotor blades began to die, the passenger unbuckled his seat belt, nodded at the pilot and eased his way back into the cargo hold.

Watched by the crewman, the passenger unzipped his flying suit and pulled it off. Underneath he wore a white uniform. He went to his bags, undid one and took out a uniform cap, and placed it squarely on his head. The crewman stiffened and then stood to attention.

Captain William F. Beckett from Covert Naval Operations, now on attachment to the *Voyager*, returned the salute and then growled at the lanky Southerner, 'Get me out of this sardine can.'

3

Saul Peters found the steel security door to the lab wide open. Inside, Herbie Kipling sat at his workbench bent over a microscope. Saul could smell formaldehyde.

Herbie glanced up. 'Good afternoon,' he said pointedly.

'Not my fault,' Saul said, crossing to his own bench. 'I hung about waiting to meet the bugger.' The air in the lab was still and sickly; the atmosphere one of ruffled concentration.

'So what's he like?' Herbie exchanged the glass slide under the microscope with another from the open slotted box on his bench.

'Made Mark look foolish. It's bad enough to lose your command without being humiliated into the bargain. Beckett ignored the welcoming party, complained to Mark at the state of the paintwork, would you believe, and asked to be taken to his quarters.'

'Any clue yet why he's here?'

'Hmmm.' Saul had begun to rifle through the in-tray of notes and report sheets awaiting his attention. 'No,' he said, looking over at Herbie, 'He's Captain William F. Beckett. That's all we know so far. I've a fair idea now what the F. stands for. He came off that chopper like a tornado. God knows what he's got in store for us. What's all this about?' Saul held up a report sheet.

'The specimen? It's like nothing I've seen before.'

'How are you checking it out?'

'Carefully.' Herbie bent his head back to the light microscope. After a moment, he straightened up, removed the slide from its clip and returned it to the box with the others. 'You're going to have to take a good look at this yourself. When you've got time. It gets odder all the time.'

'So don't keep it to yourself.'

'Give me a break. I've got to take sections for the electron. That'll tell us if it's really weird.'

Herbie moved to the microtome – an apparatus for cutting the tissue for examination in the electron microscope. The microtome stood next to the large microscope which was built into the corner of the lab behind Herbie's bench.

Saul watched his assistant settle to the painstaking task of sectioning minute tissue samples on the pyramid-shaped specimen block. Herbie sat back bent over his work facing the far wall. Saul was happy with Herbie's dedicated approach despite Herbie's moan that he was left with all the dissection. There was some truth in the complaint. He could see Herbie's dissection tray near the light microscope, now unattended on the workbench. There was stretched and pinned tissue on the cork. Saul walked up between the workbenches and the communal sinks and draining boards to take a better look.

'Is this the specimen?' he asked.

Herbie paused in his work, turned to Saul and then nodded. 'Yes,' he said, irritated at the interruption. 'Let me finish. This is tricky.'

Saul took a closer look at the specimen while Herbie turned back to the microtome. He saw a torn tail segment lying in the tray. It was cut open to the bone and covered with water. A thin translucent sliver of tissue lay pinned out next to it on the cork mat. The pins, as long as acupuncture needles, stretched the thin slice of flesh. A scalpel and tweezers lay in a small glass dish beside the tray. The lab's light microscope was at the other end of the bench.

The sections which Herbie was preparing at the microtome were for the electron microscope. This instrument enabled the study of subcellular particles in amazing detail. It could take five hundred separate sections to complete the examination of a single cell.

Saul picked up the forceps on Herbie's bench and used them to fold and close the neck of the plastic bag in which the tail had been stored. There were hundreds of these carefully tagged plastic bags in the walk-in deepfreeze. Their contents once swam, crawled or hopped on the deep ocean floor. Now they were kept in formaldehyde and refrigerated in retractable white cabinets.

The lab was quiet except for the filters bubbling in the glass bank of fishtanks which lined the wall separating them from the ship's central corridor. These tanks housed the live specimens captured from the deep. Some of the fish had bulbous eyes and spiny gills. There were giant slugs, crabs, sponges, sea cucumbers, sea worms, molluscs and some primitive jelloid creatures. The aquarium intimidated visitors to the lab. The navy crew and the two kitchen hands were always slightly ill at ease. Saul understood. He had felt the same for years about the snake house at London Zoo.

Saul smiled to Kathy Kipling when she walked into the lab. She wore a blue cotton tracksuit and her auburn hair was tied back with a ribbon. He broke into a grin when Kathy puckered her nose at the bad smell.

'Terrible isn't it?' Saul said. 'Your husband doesn't seem to notice. Tell Nicholson from me to get off his ass and do something to fix the extractor fan.'

Kathy shrugged. 'He promised me he'd do it yesterday. Listen, do you know anything about this being the last supply trip?'

'What!' Saul was astonished. Herbie looked up from his work and swivelled round on his stool.

'That's what the pilot told me.'

'What exactly did he say?' Saul asked.

'I'd been checking the delivery. As I was leaving he said he didn't think he'd be seeing us for a while. I asked why – I assumed his rota was changing – and he said he'd heard it on the grapevine back at base that flights have been suspended. Until further notice.'

'That's crazy,' Saul said. 'We need supplies. So does mining – and the kitchens. Mark said nothing.'

'He's not captain anymore,' Herbie said from behind him.

'You sure you heard the pilot right?'

'He sounded certain.'

Kathy walked past Saul into the small side room connected with the laboratory. He watched her move across a patch of scruffy red carpet, past two battered armchairs, the settee, the coffee table and its trailing plant.

She made an entry on a wall chart hanging among assorted photographs and cartoons, a well-marked map of the Pacific and some graphs. She let the pencil drop back on its short string and showed no surprise at Saul's continuing gaze when she turned around.

Saul could see the curve of her neck silhouetted against bright light streaming in through a porthole. His eyes lingered on the outline of her breasts.

'Anyone want coffee?' she frowned at Saul.

'No thanks,' Saul said. The fragile spell had broken. 'Coffee, Herbie?' he inquired.

'No.' Herbie remained bent over the microtome.

Mug in hand, Kathy returned to the lab. 'Good thing someone's here to get the gossip. You two are hopeless. I'm off for a shower. Back soon.' She departed.

Herbie slipped off his stool and, with a theatrical gesture, invited Saul to look down the viewing window of the electron microscope. 'There's no need to wait for the new sections. This is what I discovered last night.'

'Why the drama? Just tell me.'

'I want you to look for yourself.'

Herbie switched on the electron microscope. The machine began to hum as its chamber emptied. When the vacuum was complete, Herbie flicked a switch on the console. The electrons began to bombard the specimen and Saul saw a green fluorescent image appear through the viewing window.

'That's mitochondria,' Herbie said.

Saul knew about these subcellular particles. They lay outside the nucleus and burned chemicals derived from food to produce energy for the cell.

'Why are they kinked like this?' Saul asked. He was puzzled by the form and arrangement of some particles within the mitochondria. 'They look diseased.'

'Or part of a new physiology,' Herbie suggested. 'I'll know better when I look at the new sections.'

'This is from the tail?'

'Yes. Came up the mining pipe a couple of weeks ago. One of Dansk's men brought it in with a whole bag of bits and pieces. It's obviously a vertebrate but I didn't realize its significance at first.'

'I don't need a microscope to tell me it's a fish,' Saul said.

'But it was too deep.'

'How deep?'

'That's the point. Six miles.'

'Impossible.'

'Exactly why I bagged it and left it for routine examination. I thought it probably drifted down from a higher level. But the flesh is too fresh. And these mitochondria confirm my suspicions. I think it lived at six miles.'

'That's not on your report sheet.'

'Well I find it hard to believe.'

'Why wasn't I told?'

'You just have been,' Herbie said. 'Besides, I do all the work. It's time I had some of the credit. You usually make sure you take all the glory. You'll be on the lecture circuit with the stuff I've discovered this trip.'

Under pale cheeks, beneath the thin, curled black beard, Herbie's tightly knotted jaw muscles stood out like bones.

'Christ, you even hog the dives.' Petulantly, he slapped his hand down on the table. A slide fell to the floor and shattered. A flask of fixing fluid toppled over and dripped steadily on to the linoleum. Herbie went down on hands and knees to clear up the mess.

'Leave that for the moment,' Saul said.

'It's all very well for you . . .' Herbie caught himself on a splinter of glass and wrung his hand. 'Damn.'

Saul extended a hand. 'You're right about the dives. I'm sorry. The next is yours. But right now I want some answers.'

Herbie got to his feet, blood welling from the cut.

'I'll get you a Bandaid.' Saul went back to his workbench and tossed the box of Bandaids he kept in his drawer towards Herbie who was washing his hand under running water at one of the aluminium sinks.

Saul knew Herbie Kipling as methodical, meticulous and level-headed. He knew from Kathy that Herbie's goal in life was tenure at San Diego. He also knew what really lay behind this fit of pique.

Herbie had begun to suspect him and Kathy. Herbie would have to have been blind to have missed the changes which had been taking place in the past few weeks. The more Saul and Kathy tried to conceal their feelings, the less they succeeded. Even Mark Bell had guessed.

Saul went over to the electron microscope. He avoided the broken glass and withdrew the specimen holder through the airlock without interfering with the vacuum inside the machine. He returned to his own bench and sat at the keyboard terminal adjacent to it.

Herbie cursed. It was not clear whether he was protesting at the pain in his hand or at what Saul was doing.

Saul tapped the password and his personal user number into the computer. After gaining access – the words 'Good afternoon, Mr Peters' appeared on the screen – he entered the slide's code number. The screen told him that the specimen was from a fragment which had arrived on board two weeks ago, caught in the shaker-screen which separated mineral samples from the mining pipe slurry. Latitude and longitude coordinates appeared on the screen. He jotted them on a pad beside the keyboard. He wondered what the sector number was. It was a simple instruction to the computer.

The intercom on his desk interrupted him.

'Saul.' Mark Bell's voice came through the desk speaker.

Saul took the two steps across to his bench and flicked off the privacy button. 'Yes, Mark. What can I do for you?'

'Will you join the captain in the conference room right away.'

'I'll be a few minutes.'

There was a brief pause. 'No. Now.'

Mark Bell sounded strained. Saul guessed Beckett must be standing at his shoulder. 'I'm on my way,' he said and switched the intercom privacy button back on.

Saul looked over at Herbie. 'When you're feeling more yourself, I want a full report on this fish – where it comes from, cellular analysis, species type.' He tore the sheet of paper with its coordinates from the pad by the terminal and put it in his shirt pocket.

'You could tell this new captain of ours that what we need is a fresh specimen.' Herbie pointed with his bandaged hand at the tail segment on his bench. 'A whole fish, this time.'

'That may be easier said than done.'

'You can be very persuasive,' Herbie said.

Saul knew the remark was not intended as a compliment. 'What do you suggest? That I name the fish after him?'

'Sounds your style,' Herbie said. 'Serve you right if it turns out to be an ugly bastard.'

4

Saul shaded his eyes from the bright midday sun as he emerged on deck. He listened for a moment to the monotonous low roar of the mining rig at the stern mix with the dull beat of diesel in the bowels of the ship, and then hurried past the metal stairway which led up to the bridge. He knocked at the door next to the captain's cabin, and without waiting for a reply, turned the handle and walked in.

Bertil Dansk and Mark Bell sat at the oval conference table where the three of them had played poker together. Bell nodded to Saul.

'It's quite impossible,' Dansk was saying. 'We need spares all the time. The equipment is always breaking down.' Dansk turned in his chair to look at Saul. 'What do you think, Saul?'

Saul raised his eyebrows. 'About what?'

'This is the helicopter's last trip.' It was Bell who answered. 'No further supply runs. Our captain's first command. There's no knowing when it'll be back.'

'The pilot told Kathy as much. What the hell is going on?'

As if in answer, the double doors connecting the conference room and the captain's cabin were thrown sharply open. Bell and Dansk stood up as Captain Beckett made a stately entrance leaving the doors ajar behind him.

'Welcome gentlemen,' Beckett said. 'Please sit down.'

Saul pulled out his chair and sat down with the others. He avoided eye contact with Beckett. The polished table, anchored by its brass fittings to the floor, would have done a boardroom proud. Pads of paper and sharpened pencils were arranged at each man's place. The green felt for cards was now draped on a dresser top, with a tray, a port decanter and several glasses on it.

'Right,' Beckett began, his hands on the back of his chair, 'I'm Captain William Beckett and I've been assigned to the *Voyager* by CNO.'

Saul and Bell exchanged glances. Covert Naval Operations was a branch of the CIA, headquartered in Washington.

Dansk caught Beckett's eye and asked, 'Mind if I smoke?'

'No, indeed. You must be Bertil Dansk.' Beckett offered his hand to Dansk who rose and shook it. He then continued round the table to Saul. 'And you must be Saul Peters. I spent some time at Mildenhall once.'

'Pleased to meet you,' Saul said, shaking hands and taking stock for the first time. The gaze he met was steely. The uniform was crisp but the man looked gaunt and worn. His hair was wiry, flecked with grey at the edges. It was shaved close to his head and gave the face a pugnacious quality.

'This is quite a change for me,' Beckett said. 'A week ago, I knew nothing about any of you or of the *Voyager*. My active service has been front-line – Vietnam, El Salvador. . . .' Beckett looked round the table. 'Let me say straight off, my arrival is no criticism of the work you boys have been doing . . . .'

Saul watched for Bell's reaction. The young lieutenant remained impassive. He was just twenty-eight and had handled himself with surprising maturity on the trip. Bell had served several years of naval protection duty, patrolling the oil rigs up and down the California coast. A six-month ocean survey had been promotion. He had kept the crew happy by settling differences fairly and by keeping up pressure on San Diego to fly in regularly fresh food, magazines and mail, and video films.

'I'm here in fact,' Beckett said, 'because of your success. You've been sending back some very interesting samples, very interesting indeed, Mr Dansk.'

Dansk sucked calmly on his pipe.

'As a result, there's a change in the status of the mission. Effective immediately are the following measures: helicopter supply visits are suspended until further notice; the ship will assume complete radio silence – a total blackout; and we'll be heading for a new mining site by tonight at the very latest. We're on top security rating as of now and for however long it takes to get the job done.'

Beckett looked at the perplexed faces around the table. 'Let me explain. America's mineral resources are in bad shape. I don't need to remind you. That's why you're here. Every year we've been importing more. And the Third World exporters – in Africa and South America – are ripping us off. It's like oil all over again.'

Bell nodded in agreement. Saul looked at Dansk who lightly drummed the table top.

'For the past fifteen years,' Beckett continued, 'the goddamn United Nations has been trying to work out who owns what on the high seas. Their new Seabed Authority is hollering at us to ratify the treaty and accept jurisdiction. You know the line: the high seas are the common heritage of mankind, like the Arctic or the moon. Well, of course, if ocean floor mineral production really gets going, it's the Third World that'll lose out. Their ore exports will take a tumble. And that's what the whole treaty was about. But the President's made it crystal clear to those sons of bitches that the US has the sole right to mine within two hundred miles of its territory – and that includes the Pacific islands.'

'Captain?' Saul began.

'Questions later if you don't mind.' Beckett resumed. 'The United Nations and their precious Seabed Authority, based in sunny Jamaica by the way, have been squeezing pretty hard. They've stipulated parallel development of sites, half for the country or consortium that's mining, half for the Third World. That might be acceptable for manganese – outside the coastal zone. But there are strategic minerals. And when we find them, we're not about to start giving them away. No matter if they're two hundred or two thousand miles from land.

'Let me be more specific. Cobalt is one of our most vital minerals. Used in everything from steel to solar technology. Vital to the military–industrial complex. We can't survive without it, yet we have to import virtually every ton we use. We take everything Canada can spare and get the rest where we can. That in practice means one particular African country. Ninety per cent of our cobalt comes from just one tin-pot republic. And after doubling and doubling the price again, they've decided to change sides.'

Beckett took a buff envelope from his inside pocket and pulled out a computer tear-sheet of row upon row of figures. 'This print-out, gentlemen, is the best news America has had for a long time. You didn't know it when you sent off the samples, but you found treasure – cobalt-rich nodules.'

'We didn't conduct cobalt tests,' Dansk said slowly.

'You weren't supposed to. No one believed in cobalt-rich nodules. But your samples, under detailed analysis, set the alarm bells ringing a week ago. Since then I've been briefed in Geneva – that's where I was a week ago – by State Department officials, in Washington by the Coordinator, and I've been at the San Diego naval centre for the past couple of days.'

Saul had been growing more and more depressed as Beckett spoke. Mention of the Coordinator startled him. The Coordinator, Saul knew, was a shadowy figure at the top of the CIA naval bureau, widely assumed to have trained as an assistant to the FBI's J. Edgar Hoover. His reputation was for complete ruthlessness. His sharp, rasping voice had been heard more than once defending the CIA before Senate subcommittees.

'I don't like the drift of this,' Saul said. 'Are you saying we're going to lift this cobalt secretly? I joined a civilian survey, not a bloody commando unit.'

'The *Voyager* is no longer a civilian exploration vessel,'

Beckett said coldly. 'It's been requisitioned by the State Department for government work. You're all part of the American navy now.'

Beckett looked first at Saul and then at Dansk. Both remained silent. 'You were considered too senior, the two of you, to be removed. I'm unhappy with that but, for the time being, your expertise is valuable.'

Saul could contain himself no longer. 'Did anyone think of consulting us? Don't we have a say?'

'The simple answer is no. You don't. Your governments have been informed. You have nothing to fear. Our task is simply to get back to where you discovered cobalt. Cargo ships will rendezvous there in precisely ten days' time to take the first batch on board. You'll all be shipped home on schedule in about six weeks if all goes smoothly. A full naval operations unit will take over once mining is well underway.

'There can be no communication with shore. This ship's radio is too basic. It's far too public. I don't like the idea of being out of radio contact much myself. But those are my orders and we'll be sticking to them. I want the radio deadlock key from you, Lt Bell, straightaway.'

'Yes, sir,' Bell said.

'I'll spell it out later. Arrange a full turnout after dinner. Our new destination, gentlemen, is in sector 27 – about a hundred and fifty miles northeast of here. I'll give you the exact coordinates shortly, Lt Bell. I'll want to discuss your timetable also, Mr Dansk. Let me know how long it will take to finish surveying the present sector and how long to get the pipe up. And I'm afraid, Mr Peters, this means the end of your diving programme for a while. You'll have to be satisfied with what you've got so far.'

Beckett stood up. 'Thank you, gentlemen. That's all for now.'

No one spoke until the captain had disappeared through the connecting double doors to his cabin.

Dansk took his pipe from his mouth and, shaking his head slowly from side to side, said, 'I hope to hell we got our clamps.'

Saul couldn't help laughing. He admired the Norwegian

23

mining engineer's devotion to his machinery but failed to understand the response, given the series of shocks with which Beckett had left them.

'They were on the supply schedule,' Bell said. 'Check with the cargo bay.'

'He'll have to know,' Dansk said. 'The pipe assembly clamps are clapped out. He's going to lose at least a day while we change them. Sector 27 is six-mile territory. If we don't replace the clamps, chances are they'll pack up.'

Now Saul understood Dansk's concern. 'Sector 27 is six miles, is it?' he asked.

'Yes.'

Strange, Saul thought.

'I'd better go find my spares,' Dansk said, standing to leave.

'And I must get back to the bridge,' Bell said, rising. He lowered his voice, 'Let's talk later.'

Saul remained seated for a moment after his colleagues had left. From the captain's cabin he heard the strains of what he thought he recognized as Berlioz. Beckett had not struck him as classically inclined.

Saul listened carefully to the music which he liked. He went to the large map of the Central Pacific mounted on the wall behind him. The *Voyager*'s area of interest was marked in a grid of eighty sectors, each of which was 50 miles square. The small patch of ocean lay roughly midway between North America and Japan. The Hawaiian islands of Kauai, Oahu, Maui, Molokai and Hawaii lay nearly 2000 miles to the southeast. To the north, further away, were the Aleutian islands, the Bering Strait and then the Arctic Ocean. Saul took from his breast pocket the scrap of paper on which he had scribbled the coordinates of Herbie's mystery fish. He ran a finger along a latitude line until he found the correct longitude intersection. He stared surprised at where his finger rested. He checked the coordinates.

As the music built in volume – it was from the 'Symphonie Fantastique' – Saul made up his mind. He crossed the room and rapped firmly with his knuckles on the polished wood door.

5

'Enter.' Beckett's voice was clearly audible above the music. Saul found the captain seated before an open briefcase on the far side of the cabin. As he shut the doors behind him, he watched the captain swivel his chair to face him. The music crescendoed.

Beckett rose, saying 'Yes?' and fixed Saul with a look that left him in no doubt that the captain was irritated by the interruption. Beckett crossed the room and turned the tape recorder off. 'Yes, Mr Peters. What?'

'I want to report a major marine discovery.' Saul sat down on the most comfortable chair in the neatly arranged cabin. He refused to feel intimidated. 'In accordance with procedure,' he added.

The captain returned to his own chair. 'Glad to hear it. Will it mean anything to me? You may be wasting your time and mine. Marine biology is not my subject.'

'I'm sure it will interest you,' Saul said. 'We've been examining a fish tail in the lab which came up the Bottom Miner pipeline. It's unlike anything we've found before. The tissue cells have a very unusual construction. And the most exciting thing is that the fish comes from six miles deep.' He explained, 'Up to now, no one's thought a vertebrate could live permanently at that depth.'

'Congratulations. Doubtless you'll put all this in a written report.'

'Yes, but I'd like to . . . .'

Beckett interrupted. 'That's all you have to do. My only concern is with cobalt.'

'My priority must be to get a complete specimen and more information about its habitat. And there's only one way: going to catch one with the bathysphere's pressure grab.'

'Didn't you hear me in there?' Beckett pointed beyond

the double doors. 'Your diving programme is over. We're moving to the cobalt field.'

'That's precisely the point,' Saul said carefully, 'The cobalt and our fish are both within the same sector.'

'Each sector is 2500 square miles,' Beckett snapped. 'If you think I've got time to go chasing around for you and then wait while you mount an underwater fishing trip, you've got another think coming. It's out of the question.'

'The dive would take half a day – including time for the detour. The sector may be big but it's still only fifty miles long and fifty miles wide. If you tell me the cobalt coordinates I can work out how far off course it would be.'

'I don't care if it's right on our route, Mr Peters. From now on the *Voyager* is concerned exclusively with cobalt. You and your researchers are just along for the ride.'

'Captain, I must protest . . . .'

'They warned me in San Diego you were an awkward customer. Made quite a nuisance of yourself at the naval centre before you left – demanding extra technicians and all sorts of fancy safety gear. That right?'

'My brief,' Saul tried hard to keep his temper under control, 'is to conduct a deep-sea census of the areas under survey by the *Voyager*. I also have to study the environmental consequences of deep-sea mining – both on the ocean floor and at the surface. It was the entire advisory board of the Adams Institute which requested extra technicians – God knows we could use them – and sensible safety procedures.'

'You kicked up quite a rumpus from what I heard. Don't get me wrong. The Institute has a fine reputation. That's why the navy invited a team on board in the first place.'

'The Institute got invited because your government wants mining to have a clean bill of health,' Saul said. 'Let's not kid ourselves. We haven't been given adequate manpower or equipment to monitor the pollution properly. We weren't even able to insist on safety clothing to protect the miners from bugs which might survive the journey up the pipeline.'

'You must be joking. The miners would never have stood for it anyway.'

'Because no one tells them the risks. They'd wear protective suits if they knew. NASA had the sense to put astronauts into isolation after the moon trips. Why? Because they might have brought back alien bacteria.'

Beckett snorted mirthlessly.

Saul continued, 'If there are bizarre lifeforms at the bottom of the sea, some may be harmful. If any survive the change of pressure on the way to the surface – up the pipe or in the bathysphere's grab – anything could happen. That's all I'm saying.'

The captain had listened carefully. 'I hear what you're saying, Mr Peters. But I have orders and I propose to follow them to the letter.' Beckett paused. 'Maybe you'll still get a chance to look for your fish, once we're on station and pumping cobalt.'

There was nothing more to be said. Saul stood up.

'Before you go,' Beckett said, 'show me how this monitor works.' He was looking at the visual display unit next to his desk. 'I'd like to take a look at the bottom while we're still sampling this sector.'

'It's easy.' Saul patted the grey console housing the screen. 'You switch it on so,' Saul pushed a button, 'and you select the channel with these keys. One to five are Bottom Miner and bathysphere channels; the rest show you whatever's on line from the computer – course, fuel consumption, that sort of thing.'

'It's a feed from the consoles on the bridge?' Beckett asked.

'Yes. If you want to do anything more than look in, you need the keyboard upstairs. Henderson and Jennings are the whizz-kids. Second nature to them.'

The screen had brightened and then faded into a murky fog of shadows.

'Don't expect too much,' Saul said. 'It's hard to see far. The lights are on about half power at present, I would guess. If you want it brighter, we'll have to go up to the bridge. There's also a sort of joystick up there for moving the camera about.'

'What's that?' Beckett indicated some numerals in a corner of the screen.

'The depth. A little over 17,000 feet – that's three miles or thereabouts.' Saul tried adjusting the brightness knob. 'It's hard to make out much until you get used to it. The camera is pointing straight in front of the mining head. That's the seabed,' Saul ran a finger in front of the screen. 'And those are nodules – manganese mostly, around here.'

Beckett looked distinctly unimpressed. 'They look like pebbles. How big are they?'

'Only a few inches. It's hard to gauge the scale.'

'The ones I was shown at San Diego were much bigger.'

'They vary. Up to fist size is normal, like these. You must have seen the prizewinners.' Saul turned his attention from the screen to Beckett who had drawn close to the console. He saw the concentration on the captain's face. 'Bottom Miner is a sort of deep sea tractor.' Saul paused but the captain continued to stare at the screen in silence.

'The bathysphere,' Saul continued, 'is much more flexible. There's a man inside, it can carry two cameras and there's the grab for bringing things back under pressure to the surface.'

Beckett nodded.

'This all *looks* rather unexciting,' Saul pointed at the murky picture on the screen. 'It is in fact one hell of an achievement.'

'Too damn right. And that's why you'll never get our country handing over this sort of technology to any damned Third World dictatorship.'

Saul was thoroughly depressed by Beckett's crude philosophy. He tried not to show it. 'Bottom Miner is travelling across a large plateau in this sector. It's rarely this flat. The sea floor here is as varied as any land mass. There are mountains as tall as . . . Shasta.' Saul deliberately chose an American mountain. Mount Shasta was about 13,000 feet high in the northern tip of California. He had climbed it on a summer hike recently with a colleague from the Institute.

'There are valleys deeper than Grand Canyon,' Saul said, 'cliffs which drop thousands of feet, volcanoes so large they sometimes poke through the surface – little islands which come and go.'

'Incredible.'

'It is. But I guess I've been a lecturer too long, always trying to get students enthusiastic. I tell my students that deep-sea mining is like sucking peanuts through macaroni from the top of the Empire State building. It's a graphic image. But, of course, most of the time it's dull down there. All very routine.'

There was a sharp rap on the double doors connecting the cabin with the conference room, a momentary pause and then Lt Bell appeared.

'I didn't realize you were busy, sir.'

'I'm not. Mr Peters is just going. What do you want?'

'To give you the key, sir, the radio key.' The captain held out his hand and stared at the brass-handled key which Bell put in his palm.

'This is the only one?' Beckett asked.

'Yes, sir,' Bell replied.

The key was vital to work the elementary shortwave radio. When the key was withdrawn from the transmitter, the frequency control locked and the power circuit was broken.

Beckett pocketed the key. He patted his trouser pocket and addressed both men. 'If this tub had been equipped with ultra-high frequency and a scrambler, this wouldn't be necessary. We could have used a satellite. But no one's prepared to trust shortwave bouncing off the ionosphere – in or out of code. I'm sorry. How long before the helicopter can leave?'

'Anytime now,' Bell said.

'Get it away as soon as possible.'

'Understood, sir. We can plot the new course anytime you want to give me the coordinates.'

Beckett removed a buff envelope from his inside jacket pocket. 'I'll be up shortly to see round.' He took a step towards Bell and handed over a sheet of paper. 'Let me have this back.'

'Yes, sir.'

'That's all for now.'

Bell turned towards the door where Saul was standing.

'Thank you for your time,' Saul said to Beckett.

29

'I hope we understand each other better now,' Beckett said.

Saul and Bell left the captain's cabin, Saul pulling the doors firmly shut behind him.

'Mark,' he said in a strong whisper. 'Let me see.'

Bell offered Saul the sheet of paper.

'I want to see how close my fish is to the . . .' Saul stopped in amazement. 'I don't believe it, it's in exactly the same place.' Saul shook his head and scrutinized the piece of paper again. He read: '169°47′W, 38°15′N.' He felt in his shirt breast pocket and found the scrap of paper on which he had written the location of the fish find. 'The same place,' he repeated to Bell, putting both sheets side by side on the rosewood table. 'Absolutely exactly.'

'Quite a coincidence.'

'They don't make coincidences like that. There's a connection. Don't ask me what, but there's a connection.'

6

The sleek metal monster had come to rest just a few feet above the ocean floor. The propeller rotated gently, almost idly, to balance the effects of a current that swept along the seabed nearly 6 miles below the surface.

The man within had located the centre of the cobalt site. It lay about a mile ahead. His companion was still asleep. The men and their machine would wait, to observe and record, until instructed further.

A fish approached. It kept clear of the single beam of light from the monster's snout. The fish confronted the intruder. After a moment, the fish moved cautiously closer. It sensed an unexpected warmth in the chill water. With a flick of its tail, the fish shot to the side of the cylinder. It rubbed against the metal skin searching for the source of the warmth. The fish pressed against the monster's underbelly.

Cocooned in their shield of lead, the fuel rods in the

nuclear pile emitted heat. The generator emitted a high-pitched hum throughout the submersible. The pilot preferred the sound to silence. He sat in front of a cockpit of controls and fought back drowsiness. He blinked hard and once again scanned the dials and displays arrayed in front of him. He settled back in the padded chair and began to operate the keyboard set in its arm.

Powerful sonar beams radiated from the antennae set in the submersible's shell. A sidescreen showed the sonar scan read-out. The data was converted to graphics by the computer and a picture of the surrounding ocean floor appeared on the main screen. It showed details which the cameras could not pick up. The man noted a boulder 200 yards away. Further ahead the sand and mud floor gave way to a smooth hump of rock. Otherwise, the area seemed as featureless as a wind-scoured plateau and as barren as a desert.

The man was bored. For a moment, he thought of waking his commander. He dismissed the idea. He should instead report their safe arrival back to base.

The codebook was kept in a small drawer under the console. He removed it, checked day, date and time references and tapped the correct code factor into his armchair keyboard. He punched in a short message: 'ON STATION UNDETECTED AHEAD OF SURFACE VESSEL. AWAIT ORDERS.' Then he routed the signal into the computer for scrambling. It would be sent to the surface in one great pulse of energy. He despatched the message to his masters with a final stab at the keyboard.

In the water, the fish thrashed frantically when the laser beam shot from the monster's body. It stunned the creature into stillness. It began to float away from the submersible – a stray too far from home, its curiosity rewarded with strange and awful pain.

The pilot stretched. There were still several hours to the end of his shift. He addressed himself to the chess problem he had set up on one of the side display screens. He asked the computer to restart the game by suggesting his best move. It did so in seconds. Then the computer signalled its own response. It reminded the man of a classic Karpov defence in one of the Manila games against Korchnoi. He tapped his instruction back into the keyboard to bring up his knight into attack. The image of the knight changed squares and replaced a captured pawn.

From the corner of his eye, the pilot saw movement on the main display. Something was tumbling slowly across the screen. He engaged the sonar image enhancer and put the resolution control on maximum. The shape grew sharper. He moved the cursor on the screen until it was in the middle of the rolling shape and requested a distance and size read-out. The data appeared across the bottom of the screen. The object was twenty feet away and about two feet long. The man looked for signs of life, but got no positive reading. He switched off the sonar, yawned and returned to the chess. The computer had him in check.

7

The mining rig towered above the *Voyager*'s main deck. It dwarfed everything in the rear half of the boat, out of balance with its surroundings, reducing the cranes and davits around the horseshoe harbour at the stern to doll's house proportions.

The din eased as Saul and Beckett turned into the corridor and closed the soundproofed door which led from open deck into the mining quarters. They found Dansk in his office.

The head of mining operations was seated in a battered swivel chair behind a pine desk. He waved the captain to an upright chair.

'Pull out the rocker,' Dansk said to Saul. 'Or I can get you a chair from in here.' He indicated a darkened back room separated from the office by a worn velvet curtain.

'Not necessary,' Saul said. He pulled the low rocking chair towards the centre of the room. He had wanted to see Dansk alone. But the captain had insisted on coming to see the mining quarters with him after a quick visit to the bridge.

Beckett spoke. 'You seem comfortable here, Mr Dansk.' Beckett had not sat down. He stood looking round the small room.

The room reminded Saul of a collector's den. One set of shelves was filled with glass sample jars, each with a handwritten label identifying the black misshapen nodule it contained. Another set of shelves contained books and charts. They were arranged – Saul was always amused to see – in order of size as if they were so many soldiers on parade. The desk was empty apart from a polished brass compass, a steel rule and a mug containing a clutch of freshly sharpened pencils.

'You're a man after my own heart,' Beckett said. 'All shipshape. What's through there?' He nodded in the direction of the back room.

'My bunk.'

Saul observed the two men marking out their territory like cats. He admired the Norwegian's aplomb. Dansk was polite but not deferential.

'A commendable devotion to duty,' Beckett said.

'Well, I have a crew of only six. It's easier this way. Trouble can hit day or night when we're mining. And it's quieter here than in the cabins. I keep my fridge full of beer and watch your wonderful cowboy films on a video. Not such a bad life.' Dansk smiled.

'Cobalt comes first from now on,' Beckett said.

'We can finish this sector in two hours. Sector 27 is a hundred and forty miles northeast. We have to get Bottom Miner up. There are mountains in between. It could take days to get round them.'

'How long to pull it up?'

'Two, two and a half hours. It takes forty-five minutes for every mile of pipe. We're down three miles. It stays that way through to the end of the sector.'

'So you'd be finished,' Beckett glanced down at his watch, 'by 7 p.m. I'll brief the crew at 7.30 p.m. I want your men there, Mr Dansk – in the canteen. Soon as the briefing's over, I want your men raising pipe so we can be heading for sector 27 by midnight.'

'I'll see we are.'

Beckett continued, 'It should take about twelve hours to reach the cobalt site. There's a current in our favour.'

'I do have one problem,' Dansk said. 'The assembly clamps.' He explained, 'I've got to replace them before we can lower pipe again. The pipes have to be heat-moulded together and the clamp circuits are badly worn.'

'How long, Mr Dansk?'

'It's a day's job.'

'A day!'

'It *is* necessary.'

'Anything not essential can wait,' Beckett said.

'There's not really a choice, Captain. Not for a six-mile pipeline. The clamps are shot to pieces. I wouldn't be able to run them at more than a crawl. The spares came in with you on the helicopter, thank God. It's a simple job. It just takes time. We can work all night.'

'And if I say no – try it with the old clamps?'

'We could have a major accident,' Dansk said slowly. 'Believe me, it'll be quicker to change the clamps and join pipe at full speed than to limp along with worn-out equipment and risk a breakdown however slowly we take it.'

'If it breaks down?'

'The pipe can be joined manually. But it'd take weeks. I'll get some lights rigged up. The repairs will be well underway before sun-up. My men are used to nightwork. We're like a whorehouse. We never close.'

Saul kept his silence. Beckett seemed prepared to accept the mining expert's advice.

Beckett turned to Saul, 'So you get your chance after all, Mr Peters. You can map out the cobalt field while the clamps are repaired. Catch your fish if you can.' Beckett turned back to Dansk, 'I want that pipe going down just as soon as you get those clamps working. No more excuses.'

'There won't be, Captain.' Dansk reached out an arm and took a bottle and then glasses off the shelf. 'Whiskey?'

'Not for me,' Beckett said.

Saul accepted a tot. Two foreign nationals stood together and shared a silent toast. Dansk returned the bottle to the shelf, removed a pipe and pouch of tobacco from a drawer in the table.

The captain had stood throughout the discussion. He suddenly asked, 'How did you lose that finger?'

Dansk stretched the fingers of his left hand. The top knuckle of his index finger was missing. 'An accident in the North Sea.'

Beckett looked inquiringly at the mining engineer.

'An oil rig broke loose in a gale,' Dansk explained. 'A chain sliced it off as I was trying to winch back a man overboard.' Dansk drummed lightly on the tabletop with the stump of his finger. It was a nervous habit.

'No accidents with the clamps, Mr Dansk, or you'll lose more than a finger. You can depend on that.' The captain turned for the door.

Saul displayed his shock at the captain's remark to Dansk who smiled and shrugged. Saul hurried after Beckett.

Beckett had stopped in the corridor outside a door marked Security. 'What's in there?' he asked when Saul edged past him to lead the way back on deck.

'A storeroom. Bertil uses it as his filing cabinet. Some precious stones which probably pay our wages,' Saul tried to coax some good humour out of the captain. 'I'm very grateful you're permitting me the dive.'

'I'll want the cobalt clusters mapped. Don't think you're going to piss around just trying to catch your fish down there.'

Saul opened the door to the deck. The noise of the mining rig washed over them. Before leaving the gantry alongside the base of the rig, Saul pointed to a platform halfway up. He cupped his hands and shouted, 'Assembly unit.'

Beckett looked puzzled for an instant, then he nodded.

Saul pointed to a long ladder which stretched from the metal platform down into the bowels of the ship. Saul could see a man climbing down, hand over hand, leg over leg, like a spider across a web. 'Want to see the pump room?' Saul shouted his question.

Beckett shook his head and shouted back, 'Another time.'

Saul led Beckett away from the rig. Most of the noise came from the roar of slurry from the well head, which, after a journey through three miles of pipe, was gushing over giant shaking sieves. A miner, in a booth with a commanding view of the jet of slurry, manipulated the sieves in and out of position. The three-stage separation system included centrifuge, shaker-screens and settling tanks. The nodules were graded and tested before all but a few samples were dumped unceremoniously back overboard into the horseshoe harbour at the stern.

The two men passed the hold, still half-full with pipe. Most of it would be needed to make up the six-mile pipeline. First the existing pipe would be broken back into sixty-foot lengths and piled, like so much scaffolding, in the open hold. Bottom Miner would rise from the water to occupy its reserved position on the rear deck. Only after the assembly clamps had been repaired and the *Voyager* taken up its new position would the lengths of pipe be joined once again and Bottom Miner sent back into the deep.

Saul steered the captain towards the mid-decks where the bathysphere was attached to its own crane and nestled in a cradle. The diving bell was fifteen feet in diameter. A long umbilical carrying power and communications ran over pulleys on the crane and disappeared below deck.

Saul patted the bright yellow sphere as if it was a pet.

'What're those?' Beckett asked. He pointed at the outsize tubular rings lying on the deck.

'Flotation. Allows the bathysphere to surface independently.'

'And that?' Beckett pointed at a hinged steel contraption lying open on the deck with serrated teeth like a mantrap.

'The pressure grab. It gets connected to that arm over there. We catch our specimens with it. You trigger it from inside and a small charge slams the two sides together. You can scrape up rock samples in the scoop under here,' Saul indicated a mesh net, 'but for anything delicate, you need to keep a constant pressure. The grab is very sophisticated. Not like the rest of Saturn.'

'Saturn?'

'Her nickname – because of the flotation ring.'

'How deep can you go?' Beckett asked.

'The record's held by a Frenchman called Jacques Piccard. He went down nearly seven miles into the Marianas Trench off the coast of Japan in 1960. In a bathyscape – quite a bit different from this. Six miles is enough for Saturn.'

Beckett grimaced and walked round the yellow metal sphere.

'We look after this as if it was a fighter aircraft. After every descent, it needs a day's work.' Saul picked a spanner from a toolbox on the deck and rapped on the bathysphere.

From inside a voice hollered, 'Whadya want?'

Seconds later a man appeared through the hatch at the top of an inspection ladder, emerged and began to climb down towards them. He was stocky, in his early forties, with tousled hair and a craggy face which hadn't seen the blade of a razor for a couple of days. He was dressed in oil-stained dungarees and his bare arms were knotted with muscle.

'This is Carl Nicholson, Captain.'

Nicholson jumped the last few rungs of the ladder. He looked with evident distaste at Beckett's crisp, white uniform, said nothing and continued to chew the wad of gum in his mouth. He wiped his hands on the side of his dungarees. He took the spanner from Saul and tossed it back into the small canvas toolbag.

'Carl, the captain has decided to let us dive – to six miles – tomorrow.'

Nicholson grinned. 'Good, a big one!'

'We'll be moving sectors overnight, diving in the morning.'

'What's the hurry?'

The captain's face remained impassive.

'The captain will explain this evening – 7.30 p.m. in the canteen. Be there.'

Nicholson looked suspiciously at Saul and then at the

captain without evoking a response. He took a pack of Marlboro from his dungarees, tapped one out and lit it.

'Change the bulbs to quartz-iodine,' Saul said to Nicholson. 'And double-check them. Mount the second camera. I'll want you up crack of dawn for a full service – console, flotation, air tanks, communications ... the works.'

'Everything?'

'The lot.'

'Mind if I break now for a while?' Nicholson said. 'I missed my jab this morning. Sounds as though Popeye's going to need his spinach.'

The captain looked puzzled.

'You do that,' Saul said. 'I'll see you back here in an hour. There's plenty we can start on.'

Nicholson strolled across the deck. He gave a cheery wave as he turned down the steps leading below deck.

'That man is insolent.' Beckett spoke scathingly. 'You let him behave like a boat bum on a pleasure yacht.'

'You don't have to like him,' Saul replied. He chose his words carefully, not wishing to deepen the rift he felt between himself and the captain. 'He knows his job. That's what's important to me.'

'Well everyone round here is going to have to learn a little navy discipline from now on.' Becket's pompous tone suddenly dissolved. 'What on earth did he mean about Popeye and jabs?'

Saul smiled. 'He has to have injections. But don't worry, he's not a junkie. Carl has a tricky liver. All to do with an unsavoury past, I'll grant you. Dr Mendoza gives him a weekly vitamin jab. Powerful stuff. It keeps him in good shape . . . .' He trailed off.

The helicopter, preceded by a sudden wave of noise, rose into view above the bridge from the landing circle beyond. It hovered ominously for a moment, dipped away from the *Voyager* and gained height rapidly, shrinking into the blue sky until it could no longer be heard or seen.

Nicholson stood at the back of the canteen near the door. Beckett was intoning at the other end of the room about the *Voyager*'s new mission and the need to improve standards. Lt Bell stood beside a map of ocean sectors which had been stuck with tape to the wall near the service hatch. He held a pointed wooden baton in his hand. A large 'X' was visible inside sector 27 indicating the conjunction of longitude 169°W and latitude 38°N. The *Voyager*'s present position was marked with a flag.

Along with one or two others, Nicholson had arrived slightly late. He counted those assembled: there were seventeen people present, some sitting at tables, some standing. The men were hushed as they listened to Beckett announce the imposition of complete radio silence. There was a murmur of approval when Beckett told them they would be paid bonuses and their families advised of the special security status of the mission and why letters would be delayed.

The door opened and Helen Mendoza, the ship's doctor, entered quietly.

She stood for a moment beside Nicholson. 'What's happening?' she whispered.

Nicholson smiled, 'I don't like the sound of it. International piracy, I think.'

Dr Mendoza smiled. 'There's a seat by Kathy, excuse me.'

Nicholson watched her take her seat and exchange a silent greeting with Kathy. The doctor was in her fading forties and in no great shape. For the first week of the trip, Nicholson remembered, the sight of the two women pounding the deck on a morning jog together had captivated the whole boat – one overweight middle-aged woman in shorts struggling for breath and the graceful Kathy. They made an odd pair.

There were now just two crew missing. Nicholson concluded that one had to be on the bridge and perhaps a miner was in the pump room watching over Bottom Miner and the silent rig. There had never been a better opportunity. Nicholson slipped out of the room, unnoticed he hoped. The corridor was empty. He walked towards the cabins, moving cautiously but quickly. He rose to deck level and surveyed the deck.

Nicholson looked at the girders of the steel rig. They cast eerie shadows in the half-light. Without the drone of the pump and the roar of slurry, he could even hear the gentle slap of water against the ship's side. He hurried across the deck and entered the mining area. He came to the door marked 'Security' near Dansk's office, took a set of narrow steel picks from his back pocket and inserted two in the lock. He probed carefully until the lock sprang open. It got easier each time.

Once inside the storeroom, he shut the door and waited for his eyes to adjust to the dark. One side of the room was shelved. There were leaded containers of radioactive isotopes stored there, some machinery spares and Dansk's personal supply of whiskey and beer.

With a pencil torch for light, Nicholson opened the storage cabinet in the corner. In the top drawer there were several lumps of rock. He examined the selection as if looking for a ring on a jeweller's tray. There were some uncut diamonds, irregularly sized and shaped, most still encrusted in nodule fragments. There were some large pearls which rolled to the front of the drawer when he tipped it forward to see better in his thin beam of light.

It was then that he heard a sound in the corridor. Nicholson switched off the torch. He stepped behind the storeroom door and felt for the fire extinguisher. His heart beat faster. He lifted the cylinder off its hook and tested its weight.

The footsteps slowed and then stopped. Nicholson could hear the man breathing on the other side of the door. He tightened his grip on the cylinder and raised it above his head. Whoever entered the room would never know what – or who – had hit him.

There was a jingle of coins. The man was searching his pockets, presumably for a key. Then came a muffled grunt of annoyance, then the footsteps retreated down the corridor.

Nicholson replaced the fire extinguisher and returned to the drawer of precious ores and stones. He selected a handful, but not so many as might be noticed by anyone conducting a casual audit. He dropped them in his pocket, closed the drawer and storage cabinet, and left the storeroom.

Nicholson hurried back to his cabin. He locked his door from the inside, sat down heavily on his unmade bed and picked up a can of beer from the table. He pulled back the tab and poured the warm contents down his throat. Some of the beer dribbled down his chin and on to his tee shirt. His heart was still thumping.

He belched and took the stolen stones from his pocket. He held them to the light. Not of the best quality, but valuable nevertheless. He rose from the bed and crossed the narrow cabin to a large fishtank resting on a table by the sink. Lying coiled on the sand at the bottom of the tank was a dark-spotted moray eel. Nicholson tapped the glass and watched it bare its teeth. The young fish had been brought aboard in a sampler net. Saul had reluctantly allowed him to keep it as a pet until it grew too big for the tank. As a kid back in Florida, Nicholson had seen a moray take a lump out of the leg of a careless fisherman. Anyone foolish enough to put a hand in the tank would lose at least a couple of fingers. He grinned at the thought.

Nicholson dropped the stones into the water. He watched them settle on the sand bottom. The disturbed fish twisted violently in the tank. Nicholson picked up a small net and poked each stone with the handle until they were all buried from sight.

8

Saul walked to the gangrail leaving Nicholson to check the gas pressure in the flotation ring. They had both been up since dawn preparing for Saturn's deepest descent of the voyage. The sky promised another day of unbroken sunshine: it hadn't rained in a month. From where he stood, his back to the ocean, he could see two men halfway up the mining rig. He saw a shower of sparks fly. They were using oxyacetylene cutters on the old assembly clamps.

The mining head stood on deck looking like some visiting contraption from another planet. It resembled a tank with its caterpillar tracks. The body was painted with a dull red oxide paint against corrosion. The joints and moving parts were heavily greased.

Saul saw the captain striding towards the bathysphere from the bow. He hurried back to Nicholson.

'Stay civil,' he said.

As Beckett drew close, two miners shuffled across his path. They were stripped to the waist, laughing at something. They ignored the captain.

'Slobs,' Beckett said, on reaching Saul. 'They'll soon learn though.'

'They've been up half the night lifting pipe and working on those clamps,' Saul began to explain.

Saul was neatly dressed, wearing a tee shirt, khaki slacks and canvas sailing shoes. Nicholson, however, was crumpled and still unshaven. His singlet was stained and his cotton work trousers streaked with oil and paint. Saul was more than prepared to defend Nicholson from the captain's disapproval. He had been impressed by the engineer's capacity for hard work and by his interest in the mission – in the fish and in the nodules.

'I want you ready to dive in half an hour,' Beckett was saying.

'We're almost on station.'

'We'll be ready,' Saul looked towards Nicholson who nodded agreement.

The klaxon sounded from the bridge and a moment later the *Voyager*'s engine noise dropped.

'I'd better get him up,' Saul said.

'I'll be on the bridge.' Beckett strode off.

'What a jerk!' Nicholson said to Saul.

'Never mind, we have our dive,' Saul said. 'I'll get Herbie.'

When Saul entered the lab, Herbie was in the rest area putting on a thin one-piece insulation costume.

'Everything OK?' Saul asked.

'Fine,' Herbie said. 'With you in a minute. Take a look at the fish models.'

Saul turned to the computer terminal. He knew Herbie had spent most of the morning keying in the analysis of the tail fragment. He had then crosschecked the computer's species file, but without any success. Saul punched his way across the keyboard.

The eel-like tail was the only constant on the terminal screen. For every set of hypotheses Herbie had fed in, a different outline built up in front of the tail. Sometimes it was recognizably fish-like with conventional fins. One image was almost conical with a huge and grossly distended mouth. Another curled like a snake showing two primitive limbs – no more than stumps – near an eyeless head.

'I'm ready,' Herbie said.

Saul turned from the terminal and saw Herbie in the doorway between the lab and the rest area. Herbie was bearded, balding and short. Yet when he wore the foil suit, he changed – like Clark Kent into Superman.

'My, don't we look groovy,' Kathy said, coming into the lab from the corridor. She wore corduroy slacks and a faded University of California sweatshirt.

Saul watched Herbie's reaction. Herbie was devoted to his wife, unable to accept that she was drifting away from him.

'Well, let's go,' Saul said, breaking into the silence. 'Nicholson has Saturn all spruced up for you.'

Kathy accompanied the men down the corridor and up on to deck. The ship's engines were now strangely quiet. The *Voyager* was in position. The bathysphere awaited.

Nicholson stood at the front of the access ladder. 'Good hunting,' he said to Herbie. 'Look after my baby.'

Herbie put an arm round Kathy's waist and pulled her to him. Such public displays of emotion were rare for him. He kissed her, then began to climb the ladder. At the top step he turned, looked briefly back down towards Kathy and waved his Superman wave before disappearing inside.

Saul helped Nicholson to swing the hatch closed as soon as Herbie had dropped into the bathysphere seat. They spun the wheel entombing him. Herbie's only way out was

43

through the hatch which could only be opened from the inside in an emergency by exploding the hinges.

Saul left the bathysphere and went to the base of the crane. He picked up the cordless phone and punched the code for the bridge and then for Herbie inside Saturn. Bell answered from the bathysphere control desk on the bridge.

Herbie's voice joined the three-way link up.

'Do you want to raise her using the deck controls?' Bell asked Saul.

'I'll watch. You take her over the side,' Saul said. Then to Herbie, 'Good luck. Enjoy yourself.'

The winch began to turn slowly and the bathysphere rose away from its cradle. The arm of the crane swung gently out over the side of the *Voyager* until the bathysphere was held suspended over the sea. Then, still operated from the bridge, the winch cable began to lower the bathysphere into the water.

Saul kept the receiver to his ear listening to Bell and Henderson on the bridge run through pressure, air, power and communication checks. He walked to the ship's rail, carrying the receiver with him. The bathysphere was dropping as gently as a balloon towards the water. The sea swallowed it whole. The winch stopped. Saul could still see the outline of the yellow bathysphere below the surface.

'Can we get going?' Herbie's voice already sounded tinny and a little anxious.

The winch cable began to clank steadily out. Saul heard Bell say, 'You're on your way. Keep an eye on the sonar.'

In a matter of moments, Herbie would be through the euphotic zone. This was as deep as sunlight penetrated – 300 feet – the limit for the formation of plankton by photosynthesis. This top layer of Pacific deep ocean was, in fact, largely a biological wasteland. There was little upswell of minerals from the seabed to act as fertilizer for plankton growth. Without the plankton at the base of the marine food chain it was inhospitable water for fish. There were a few tuna, some whales, dolphins and porpoises. But there were none of the huge shoals of mackerel and herring found in the Atlantic.

Saul cut his contact with the bathysphere but directed

a message to Bell on the bridge. 'Mark, sound the klaxon when we're within three hundred feet.'

'Right. It'll be a couple of hours,' Bell said.

'I'll be below,' Saul said and returned the receiver to its hook at the base of the crane.

Saul had spent the interval reading from his small shipboard library. It occupied a single shelf in his cabin. His concentration was broken by the sound of the shower running in the cabin next door. Kathy was in the shower. He shut the book on the table in front of him. It was an account of the *Challenger*'s voyage in the Pacific more than a hundred years before when metallic nodules were first discovered on the ocean floor. He stood and paced his narrow cabin.

The Kiplings were the only married couple on board and the arrangements devised for their living quarters had been ingenious and simple. The dividing wall between two single cabins had been removed. It meant there were two of each fixture: two lavatories, two basins, two showers. There were still two doors to the corridor outside although one was permanently locked. There were twin beds, side by side. The San Diego suppliers didn't run to doubles.

The shower ceased after a few minutes. Saul left his cabin, rapped on the next but one door along the corridor and, without waiting for an answer, turned the handle.

'Me,' he shouted round the open door.

A moment later Kathy's head appeared in the misty bathroom doorway, her neck craning round the corner. The sight of Saul standing sheepishly half in the cabin and half in the corridor gave her pleasure. She felt a slight shock run through her body.

'Are you coming or going?' she asked. 'Make up your mind. There's a draught.'

Kathy wore a white towelling dressing gown. Her auburn hair, shining damp, cascaded over her shoulders. He shut the door behind him.

Kathy sat at a chair in front of the small dressing table and stared at herself in the mirror. She began to search through her bag for make-up.

Saul approached and put his hands under her damp hair and on to her shoulders. She smelled sweet.

'Will you leave him?' he asked, after a pause.

Saul rubbed Kathy's shoulders, working under the blades and then moving his thumbs further down her back. He kept his hands outside the towelling.

'Yes,' she said, in a subdued voice.

'When will you tell him?'

'Not before the end of the trip. I must wait. It's harder for both of us, but I'm not going to hurt him more than I have to. It would be wrong to have it out in the open while we all still have to work together.'

Saul turned Kathy's face towards him. He pressed his lips to hers and pulled her to him.

'No, Saul, not now,' Kathy pleaded softly.

Saul ran his tongue gently around her inside lip and parted her teeth. She did not try to pull free. She responded. The tie to her towelling wrap had loosened. The top front edge of the towelling revealed a soft, rounded breast, nipple swelling. Saul moved his hand towards the gap between towelling and skin.

The ship's klaxon blared.

Saul withdrew his hand and smiled at Kathy. 'Wouldn't you know it? Herbie, right on cue. We'd better get up to the bridge.'

9

Saul closed the sliding door behind him and Kathy. Beckett was sauntering slowly around the bridge, hands clasped behind his back.

The bridge was dominated by a panoramic window that overlooked the bow. Lining the rear wall, either side of a hatchway down to the captain's quarters, were two separate banks of instruments, each with three shallow-backed tall stools fixed to the floor in front of them.

The sailor who usually navigated *Voyager* sat in the centre seat at the bathysphere control console to the left of the hatchway. Bell sat beside him. The sailor spoke into a microphone which rose on a flexible arm to just below his chin. 'I'll leave the line open.'

Saul crossed to the bathysphere controls, and slipped into a vacant chair. 'Any problems, Henderson?'

'He's here,' Henderson said, pointing at a screen of sonar-graphics superimposed with markings to indicate the original mining head track and Saturn's position.

'Come to keep an eye on your husband?' Beckett asked Kathy. He wiped a finger across the top of the radar desk in the centre of the room as if looking for dust.

'Yes, thanks.' Kathy felt uncomfortable under the captain's scrutiny. She turned towards the control console.

Beckett watched her move. He thought of his encounter with the French girl in Geneva less than two weeks ago. Since his divorce, he had grown used to paying for his sex whenever his need flared. That way he usually got what he wanted. But not with the French girl. In excellent English, she had told him he was sick, enjoyed violence because he resented being aroused by a woman and should get professional help. Kathy would doubtless take the same view of him.

Saul felt Kathy put her hands on the back of his chair. He was studying a dial which recorded the rate of Herbie's descent. The needle hovered at the three-knot mark.

'How about pictures?'

'He's setting that up.'

Saul pulled the mike towards him. 'Herbie? It's Saul. We'll take the last few feet nice and slow. Use full lights.'

'Roger.' Herbie's voice came from a speaker on the console.

'Do you want to watch, Captain?' Saul asked, looking over his shoulder.

Beckett ignored Saul's question. 'Increase the field,' he told Jennings, the rating at the radar display.

'Yes, sir.' Jennings switched the scale from thirty to fifty miles. A single blip appeared at the edge of the green screen. It reappeared on each sweep of the arm.

'What's that?' Beckett asked.

'We passed it last night,' Jennings replied. 'Might be a Japanese trawler.'

'So long as it isn't Russian,' Beckett said. He walked towards the three men seated at the bathysphere controls. 'Right, Mr Peters. You have my full attention.'

Saul spoke into the mike. 'Herbie, we're all ready for you.' Henderson put an arm into the mass of dials in front of him. He flicked one switch and then another.

'You're on screen,' Saul said to Herbie.

'Light enough?'

'Yes. How far can you see?'

'Thirty to thirty-five feet.' Herbie's voice held uncommon assurance.

Saul looked at the altimeter. The hand swept slowly and steadily round the dial. As it completed each rotation, the digital read-out changed. It passed 31,000 feet.

'Seventy . . . Sixty-five . . . Sixty . . .' Bell read from a dial indicating distance from the seabed.

A picture from the second camera flickered on to a second screen in front of Saul. He saw Henderson switch the image up to the captain's monitors.

'The stabilizers are cutting in,' Bell said. 'There's a slight drift east.'

'Nice 'n smooth,' Saul said. 'I don't want to scrape him . . . .'

'Seabed visible,' Henderson interrupted.

Bell read from his dial, 'Thirty-three feet.'

'Hold at fifteen feet,' Saul said. He watched the distance drop and then addressed Herbie on the mike, 'You're free to use your jets and scout around.'

Henderson was trying to improve picture contrast. The eerie light from the bathysphere's full battery of bulbs illuminated a sandy surface.

On one screen, Saul could see a smooth swathe which was Bottom Miner's track. To either side lay a jumble of underwater debris.

'That's as good as we'll get from the wide-angle,' Henderson said.

A blurry cloud swirled across both screens.

'What's happening?' Beckett asked.

'Sediment,' Saul said. 'From the jets. It takes time to settle.' He watched the depth of vision increase. 'There are some nodules.'

Beckett studied his monitor with interest.

'And those are sea cucumbers.'

Beckett stared silently up at the misty picture.

Henderson spoke. 'There's a slight depression and a ridge of some sort coming up on sonar.' He put the sound map taken by Saturn's sensors on to a third screen on the console.

'I'm going closer,' Herbie said. 'The seabed seems to dip.'

'There may be a cliff ahead. Take it slowly,' Saul said.

'Lower me ten feet, repeat ten feet.' Herbie didn't sound six miles away.

Henderson made the adjustment after a nod from Saul.

Suddenly jagged lines like forks of lightning began to run across one of the screens. Henderson twiddled with knobs on the console to no effect. Pictures from the second camera began to break up. Only the sonar map remained intact.

'I can't get rid of this,' Henderson said.

'A fish.' Herbie's voice sounded animated. 'Incredible – about two feet long. Hovering on the edge of boulders. And, nodules everywhere.'

'Herbie, we've lost vision,' Saul said. 'Take a quick shot with the grab. Then you're coming up.'

The captain leaned forward and shouted towards the mike, 'Nodules first, Mr Kipling. Understand?'

Herbie's voice emerged firm and steady. 'I can get them both at once. It feels like a sauna in here.'

Henderson tapped Saul's arm and drew his attention to a dial towards the back of the console. 'Do you think that can be right?' he asked.

Saul returned to his microphone link with Herbie. 'Give me your temperature readings. We have you overheating.'

'Hang on, Saul, I can't do two things at once. The grab is nearly ready.'

'Temperatures!' Saul was alarmed. 'At once – cabin and external.'

The answer was confused. 'One gauge seems broken. Something's wrong. The cabin is 33 degrees and rising. I'm sweltering.'

Saul immediately knew what he had to do. 'Bring him up, Henderson.'

Henderson pointed at the console. 'I can't. He's using the jets. I need authority to override.'

'Get him up,' Saul said more urgently. 'At once.'

'Do I have authority?' Henderson looked instinctively at Bell.

'Yes,' Saul said urgently.

'No,' said the captain.

Saul swung round and stared up at Beckett. 'He's in trouble. We must get him up. Now.'

'Not yet,' Beckett snapped.

Saul turned back to the mike. 'Stop your jets, Herbie.'

There was no reply.

'Herbie?'

Still no reply.

Beckett's face was impassive. Yet behind his eyes, images flashed garishly. Bodies, blood and jungle green. A cascade of sound invaded his ears. Not even the chatter of machine guns from somewhere in the recesses of his mind could ruffle the cold composure. The seconds passed.

The captain spoke slowly, 'He's had time to use the grab. Wind him in.'

Henderson looked relieved. He pulled the lever which operated the vertical hoist.

Saul had slipped out of his seat. He stood beside Kathy who stared blankly in front of her, eyes unblinking. 'It'll be all right,' he said. 'He's on his way. It won't take long.'

The man sitting at the controls of the deepwater submersible was puzzled. The *Voyager*'s bathysphere seemed to be on its way up barely ten minutes after it had reached the ocean floor. He stared at the screen which showed him a telescopic sonar image of the bathysphere a mile away. He was under instructions from the senior pilot not to move any closer for fear of detection by the *Voyager* or its bathysphere.

This was the second big surprise of the copilot's watch. He had been told to expect to see the *Voyager*'s mining pipeline lowered to the cobalt site. Instead he had picked up the shape of a sphere on its way down to the seabed, suspended by a fragile umbilical from the ship.

The data now displayed on a sidescreen told him that the bathysphere was moving up at four m.p.h. That struck him as fast for an old-fashioned McDonald diving bell. He was unsure what to do in the circumstances. He made a note of the time and speed of the ascent. But he still had nearly ten hours of his shift left. The senior pilot would not wake for another five or six hours. With only the familiar hum of the generator to comfort him, the copilot settled back in the padded chair and followed the bathysphere's steady progress towards the surface.

Then he had an idea. He targeted the sonar towards the spot on the ocean floor where he had last seen the bathysphere. Because his own submersible lay so close to the seabed, he could get no bearing on the surface of the seabed a full mile away. He could see a cliff face beyond, but that had not caused the bathysphere any problems. He was sure of that.

He sat forward in his seat and took the controls. Slowly and gently, he lifted his nuclear-powered submersible away from the bottom. Then, with sonar antennae extended and infrared cameras peering through the black wall of water, he tried again. Apart from the steep cliff face beyond, the surface of the seabed appeared smooth and without obstacles.

He set off in a great circular loop, 500 feet above the seabed at the regulation mile radius from the cobalt site. Nothing changed except that he was able to build up a 3-D image of the cliff face. In a last attempt to unravel the mystery, he directed the heat-seeking thermopile at the site.

At first he got readings of 1° and 2°; then slightly higher which surprised him. He panned slowly back and forth across the cobalt site. Suddenly the needle shot up and disappeared off his temperature dial. He changed scales. What he saw was scarcely credible. The highest temperatures affected a very small area of seabed. But they were so remarkable that he now knew what had caused the bathysphere's sudden departure. He also knew that he would have to rouse his commander. He pressed the wake button and prepared to explain.

10

Saul paced the deck. He glanced at his watch. It was nearly 4 p.m. – almost an hour and a half since Beckett had given permission for Saturn to be raised. Saul watched a sailor hosing water over the main weight-bearing pulley. The winch was running hot but the extra speed had saved nearly half an hour on the lift.

Saul looked along the gangrail to where Kathy stood staring into the water beside Helen Mendoza. A black Gladstone bag was at the doctor's feet – just in case. Bell and Henderson, on the bridge, had not been able to re-establish contact with Herbie. Saul's fervent hope was that, with the bathysphere safely back on board, they would discover that the jets had malfunctioned burning out the picture and sound links with the *Voyager* but leaving Herbie safe and sound.

Most of the ship's complement were now on deck. Saul saw miners standing side by side navy crew. Dansk had ordered a halt to work on the assembly clamp replacement without reference to Beckett. So far Beckett had not countermanded the order.

The captain leaned against the gangrail puffing on a cheroot clamped between his teeth. His shadow stretched across the deck.

The ship's klaxon sounded a warning blast. Saul raced for the rail. He was in time to see the bathysphere loom in the water. The winch slowed and the diving bell emerged from the sea, water cascading off its yellow steel. Someone cheered. But then an anxious silence fell over those on deck as the crane swung Saturn above its cradle. As Saturn was lowered, Nicholson signalled the bridge like a runway worker guiding an aircraft to its berth.

Saul was on the access ladder when the bathysphere came to rest. He attacked the hatch, furiously spinning the wheel to break the air seal. He swung the hatch cover back on its hinges and leaned inside.

Herbie sat strapped in the swivel seat. He was motionless, his head flopped to one side. Saul swung himself into the bathysphere. He squatted down beside Herbie and lifted his head. The eyes stared blankly at him. The head was limp and heavy. The foil insulation suit was unzipped to the waist. There was no sign of breathing. Herbie was dead.

Saul met anxious faces outside. He saw Kathy's worried expression, and shook his head slowly. 'I'm sorry,' he said.

Kathy stared up at him numbly, unable or unwilling at first to comprehend. She moved to the foot of the access ladder oblivious to all but Saul as he came down the steps.

'There's nothing you can do,' Saul said. 'Nothing at all, I'm afraid.' He put a hand on her shoulder, steering her aside to make room for Nicholson and Helen Mendoza to squeeze past.

Kathy couldn't speak. She felt as if she had been badly winded. She drank in air, clutching at her stomach, turning first one way and then another.

Saul looked around for Dansk. The knot of men around the bathysphere had loosened and Saul saw him at the base of the crane talking to the captain. He called Dansk over.

'Please go with Bertil,' he said to Kathy. 'Helen will be down very soon. And so will I.'

The Norwegian mining engineer put a comforting arm around Kathy and walked her to the main stairway which led below deck.

With the doctor's help, Saul and Nicholson lifted Herbie's limp body from the bathysphere. Saul noticed a dried trickle of blood from his nose and blistering around the mouth. He helped to lay Herbie down on the deck while Nicholson went with a miner to fetch a stretcher from the stern.

Nicholson and the miner lifted Herbie on to the stretcher. The doctor, black bag in hand, helped them to negotiate the stairs. The small, sad party made their way below deck.

Saul had a sudden thought. He looked at one of the television cameras sticking out on an arm like an insect's leg from the underside of Saturn. He circled the bathysphere noticing that the scoop was empty. The pressure grab also remained open and unfired. He saw the second camera pointing at him from the end of its gantry. The lens looked cracked and clouded.

Beckett looked at his watch and said, 'I'll open the inquest in an hour's time. I want cause of death from Dr Mendoza and, for a start, you could find out why we lost communications.'

'An hour?' Saul protested. 'I don't think we should rush this.'

'I want to know if that no-good Nicholson is the one at fault. Don't try to protect him.'

Saul tried to keep calm. 'You can rest assured I don't approve of cover-ups – or of looking for scapegoats.'

'Let's get started, shall we?' Beckett sat at the conference table surveying the small gathering of his senior crew. 'The doctor's late.'

Saul, Dansk and Bell exchanged looks. Saul fingered the book in front of him which had paper markers in it for reference. Dansk took a pipe from a pocket and began to prepare a plug of tobacco.

Beckett cleared his throat. He switched on the tape recorder in front of him, adjusted the microphone towards the centre of the table and opened proceedings. 'Preliminary inquest, 15 July at . . .,' he checked his watch, '. . . 5.15 p.m., on board the *Voyager*, into the death of Herbert Kipling . . . .'

The door from the deck opened and Helen Mendoza appeared with Kathy by her side. Beckett pressed the recorder's pause button.

The doctor led Kathy to the table and pulled out a chair for her. 'She wants to be here.'

'I'm sorry Mrs Kipling about your husband's death.

We're here to try and find out how it happened. You can stay if you wish.'

Kathy stared blankly at the captain.

Saul could find no response in Kathy's eyes when he met her gaze. Her eyes, unblinking, seemed to see straight through him.

Beckett restarted the tape recorder. 'Present are,' he spoke at the table mike, 'Captain William F. Beckett, Covert Naval Operations, Lt Mark Bell, second-in-command, Helen Mendoza, ship's doctor, Mrs Kathy Kipling, wife of the deceased, Mr Bertil Dansk, chief mining engineer, Mr Saul Peters, senior marine biologist. The recording will be accompanied by a full written report. First, the cause of death. Doctor?'

Saul was fond of Helen Mendoza. She was one of the oldest members of the ship's crew, with good reasons, he knew from Kathy, for choosing a shipboard life. There had been very little for her to do on the trip – a broken arm required setting, a bad cut needed stitches and a precautionary tetanus shot. She appeared to enjoy helping out in the lab from time to time.

'I'm not a pathologist, I'm afraid,' the doctor began. 'I'm used to people *telling* me what's wrong with them. But there's not much doubt. The immediate cause of death was almost certainly a stroke. The most likely cause of that on the seabed is a sudden change of pressure. But I don't think it was that.' She paused. 'It doesn't make much sense to me, I warn you. It may to you,' she looked towards Saul. 'How hot is it at the bottom of the sea?'

Saul frowned. 'It isn't, usually. 1 or 2 degrees, that's all.'

'Well,' the doctor looked round the table, 'Herbie died because he got too hot. His lips and mouth were badly blistered. His lungs were also burned. They don't blister but they fill with fluid which leaks out from blood vessels. As that began to drown him, the blood in his veins was thickening and suddenly clotted somewhere in his brain.'

For a moment no one spoke.

Then Beckett said, 'Mr Peters, can we hear from you?'

'Yes, Captain, I have a theory to explain the heat and I have some of the evidence.' He took a small reel of magnetic tape from his breast pocket and laid it on the table. 'This is the instrument recording tape from Saturn's black box. I've only had time to scan the few minutes we were out of contact with the bathysphere. The tape records a variety of instruments throughout the duration of every dive. It shows, quite conclusively, that as Herbie moved along the seabed, the ambient water temperature reached 250°C.'

'Are you seriously trying to tell us the sea is boiling down there?'

Dansk began to nod his head in understanding and sucked calmly at his pipe.

'Water boils at 100°C at ground pressure,' Saul said. 'As the pressure goes up, so does the boiling point. So, captain,' there was an edge of irritation in his voice, 'the water won't boil in the sense of bubble. But it's every bit as hot as the black box says it was.'

'So was it the jets?' the doctor asked.

'No,' Saul said. 'They couldn't heat the ocean like that, not even if Saturn had been trapped in a small pocket of water.'

'Can the black box be wrong?' Beckett asked.

'It doesn't know how to lie,' Saul replied. 'There's also other evidence to corroborate it which explains why we lost communication with Saturn. There's a small metal housing at the base of the bathysphere. It's a junction box really – the communications link with Saturn. The metal housing was warped when we pulled Saturn up. It's a strong alloy, resists water pressure but clearly couldn't take the heat. There's about a three-inch section which warped and melted on the connections. First it shorted our picture reception. Then we lost voice contact. The sonar transfer cable escaped.

'There's one other thing,' Saul continued, 'I couldn't understand when I first saw the bathysphere. One of the camera lenses seemed to have glazed over. The lenses are made from a highly refined sort of perspex, developed for orbital spacecraft. In space they carry heat shields which enclose them on re-entry. But, of course, the shields weren't fitted on underwater cameras.'

'How did it get that hot?' The captain had accepted Saul's authority on the matter.

'I'll quote you chapter and verse,' Saul said. 'The *Alvin* – a navy sub, operated by the Wood's Hole Oceanographic Institution – found vents of hot water in 1977 during a dive off the Galapagos. A couple of years later they came across a lava landscape on the seabed 250 miles west of the Mexican coast. There they recorded temperatures of nearly 400°C.'

'Why haven't I heard about this before?' Beckett asked Saul.

'It's not a secret,' Saul said. 'It's been fully reported – in the scientific journals, even by *Time* and *Newsweek*. The vents are very rare, but they do occur.'

'They're some sort of underwater volcano?' Dansk asked.

'That's right. The water pressure down there is enormous. So they don't seem to erupt in quite the same way.' Saul explained further, 'They're thermal vents in the sea floor where magma, the molten lava from the earth's core, leaks out. Some vents look like chimneys according to the *Alvin* reports. They're called hotspots.'

'Sounds like an understatement,' Dansk said.

'Haven't you come across them before during mining?' Beckett directed his question at Saul and Dansk.

Saul answered. 'No. The *Alvin* hotspots were associated with high densities of mineral deposits. As part of the volcanic rock. There was no reason to expect hotspots out here. It's a most important discovery,' Saul said, adding, 'and Herbie paid for it with his life.'

There was a brief silence, broken by Saul. 'The hotspot may be responsible for the concentration of cobalt nodules. And be the reason our elusive fish can survive down there.'

Beckett put his hand out to the tape recorder and switched it off. 'Believe me, Mrs Kipling, the loss of your husband is a tragedy. However, we still have a job to do, and there is still the matter of the cobalt to be discussed. Would you like to leave?'

Kathy shook her head.

'Very well,' Beckett said. 'How are we going to get the cobalt up?'

Saul found the question distasteful. He exchanged looks with Dansk and asked, 'Any ideas, Bertil?'

'I don't think we yet have enough information. I'll want to study the black box read-out carefully.'

'I agree,' Saul said. 'But even the black box can't tell us how the cobalt is distributed. Some must lie clear of the hotspot otherwise we wouldn't have got samples up without wrecking Bottom Miner.'

'So what do you suggest?' the captain asked.

'You really want to thrash it out now?' Saul said.

'I'd like the advice of a scientist and my mining engineer,' Beckett said.

'Well, we've only got the one mining head,' Dansk said to Beckett. 'It would never survive temperatures of 250°C. So I couldn't advise sending it down until we have a good idea of heat distribution.' Dansk looked at Saul for confirmation.

'Any idea what temperatures it can work in?' Saul asked.

'Not really. There'd be trouble for sure about 150°C. The caterpillar track for a start. I'd have to check the specifications but the rubber compound must melt at that sort of temperature. The camera – that's the same as on the bathysphere. The lining in some of the suction joints is a special toughened plastic product. The nodules don't even scratch it, but as for heat . . .' Dansk trailed off.

'If Bottom Miner packs up, the mission is over. The cargo ships will rendezvous with a crippled mining vessel,' Saul said.

'You could fly in a new mining head,' Dansk suggested.

'No time. Anyway, you're no better off with a second one.'

'It's out of the question,' Beckett said.

'There is one way,' Saul said. 'I could go down again in Saturn.'

Everyone at the table except Kathy was startled at the statement. The doctor reacted by putting a hand out to soothe Kathy who showed no outward sign of having registered Saul's suggestion. Bell shook his head vigorously.

'Very interesting,' Beckett said very slowly.

Dansk remonstrated, 'I won't hear of it. We can send

Bottom Miner. If we lose it, at least we tried. It doesn't put another life at risk. Who knows, with the black-box information, we could be lucky.'

'Thanks, Bertil, but no. Assuming Saturn can be repaired, I'd like to make the descent. I'll map out the heat distribution, wherever it's safe for me to go, and then Bottom Miner can come down for whatever cobalt's safe to lift.'

'I admire your courage, Mr Peters,' the captain said.

'I hate to disappoint you, Captain, but I have my own reasons for making the trip – neither of them to do with cobalt. First, unless I go down, there's no chance of getting a specimen of the fish. Second, unless I get the fish, Herbie will have died for nothing.'

Mendoza, Bell and Dansk each gave Saul a silent look varying between incredulity and respect. Kathy still looked totally vacant.

'Something still bothers me,' Beckett said.

'Yes, Captain.' Saul softened a little. Perhaps Beckett deserved some sympathy in this predicament.

'If the water is so hot, how come Mr Kipling didn't realize something was wrong?'

'There'd be a time lag – a minute or two – before heat built up inside the bathysphere.'

'Well that's what bothers me. Why didn't Mr Kipling fire the pressure grab or at least use the scoop?'

Saul could hardly believe his ears. Beckett was blaming the dead Herbie for failing to collect cobalt samples.

'Captain, if you hadn't overruled my instruction to bring Herbie up as soon as we saw the temperature dials rising, you could have asked him yourself.'

'Mr Peters, my question still stands. If he had the couple of minutes he himself asked for, why didn't he use them?'

'I don't think you understand the scene down there.' Saul was trying to remain even-tempered but it was an uphill struggle. 'Herbie was trying to get your precious nodules and his fish – above all else.'

'But he didn't.' Beckett remained insistent.

'No, and do you know why?' Saul gave way to long-suppressed rage. 'Because when he realized he was in trouble, he had no way of making us hear him. You insisted on leaving him down there screaming his head off for us to get him out!'

Kathy leapt to her feet knocking her chair on its back. She stared wildly at Beckett. 'You killed him, you killed him . . . .'

Dansk and the doctor rose to restrain her. As they did so, she burst into tears.

Beckett remained impassive. 'Take Mrs Kipling to her cabin. Maybe a sedative would help.' He addressed his dismissive remark at Helen Mendoza.

The doctor gave Beckett a withering look before, with Dansk to help, she guided Kathy away from the conference table and out of the door.

The atmosphere in the conference room remained tense. The captain showed no indication of resuming a civil tone.

'Bell, don't just stand there like some puppy messing itself. Get back to the bridge.' Bell obeyed like an automaton. He hurried up the connecting ladder, visible for a moment only from the knees down while he opened the hatch door and then disappeared.

'I'd like a word with you, in private,' Saul said as calmly as he could.

'Go ahead,' said Beckett, sweeping a hand around the empty conference room.

'What about the body?' Saul said.

'What *about* the body?' Beckett replied.

'How are you going to get it back? His parents live in San José – Kathy has the details. Doubtless the navy has a ready-made procedure to cope with this disaster.'

'It does, Mr Peters. Anything else?'

Saul hesitated. This didn't seem the best moment to ask what also amounted to a personal favour. He ploughed on regardless, 'Kathy should fly back with the body. She shouldn't have to stay on board.'

'I thought you were short-staffed.'

'I'll make do with Dr Mendoza's help,' he said quietly. 'She knows the lab.'

'It's a tempting idea – flying Mrs Kipling out. She'll be

60

a pain in the ass if she stays.' There was a strange look on Beckett's face. 'But I'm afraid it's out of the question.'

'Why?'

'Because I'm not calling in a helicopter. The man's dead. There's time enough for his parents to learn how, when and why. You seem to have forgotten something, Mr Peters. No shore contact. That means exactly what it says.'

'But this is different. There's been an accident.'

'I told you when I first arrived on board, in this very room, just a couple of days ago. No shore contact of any kind. We're incommunicado. No signals leave, no one and nothing comes or goes for the duration. Those are orders. It's the end of the matter. And in case you think I'm acting unreasonably, Mr Peters, I'd like to show you something.'

Beckett went into his cabin and returned a moment later. 'Herbert Kipling,' he was saying as he strode through the double doors, 'will be buried at sea tomorrow morning according to provisions set out in this.' Beckett pushed the document across the table to Saul. 'Please study it, Mr Peters. You'll see I'm following procedure to the letter.'

Saul glanced at the thin pamphlet on the desk and turned it to face him. It was headed 'COVERT NAVAL OPERATIONS – EMERGENCIES ON MISSION.'

'The ship's company,' Beckett said, 'will be informed that the ceremony will be performed shortly after first light at 6 a.m. tomorrow morning.'

11

It was early morning. Saul stood in a semicircle of men at the bow with a dull ache in the back of his head. He could see Bell looking green around the gills. They had drunk heavily together the previous evening, each cursing the captain. The way Bell told it, Beckett's behaviour on the bridge seemed calculated to provoke a mutiny.

Saul shivered. The sky was sunless. Grey, threatening clouds were building fast. There were white caps on the ocean. The *Voyager* lay at the edge of a storm, the first in four months at sea. It was as though the gods had been made angry at Herbie's death and at the manner of his despatch.

Herbie lay on a stretcher on the deck wrapped in the American flag. Four sailors in dress uniform stood at attention. The service was approaching its grim conclusion.

'Let us pray . . .' Beckett said. His words were snatched by the wind as a sudden squall passed across the deck. Saul saw the pages of the prayer book in the captain's hands flutter furiously.

Saul looked around the semicircle. Dansk stood impassive, head slightly bowed, alongside his mining crew. Nicholson blew his nose in a handkerchief. Saul watched Nicholson fold the handkerchief slowly and with care, instead of stuffing it as usual like a rag into his pocket.

Saul turned to Kathy who stood between him and the doctor. She wore no make-up or jewellery. Her eyes were puffed and red, staring straight ahead towards Beckett and then dropping to focus on the wrapped bundle lying on the deck. The gusty wind silhouetted the body under the rippling flag.

'Man that is born of a woman hath but a short time to live and is full of misery.' Beckett turned the page. 'In the midst of life we are in death.' Beckett snapped his fingers at the guard of honour. Two sailors stepped forward and pulled back a section of guardrail. They returned to lift the stretcher with their two colleagues. They put it down with the handles of one end over the edge of the deck. Two of them gradually raised the other end of the stretcher until the shrouded body began to slip.

'We therefore commit his body to the deep . . .' Beckett said.

The corpse hit the water. The stars and stripes billowed slightly and sank from sight.

'. . . to be turned into corruption, looking for the resurrection of the body, (when the sea shall give up her dead), and the life of the world to come through our Lord Jesus Christ. His coming shall change our vile body, that it may be like His glorious body.' Beckett shut the prayer book.

Saul thought of the weighted body swallowed by the ocean. By the time it reached the bottom, the body would be crushed by the pressure into a pancake of flesh and bone – if it survived the predators on the journey. Only the flag would reach the seabed intact, an unseen marker for the unfulfilled scientist. It would fade and dissolve with the memories of Herbie Kipling.

Saul was jolted back to the present. The gathering had begun to break up and he needed to speak to Nicholson. He left Kathy in the doctor's care and hurried across the deck to where Nicholson was talking to one of the miners.

'Carl, I'm sorry to interrupt,' Saul said, breaking into the conversation.

'Bob, you go on ahead,' Nicholson said to his friend.

Bob Wilkins nodded, said 'Good morning,' to Saul and, 'I'll see you down there,' to Nicholson.

'What's so important?' Nicholson asked Saul.

'I need your help. Soon as possible. Where were you off to?'

'Breakfast. And a stiff drink. I'm not great on funerals. Certainly not that way, Mafia-style with weights, food for the fishes.' Nicholson spoke with distaste. 'I need to get it out of my mind. Join us. Come have a drink.'

'Go easy on the booze. I want Saturn thoroughly checked out.'

'That'll take hours.'

'So eat a good breakfast.' Saul smiled.

Nicholson pulled a pack of cigarettes from a pocket, tapped one out and lit it. He exhaled. 'You're really serious. You're going to take her down again. She's in terrible shape.'

'Nothing you can't handle. I'll go down unless it's beyond repair.'

'All the wiring's suspect and most of the gauges are bust. Some can be replaced, a few recalibrated. We have spare cameras but not much else.'

'See what we need and what we've got. We'll know soon enough if it's going to be possible. I want Saturn to cope with up to 140°C. Above that and the camera lenses will melt.'

'How long have I got?'

'As long as it takes,' Saul said. 'But I'd like to go down tomorrow, if it's at all possible. I don't know how long Beckett will wait before he decides to try Bottom Miner.'

Nicholson looked at Saul. 'You're as crazy as he is. Christ, people used to call *me* unhinged. But I can't compete. I'm not in the same ball game.'

Saul spent all day working on the bathysphere alongside Nicholson – inspecting, repairing, resoldering cables, replacing instruments. The simple technology of the old-fashioned diving bell allowed Nicholson to improvise. But anything badly damaged, not vital to safety and for which there was no spare was shut off, its dial or lever taped over to prevent confusion. Beckett appeared on deck in mid-afternoon, and greeted with relief the news that Saturn would be able to dive the following day. Towards dusk, Saul pronounced himself satisfied.

After dropping Nicholson at the canteen, with a promise to join him later, Saul settled at the lab terminal to ponder the black-box information fed to the computer. He correlated the bathysphere's movements on the seabed with the cabin and water temperatures. The outside temperature had reached 250°C; inside an incredible 73°C about two minutes later. Herbie had suffered the same ignominious fate as a lobster thrown into a pot of boiling water. His unzipped insulation suit would only have made matters worse and exposed more of his body to the murderous heat.

Saul switched off the terminal and paced around the lab. The gurgling of the fishtanks irritated him. He was depressed by the sight of an unfinished experiment on Herbie's workbench. Saul checked his insulation suit, kept in a cupboard near the deepfreeze, and was shocked to see Herbie's limp and crumpled suit hanging in front. He concluded Dr Mendoza had replaced it sometime since peeling it from Herbie's body to perform the autopsy.

Saul did not want Kathy upset by chancing on the headless outer skin in which Herbie had died. He looked for a suitable hiding place, pulled open the deep bottom drawer in Herbie's workbench and tucked the foil suit out of sight under a neatly folded, white lab coat and some notebooks. Saul felt ready for a stiff drink when he left the lab.

A crate of empty bottles and a black plastic sack brimming with beercans testified to the day's main activity in the canteen. A poker game, which Saul had seen start more than twelve hours earlier at breakfast, was still in progress. Players had come and gone and grown more boisterous during the day, but he felt no one was having much fun. A wake was underway. Instead of a muffled drum, the sounding of the last post or some elegant elegy, there was country music on the jukebox.

Nicholson was sitting by himself, a bottle of bourbon, cans of beer and a half-eaten chicken sandwich on the table in front of him. Nicholson beckoned him over. 'Sit down. Have a drink.'

Saul took a water tumbler from the centre of the table and pulled the bottle towards him. He said, 'Thanks,' and poured a couple of fingers of bourbon. He dropped in some slivers of ice floating in a waxed bucket.

'Finished in the lab?'

Saul nodded, picked up the tumbler, and drained it in two gulps.

Nicholson raised an eyebrow. 'Take it easy, that's not Dr Pepper,' he said.

Saul grimaced, and recharged the glass. As Dolly Parton gave way to Tammy Wynette on the jukebox, one of the miners at the poker table went to turn up the volume. A poker player whooped and hooted as he pulled a pile of dollar bills towards him. Another remonstrated at the outcome of the hand.

'How can you stand this?' Saul asked. He had begun to feel the pressure of the impending dive. 'If you don't mind, I think I'll be better off getting some air.'

'Sure,' Nicholson said. 'This racket doesn't help.'

As Saul left the canteen Tammy Wynette was dolefully singing, 'D.I.V.O.R.C.E.'

It was quiet on deck. Saul walked around the foredeck and then sat, under the moon, his back propped against a locker. The morning's threatened storm had never arrived. He closed his eyes.

Meditation brought him peace and calm, and renewed energy. He concentrated on his breathing, regulating the flow of air in his nostrils, making it even and smooth. He put a slight emphasis on the out-breath and let the in-breath take care of itself. He sat cross-legged, back straighter now but still supported by the lifeboat. He tried to quieten the tumbling images released in his head – and he let the breaths grow longer.

Two or maybe twenty minutes later, he sensed another presence. He opened his eyes and blinked. Kathy stood in front of him bathed in the white light of the moon. She wore a tracksuit and her hair was tied back.

'I didn't mean to disturb you,' she said.

'You're not,' he said. 'What brings you out here in the middle of the night?'

'It's not late. I was going to take a run and get rid of all that Valium and crap Helen's been giving me.'

'I'm glad you feel up to it.' Saul was relieved to see Kathy's face animated and expressive again. 'I came out for fresh air and a quiet think. The rest of the ship is boozing.'

'Do you want company?'

Saul smiled and shifted position. He pulled a life belt from behind him and put it on the deck. 'Try this. It takes the chill off your bum.'

Kathy sat down in the ring, stretched her legs in front of her and wriggled her back against the locker until she was comfortable.

'Do you have to take the bathysphere down?' she asked.

'Tomorrow.'

'Why so soon?'

'Beckett's the one in a hurry,' Saul said. 'I have to take the chance while it's on offer. I've got to get to that fish and see whatever else is down there. It may be part of a whole new food chain based around the hotspot.'

'I thought it was like a desert six miles down – very little life.'

'That's right. Not enough water in the desert. And not

66

enough food in deepwater. There's only a light rain of organic matter falling from the sea overhead. As you know, if the sun stopped shining we and every green plant on the planet would die. But not that fish.'

'How do you mean?'

'I think it depends on the earth's internal heat as its energy source – on sulphur compounds generated by volcanic heat. The process is called chemoautotrophy. Like photosynthesis, it produces organic compounds out of inorganic ones. But the energy comes from chemical reactions instead of sunlight.'

'Which means?'

'Which means,' Saul said, 'there really could be life inside other planets – say, Jupiter or Saturn. The internal heat of any other planet could supply exactly the same sort of energy and chemical food to create life.'

'Amazing.'

'It's already more than a theory – thanks to the *Alvin* dives off the Galapagos. But we've gone one better: the first animal with a spine depending on an energy source other than sunlight. Herbie will get the credit too, I promise you that. It's a major discovery.'

'It's sad he didn't live to enjoy it,' Kathy said. 'I felt guilty for not feeling anything but shock when Herbie died. I kept thinking to myself – is this all there is to it? I wanted to feel grief but it just wouldn't come.'

'It may get worse before it gets better. It comes in waves. I remember with my mother. The initial shock is that the world just keeps on going. The pain follows.'

'You loved your mother,' Kathy said. 'But I can't play the grieving widow. I can't fake it. In the early days I was convinced I loved Herbie. But not for a long time now. And there's no point pretending. Or feeling guilty. That doesn't mean I'm not sad he's dead. I wish he was alive – but for his sake and his family's. Not for mine.'

Saul looked at Kathy without speaking.

'What I still have to come to terms with,' Kathy continued, 'is that I was a lousy wife to him when he was alive. I should go and see his folks, give them a little comfort.

And then mine. I haven't been home in such a long time.'
Kathy sighed.

'I'd like to meet Herbie's family. Make sure they understand how important his work was. And then some time
in Manhattan, what better?'

'My family is tough to take,' Kathy said. Kathy looked
into Saul's eyes. 'They'd both approve of you, though, I
know.'

'You're the most important person in my life,' Saul said
softly.

'I'm glad.'

For a few minutes neither spoke. They breathed in the
cool night air under the stars. Their shoulders touched as
they sat side by side.

'I know there's no way I can talk you out of your dive,
so I won't try.' Kathy turned her face to his. 'But I couldn't
stand losing you.'

12

Saul walked around the outside of the bridge scanning the
deck below for a sight of Dansk. The foil insulation suit
was cumbersome; it creased and crackled as he moved.
The short briefing with Bell and Henderson was over and
the *Voyager* had already taken up its new station – half a
mile east of the spot at which Herbie had dived.

Saul saw Dansk and Nicholson appear around the blind
side of the yellow bathysphere. As he went to the steps
leading down to the deck, he caught a last glimpse of Kathy
gazing forlornly at him through the tinted glass of the
bridge. Saul smiled to reassure her. She gave him a weak
smile back and mouthed, 'I love you,' through the window.

Saying goodbye to Kathy had been public and undemon-
strative. Saul felt relieved that she had decided not to
remain on the bridge after he was safely launched on his
journey into the deepwater. He had convinced her she

would find it less stressful to work with Dr Mendoza on the backlog of pollution sample tests.

When he reached the bathysphere, Saul took Dansk by the arm and walked him to the gangrail.

'Bertil, I want a favour,' Saul said. 'Take my seat on the bridge. Just in case there's trouble. I'd feel happier knowing you were there. And I'm sure Bell and Henderson would appreciate it too.'

'And if he plays at being captain, what then?'

'Your simply being there will help to stop him inter-fering. In his heart, he knows he was wrong over Herbie.'

Dansk looked doubtful. 'Saul, I'm really against this dive . . . .' He spoke hesitantly. 'If you listened to any of us you wouldn't go.'

'I'll be careful. I promise.' Saul put his hand on Dansk's shoulder as they walked back to the bathysphere.

'Thanks for everything,' Saul said to Nicholson. They shook hands.

'Good luck to you,' Nicholson said. He slapped the flotation ring which encircled the bathysphere like a life belt. 'She's fully gassed. And I've primed the pressure grab.'

Saul climbed the steps to the bathysphere hatch. He got his legs in and sat for a moment on the rim. He turned to Dansk and Nicholson who had climbed the cradle steps with him and said, 'See you later,' before dropping down into the bathysphere control seat. The small circle of sky above him narrowed and then disappeared as the hatch was swung shut with a loud metallic clunk which reverber-ated in his ears. The inside of the bathysphere was plunged into darkness. Saul felt for the light switches. Three of the four were working; the fourth was taped in the Off position. Saul heard the wheel squeak as the hatch was sealed and then the comforting double knock on the hatch cover which was Nicholson's customary farewell.

Saul turned his attention to the console which spread three-quarters of the way round him. About half of the dashboard of dials and instruments were masked in tape. Saul opened communication with the bridge by slipping a body mike over his neck and clicking a switch on the console in front of him.

'Are you reading me?' he asked.

'Loud and clear,' Bell replied, his voice coming from a speaker in the console. Saul found it comforting to have another voice join him inside the small sphere.

'I want a moment to see what I've got here,' Saul said.

'Take your time.' This time it was Henderson who spoke. Saul imagined Henderson slipping into the centre seat at the bridge console, preparing to take charge. Saul could hear the pins securing the bathysphere to the cradle being knocked out. He looked around the patchy instrument console. The camera arm controls had been stripped, overhauled and rebuilt, some of the screen circuitry had been replaced. Water temperature monitor, echo sounder and precision depth indicator dials each responded to Saul's checks. He stared for a second at the empty hole in the console where the tape recorder should have been. The magnetic and gyro compasses were taped over as was the horizontal scanning sonar system, ground detector and speed meter. Saul felt behind him for the chemical fire extinguisher. It was in place in front of the bank of three emergency power batteries. The mouthpiece from the closed circuit rebreather hung above and behind his head in easy reach in case of noxious fumes from a fire in the sphere.

Saul pronounced himself satisfied.

'So are we,' Henderson said from the bridge.

Saul heard the winch turn and felt Saturn sway as the crane began to lift the yellow sphere from its cradle. Saul imagined himself dangling like a ball at the end of a chain as he swung across the deck. Saturn rocked backwards and forwards as the crane slowed and came to rest. A moment later the winch started to release cable and Saturn was moving downwards. Saul felt Saturn kiss the water, be swallowed and then a quiet stillness.

Bell's voice addressed him, 'We have you at thirty feet and holding.'

'Let's go,' Saul said. 'Gently all the way.'

'You are cleared for diving. Here we go,' Henderson said.

In little more than a minute Saul travelled the 300 feet which took him beyond the euphotic zone. Saul then passed through the thermocline – the point at which the sea's temperature suddenly dropped. Some twenty years before, huge schools of humpback whales would crisscross the ocean at this level on their way to feeding grounds. They had been almost eradicated by greedy whalers.

The bathysphere moved steadily downwards at 3 m.p.h. – more than 4 feet a second. The outside pressure increased by one atmosphere every 33 feet – an extra 15 pounds on every square inch.

At a little over half a mile Saul entered the mesopelagic zone, home of the octopus and squid, scarlet prawns, angler fish, lantern fish, hatchet fish, viper fish. It was a long list. Saul remembered the early lectures in marine biology at Bristol which had first enthused him about the subject. His teacher had been inspiring, graphically describing how fish emerged from this level like bats from caves to feed in the upper, lighter regions of the ocean, and explaining how man's knowledge of fish life at this level depended for many years on the sperm whale.

Saul needed the thick steel of the bathysphere to protect him from being crushed to death. At 3000 feet, pressure was already more than 90 atmospheres – a total weight of 6000 tons on the surface of the sphere. Yet the sperm whale, the world's greatest diver, was capable of descending to three-quarters of a mile for an hour at a time without suffering any ill effects. The story of its travels could be read in the contents of its stomach.

Throughout his two-hour journey, Saul was assaulted by eerie sounds. The groans, moans and cackles in the 200–150,000H_z range were amplified by Saturn's steel skin. Some of the noise came from dolphins or long-toothed whales using long range hunting sonar to detect food. There were sharks which used noise to stun their prey. Many sounds had never been explained, merely observed and noted during diving bell descents. They combined into a cacophony of low level noise – an endless underwater Stockhausen concert.

The bathysphere plunged steadily deeper. When Saul

71

eventually reached the edge of the benthic zone, close to the seabed, he switched on Saturn's floodlights and cameras.

'Have you got vision?' Saul asked the bridge.

'Receiving – both cameras,' Henderson said. 'Picture quality is good. No interference.'

'Thank Nicholson for that. He did a fine job.' Saul stared hard at the screens in front of him.

'I'm slowing your descent,' Henderson said. 'Our sonar suggests that cliff could be coming up.'

'I should be well east of the edge.'

'You should be. But you're short on instruments.'

'It is a bit like landing in thick fog on autopilot. I never thought I'd miss a speed meter or ground detector.'

'We have everything under control.'

Saul knew that Bell and Henderson would be scouring their screens and instruments even more carefully than usual. The shared sense of danger was strong. Although separated by nearly 6 miles of cable, Saul sensed the concentration and alertness on the bridge.

'Is Bertil there?' Saul asked.

Dansk answered for himself, 'I'm here.'

'And the captain?'

'At the radar table,' Dansk said.

The seabed swam mistily into view on the screen. 'Brakes on,' Saul said quickly.

'Already done,' Henderson said.

'I show thirty-one thousand feet, just over,' Saul said. 'That's seventy feet higher than where Herbie was.'

'Looks like you're there,' Bell said. 'We're on the higher of the two tectonic plates.'

'Temperature readings are still normal?' Henderson asked.

'Confirmed,' Saul said. 'The seabed is mainly volcanic. Not much of a covering of mud and sand. It's quite a sight. These tectonic plates make continents drift and mountains rise. The lava is in incredible shapes. There are long sheets of it. See that worn slab on camera one? It looks like a tombstone.'

'Don't *say* things like that,' Dansk said.

Bell said, 'I make you eight hundred yards east of Herbie's last position.'

'The hotspot is somewhere in between,' Saul said. He swept the sculptured landscape with his cameras: jumbled mounds of lava which, not so long ago, had been part of the earth's molten core.

'Saul?' Henderson's voice broke into Saul's thoughts. 'Are you using jets? I show you drifting north.'

'It must be current.'

'Shift back in position.'

'Whatever you say,' Saul said. He pressed two buttons on the console for a count of three. He felt the jets swing him backwards. He said, 'Start moving *Voyager* west. Ten yards a minute. Drag me across the lava field. If it gets too hot, I can back off with the jets.'

There was silence for a moment and then Dansk said, 'Yes, Saul. The captain agrees.'

Ten minutes later and 300 feet further west, Saul saw the first signs of life. On the right-hand screen, a spaghetti-like worm appeared and then swayed in the displacement created by Saturn's movement at a constant 15 feet from the seabed – maintained by the echo sounder and the shipboard computer together.

'An acorn worm. On camera one,' Saul said and noted that the water temperature had risen to 10°C.

'We can see it,' Henderson said.

'I'm going into stereo,' Saul said. He trained the second camera on to the same frame as the first, halving the amount of seafloor under inspection, but increasing picture quality sharply with an elementary 3-D effect. Saul pressed the automated locking device to coordinate the bathysphere's two camera eyes.

Further forms of underwater life began to appear. He saw limpets, mussel-like crustaceans and clams sharing the underside of one huge slab of lava. Then Saul spotted tube worms sheathed in protective tubes. They resembled their shallow water cousins in every respect but size.

Saul described them to those watching above. 'Long, pinkish bodies. You see them in coastal waters – but nothing like these. Some could be up to ten feet long. The tubes are made up of chambers. The worm seals off the old ones behind it and lives in newer sections of the tube. How it manages to detoxify the hydrogen sulphide out there, I've no idea. I'll collect one in the sampler.'

Saul saw the red tentacles shrink as he brought the scoop around the worm.

'What's that?' Saul could hear wonder in Dansk's voice. 'It looks like a dandelion.'

Saul manipulated the scoop towards the dandelion shape. It disintegrated as the netting brushed against its myriad antennae. 'Sorry,' Saul said. 'That'll need the pressure grab. Some other time.'

'What are your temperature readings?' Henderson was businesslike.

'It's 20°C inside – and ambient water temperature is up to 65°C.' Saul's voice was firm in reply. 'It's warming up out there.'

'You're less than 300 feet from Herbie's last position,' Henderson said. 'But a lot higher.'

Saul heard Dansk's instruction to Henderson, 'Halve the rate of drift.'

Dansk addressed Saul, 'Did you hear?'

'Yes, that's fine.'

'The sensors show a sharpening incline,' Bell said. 'I'll continue to keep you at a constant fifteen feet. Until you're ready to switch to manual.'

'Understood.' Saul studied his depth indicator and saw it now read 30,850 feet – 220 feet higher than Herbie had been at the time of the accident. And Herbie had been another 200 feet further east.

'This is some cliff,' Saul said. 'The plates must have really buckled. Temperatures should stay bearable if I keep myself protected behind the higher plate.'

'You sure?'

'That's what I'm banking on,' Saul said. 'It'll be hotter than Dante's inferno over the edge, that's for sure.'

Saul's attention was caught by a sudden movement on the screen. He zoomed in with the cameras to pinpoint the cause. The creature had the shape of a crab – but no eyes and a totally white shell showing pink flesh beneath.

'That's interesting,' Saul said in wonder. 'Who'd think it possible? There's no body pigment because without sunlight there's no camouflage advantage to be gained. And there are no eyes for the same reason . . . .'

'Saul!' Henderson's voice had a note of urgency. 'The temperature.'

'I have 25°C inside and nearly 80° outside. I feel a lot hotter myself.'

'I'm handing you manual control,' Henderson said.

'Understood,' Saul said. 'My temperature limit is 140°C, as agreed. Hey, see what I do?'

'Bingo!' Bell said. 'Nodules.'

'Most definitely.' Saul played the cameras over his thirty-foot horizon. He could now see what he was sure was the cliff edge. The lava seemed to stop abruptly about twenty to twenty-five feet ahead. In one place the lava seemed to protrude like a tongue beyond the edge. Nodules lay clustered thickly on the lava like a child's box of bricks tipped on a carpet.

Saul suddenly saw the fish appear. It hovered above the top of the cliff, above the tongue of lava, and then disappeared.

'That's it!' Saul exclaimed excitedly. 'I recognize the tail.'

'Be careful,' Dansk warned.

'I'm going closer to that tongue of lava,' Saul said. 'Nice and slow.'

Saul fired the jets in tiny bursts to move nearer the tongue. The needle on the dial passed 110° . . . 120° . . . 125° as the bathysphere, propelled by its underwater jets, inched closer and closer to the edge. It crept into the centre of the tongue of lava and hugged the smooth surface for protection from the heat.

'I think we'll just make it,' Saul told his anxious comrades six miles above him. Saul manoeuvred Saturn until its pressure grab could be fixed in position above the tip of the tongue where Saul had seen the fish.

The temperature gauge had reached 132°. Saul maintained his position and the temperature outside stopped climbing. He took stock. It was getting hotter in the cabin.

The needle pointed to 30°C. He wiped the sweat from his brow with the back of his hand. He resisted the temptation to unzip the insulation suit. It would only expose more of his body to the fierce heat.

The fish appeared again, snout first, from the unseen water beyond and below the edge. It was about two feet long, without eyes, humped in its body with a hollow underside from which two short stumps protruded as in one of Herbie's speculative computer models. The stumps looked more like truncated limbs than gills. Saul moved closer to the fish.

The bottom of the bathysphere suddenly scraped the lava and, with a lurch, tipped the chamber to one side. The noise echoed inside the spherical bell.

Saul swore, 'Shit.'

'What happened?' Dansk asked.

'I've hit the lava. I got too close. It's been protecting me from the heat over the edge.'

Saul used the jets and the mechanical arms to correct Saturn's position. He straightened the bathysphere until it rested upright and stable supported by its arms on the tongue of lava. He checked his instruments. All seemed normal and both cameras were working. The fish was still there too – hovering close to the edge above the cluster of nodules.

Saul eased the pressure grab open. Its jagged claws filled the screen with menace. First he manoeuvred the lower jaw across the rock face scooping up some nodules. Now it was just a case of waiting for the fish to swim into the clutches of the pressure grab. There was no conversation to or from the bridge. The anticipation grew. Saul did not have long to wait. A second fish appeared at the lava rim and the first fish moved closer to the grab and then within its bite. Saul did not hesitate. He plunged the fire button and the pressure grab snapped shut.

'Mission accomplished,' Henderson said.

'Let the captain know I have his nodules – and my fish – safe and sound.' Saul was sweating heavily. 'I'm going to get the hell out of here.'

'We can lift you from where you are,' Henderson said.

'I want to use the open scoop to get one of those crabs,' Saul said and began to redirect his cameras. As they tracked back, he experienced instant horror.

It seemed to happen in slow motion. The bathysphere had been resting on the tongue of lava which extended beyond the edge of the main ridge. Now a fissure creased the base of the tongue. It was spreading as he watched. The cracked veins grew wider and more numerous. They joined one another and the tongue of lava creaked as the fracture grew more pronounced.

Saul said with urgency, 'Start the winch. Hurry.'

Before there was a reply, Saul heard a horrendous sound. It was the deep report of the tongue of lava snapping free of the ridge. The bathysphere tipped and dropped. The noise continued to reverberate and shiver through the metal skin, like a gong struck too hard.

'Get me out of here!' Saul shouted.

'Right away.' Henderson's voice remained unruffled.

Saul was reassured. But only for an instant.

'We show no lift,' Henderson said.

The bathysphere was still rocking and Saul also saw no evidence that he was rising. The temperature gauges continued to alarm him. The tongue of lava had protected him from the full force of the heat from the hotspot below. Now, with the lava gone, he was exposed to its full blast. Already the outside water temperature was up to 170°C and the internal thermometer showed 35°C. Saul was sweating from heat and from fear.

Saul saw the picture on his screen buckle. He switched out of stereo. The out of focus image separated on to two screens but remained as distorted as reflections in a funfair's freak mirror. He switched to the wide-angle lenses and within seconds the same happened. The lenses melted under the intense heat as if they were made of celluloid.

The depth indicator showed exactly 30,900 feet. He had dropped fifty feet, suspended now about 170 feet above the lower tectonic plate. He was burning up like a moth above a lit candle.

'Henderson, get me out of here!' Saul felt weak and

77

faint. He had increasing difficulty breathing. His windpipe burned with the heat of the air he was inhaling.

Saul struggled to reach the mask behind his head. His muscles cramped as he searched. Then he found it, jerked it towards and over his mouth and nose and heard a low comforting hiss. He inhaled deeply. The closed circuit rebreather had a six-hour capacity to filter out fumes. Saul knew it would bring only temporary relief from the temperature.

After several inhalations, a wave of nausea swept through his lower abdomen. He struggled for a firm footing in the tipped chamber to reach the underwater jets. He fired a long burst to move the bathysphere sideways. The bathysphere responded but a second later crashed into a solid rockface.

With mounting horror and failing strength, Saul realized how bad his predicament was. The bathysphere was stuck fast on an overhang, dangling towards the hot vent, unable to be raised until he was unsnagged.

Only one more thing could go wrong. Saul himself had set the final catastrophe in motion with his plea to be winched up. As the *Voyager*'s lifting mechanism struggled to lift the bathysphere, the tension on the cable would increase until it snapped. He would then be unreachable. He would die, boiled in the cauldron, six miles deep.

Saul tried to drop the weights set in the underside of Saturn and to rise with the help of the flotation ring. Nothing happened. He pulled the lever again. The release mechanism on the outside of the bathysphere had jammed either when he hit the tongue of lava or when he crashed into the rock face.

Then Saul heard another noise from the outside surface of the bathysphere. It was rhythmic and metallic like the regular beat of a metronome. Then it started echoing inside his head. The bathysphere tipped once again. Saul slipped into oblivion.

The three men in front of the bathysphere controls on the bridge worked furiously. Henderson was flanked by Bell on his left and Dansk on his right. Dansk sat in the chair usually occupied by Saul. The men were grim-faced. Beckett stood hovering behind them – silent but censorious. Bell was calling out temperature readings from the console dial in front of him. '180°C ... 185°C ....' Both screens were blank. The voice relay from the bathysphere had failed shortly after vision was lost.

Bell implored Dansk, 'He can't last at these temperatures. We have to try the winch again.'

'The cable will snap,' Dansk said. 'I've got an idea. Move Saturn west, Henderson.'

'It might work,' Henderson said. He moved to the navigation terminal and began punching in instructions.

'Keep a close eye on the cable tension, Mark,' Dansk said.

Captain Beckett slipped into the central seat at the bathysphere console. Bell looked nervously past him at Dansk.

Dansk snapped at Bell, 'Sing out temperatures.'

'195°C. This is hopeless.'

The captain pointed to the cable tension gauge. The needle was nudging into the red.

'The cable's overstretched,' Bell announced with alarm in his voice to Dansk. 'There's still no sign of any upward movement.'

'When will it snap?' Beckett asked Dansk.

'I don't know, Captain. There's some safety margin – not more than ten or fifteen per cent.'

'So it could still pull clear.'

'It may, and it may not.'

'Over 200°C now,' Bell's voice was rising with the temperature. 'Twice boiling,' he said to the captain.

'I'm ready,' Henderson said. 'Whenever you are.'

'Good man,' Dansk said. He turned to the captain, 'This will take time. And we don't have much.'

'You seem to know what you're doing, Mr Dansk. Go ahead.'

Dansk said to Bell, 'Mark, let out fifty feet of cable. But be ready to winch if I tell you.'

'It's done,' Bell said a moment later. 'Nothing yet. Saturn's weight doesn't register. It's stuck.'

The ship moved steadily west. Henderson and Bell coordinated the release of the steel cable with the ship's movement west. The studied concentration added to the tension on the bridge. As the computer converted feet per second travelled into lengths of cable per second to be lowered, Bell set the release mechanism accordingly and studied the tension gauge.

Three separate times, Dansk instructed Bell to stop releasing cable to see if the bathysphere would tug clear. On the first two occasions the tension gauge rose rapidly into the danger area and Bell was forced to begin paying out cable once again. At the third attempt, with the men on the bridge now physically and emotionally drained, the bathysphere came free. It had taken nearly twenty minutes. The ship lay one and a half miles from its original position. The angle of pull on the bathysphere had altered by a little over 11 degrees.

The final temperature outside the bathysphere registered 235°C. The cabin temperature had risen to 65°C and then suddenly dropped. The bathysphere was now moving smoothly upwards, coursing to the surface on its shortening cable. The *Voyager* was reeling in its damaged probe.

Dansk said quietly, 'Now we need a miracle.'

Captain Beckett slipped out of the centre seat at the console and announced, 'I'm going below.' He opened the hatch which led down to the conference room and his cabin and disappeared.

Dansk and Bell exchanged looks of mutual disgust for the captain. Dansk added to the gloom, 'What do we tell Kathy?'

―――――――――― 13 ――――――――――

Captain William Beckett sat at the small leather-topped desk in his cabin completing an entry in the log. More than two hours had passed but the bathysphere was still not out of the water. He shared the gradual resignation which had settled on the ship that the news would eventually be bad.

The music brought back memories of his aunt at the grand piano in the bay window of her musty Massachusetts boarding house which overlooked the Atlantic. He had realized only long after she was dead how much love she had offered and he had spurned. He derived some solace from the music she had played. The piece ended, the memory faded and Beckett turned back the pages of the log wishing it was as easy to roll back time.

The intercom buzzed. Beckett leaned across the desk and switched it on.

Bell said, 'Still no contact with Saturn, sir. Another thirty minutes before she's up.'

'Where's Dansk? I asked to see him.'

'He should be on his way. He's been to talk to Kathy.'

'I want him here, now.'

'Yes, sir,' Bell replied.

Beckett ended the conversation by punching the privacy button back on. He felt himself surrounded by undisciplined civilians and a naval crew untrained for a top-secret mission. He studied the previous day's log.

He had written that the Englishman was keen to dive and that this coincided with his own wishes. But, with the ominous silence from the deep, he was glad he had also recorded that Peters and Nicholson had rigorously tested the bathysphere and declared it safe to make the dive.

Beckett was disturbed by the turn of events. It was not that he feared a further death. Since early childhood when his parents had both been killed in a car crash, and through a long, tough naval career, he had become hardened to the sudden quirks of fate which end lives abruptly. What upset him was the threat to the success of the mission. He was in no doubt that his career was on the line.

The dilemma remained unresolved: how to bring the cobalt to the surface in time for the rendezvous with the cargo ships.

There was a knock on the door to the deck.

'Enter,' Beckett said, swinging round in his chair.

Bertil Dansk, the mining engineer, appeared.

81

'You wanted to see me?'

'The excuse from the bridge is that the bathysphere has got heavier. What's yours?'

'I wasn't prepared to leave Kathy by herself. Not after preparing her for bad news about Saul. The doctor's with her now.'

Beckett backed off. 'A sensible precaution,' he said. 'There's still time for you to show me the mining rig. Your clamps are finally working, I understand.'

'Yes, we finished this morning.' Dansk drew breath. 'You're not thinking of sending the mining head down?'

'That's always been the only way we'll ever get the nodules up, Mr Dansk.'

'I'd advise against it in the circumstances.'

'I'll be the judge of that. Your job is to keep the mining rig in working order. And you haven't overly impressed me.' Beckett stared coldly at Dansk. 'When I want your views – if I want your views – I'll ask for them. Until then, keep them to yourself.'

'What's it going to take before you abandon this mission?' Dansk asked. 'How many more deaths?'

'I don't have to explain myself to you,' Beckett said. 'Remember that. We're part of a war – a resources war, maybe – but a war nevertheless. It's fought around the world in many ways, with guns, with politics, with aid. You may prefer to leave it to others to protect your freedom. Now, are you going to show me the rig or aren't you?'

Dansk turned and led the way out on deck into sunshine, past the winch noisily reeling in Saturn and towards the ungainly shape of Bottom Miner which sat on its caterpillar tracks, snout dangling forward to the deck like an animal feeding. He reached the bottom of the 120-foot mining rig beside the open hold stacked with pipe. Without turning back, he climbed the metal ladderway to the first platform and then started on another long perpendicular ladder to the second platform, about halfway up the rig, where the assembly clamps heat-moulded lengths of pipe together. Dansk moved lithely for a heavy man.

Beckett gripped the metal handrails on either side of the

steps and set off, hand over hand, foot over foot, following the mining engineer. Beckett's commando training had been more than twenty years ago in the mid-West. But he had stayed fit. His first active service had been with an elite hovercraft recce team in Vietnam. He had become a tough and ruthless fighter, able to kill without compunction ever since he had seen a colleague catch the full force of a grenade thrown by a boy no more than ten years old.

He reached the first platform and looked at the ship below. The automatic pipe feed rose from the hold to the platform. He began to climb the second set of steps. When in Vietnam, he had been recruited to a secret naval force operating under CIA command. He had taken part in the mining of Haiphong harbour. Thereafter he had gone wherever the naval force went. He had travelled the world and won promotion. Recently he had found himself leading secret landings in El Salvador.

He gripped the metal handrail tightly and stopped climbing for a moment. The images swept over him – blood, bodies and jungle green. They were vivid and he concentrated to control the horror hammering in his head. He had led a small group of men from a landing craft to ambush rebels in a jungle village. Unknown to him, local government troops had just taken over the village. He had guessed the truth seconds too late – after giving the order to attack. Once the massacre had started, he let it continue. His decision was logical and inhuman. Americans were not supposed to be in the country except as advisors. Survivors would embarrass American interests.

At the subsequent investigation, held in camera, he was befriended by the Coordinator. He escaped censure for the fiasco and readily acceded to the Coordinator's suggestion of a quiet job in intelligence in Geneva. His exile had lasted almost exactly a year.

Beckett's giddy spell had passed. He climbed the last few steps and found Dansk waiting for him on the second platform.

'Are you all right?' Dansk inquired.

Beckett nodded.

'These are the assembly clamps.'

Beckett looked where Dansk pointed.

'That's what stopped the mining head going down?' Beckett asked, astonished.

'Yes, the heat elements are inside here,' Dansk pulled open one half of the gleaming, thick circular band. 'They join the lengths of pipe with a heat seal. The pipe is fed in from the hold to the first platform, and then raised up there.' Dansk pointed above them to the top of the rig. 'And then it's moulded to the top of the previous length waiting here. It's an automatic process – and a lot more complicated than it looks. There are two men on this platform to supervise. Just in case. They keep an eye on speed and temperature and the hoist. On that.' Dansk indicated a control panel enclosed in a booth in one corner of the platform.

Beckett looked around him. He was only halfway up the rig but the deck seemed a very long way down. He gazed around the empty horizon.

'Why won't you radio?' Dansk suddenly asked.

'Not that again,' Beckett said. The question surprised him. The mining engineer persisted despite all efforts at dissuasion. Beckett took a direct tack. 'It would broadcast our presence to anyone listening in. The cargo ships are less than a week away. I'll be happy to ship the Kipling woman out then. Satisfied?' He felt inside the neck of his short-sleeved white cotton jacket and pulled out a couple of inches of gold chain hooked around a finger. 'Until then, this should make my position crystal clear. The transmitter key is on this chain. Anyone who wants to use the radio has to take it from me.'

Beckett didn't like the look of contempt he saw spread across Dansk's face. He was startled for a moment when he saw Dansk dig deep in his pocket.

Dansk produced a pipe and then a lighter. This was not Beckett's territory. Up here, the captain lacked confidence.

The klaxon on the bridge sounded.

'At last,' Dansk said. He stuffed pipe and lighter back into his trousers and started down the metal ladder without waiting for Beckett.

Beckett followed more slowly. He glanced down and saw

Dansk on the first platform. When Beckett reached it, Dansk was almost back on deck. Beckett stared at where the winch cable met the sea. He saw a dark shadow rise, quickly grow larger and then the bright yellow bathysphere came clear of the water.

Beckett went down the second metal ladder as the crane swung Saturn, dripping seawater, across the mid-decks. Two sailors stood by the cradle waiting to secure it. As Beckett moved closer, he saw Dansk gesticulating vigorously to Nicholson. Beckett could not at first hear what the mining chief shouted. Crossing the deck, he saw Kathy sheltering close to the doctor who had her arm protectively around the woman.

'It's open,' Dansk was yelling to Nicholson.

Beckett understood. He saw water slop out of the open hatch as the bathysphere was lowered, swinging gently, towards the cradle.

The doctor understood too. She pulled Kathy tighter.

Nicholson was first up the cradle steps and peered inside. The engineer lowered himself three-quarters of the way in, paused to take a deep breath and then dropped from sight. A few moments later, Nicholson's head appeared through the hatch, his hair matted with water. He conferred with Dansk who stood on the top step and Dansk took Nicholson's arm to help him out. Water dripped from Nicholson's clothes.

Beckett waited grimly at the bottom of the steps.

'It's full of water,' Dansk said, approaching the captain. 'There's no body.'

'You'd better tell the women. Get them out of the way below deck,' Beckett said. He went up the steps towards Nicholson who looked wet and miserable. 'You're sure he's not inside?'

'Certain,' Nicholson snapped. 'You can't lose a corpse inside a diving bell.'

Beckett lifted the hatch cover which hung quite normally against its hinge. He let it fall back with a dull clunk against the sphere.

'There's no way Saul could have opened it,' Nicholson said. 'It's impossible because of the pressure.'

'What's this here? These marks.' Beckett pointed at some gouged metal a couple of feet from the hatch rim. 'That looks fresh.'

'It wasn't like that when it went down,' Nicholson said.

'I want a report on the damage. In twenty-four hours.'

'Yes, Captain.'

'Now, get yourself some help,' Beckett said. 'Do whatever needs to be done with the pressure grab.'

Nicholson called to two miners standing at the foot of the crane, 'Hey Wilkins, and you, Butcher. Here a minute.'

Beckett watched the men move forward. He saw Nicholson jab a finger towards the underside of the bathysphere and disappear from sight to join the two miners on the far side.

Beckett turned back to the open hatch and looked inside. The wrecked compartment lay under water which came to within a few inches of the hatch rim. The stark skeleton of the empty central seat rippled before his eyes.

There was a metallic thud and then a curse from the deck below. Beckett withdrew his head from the hatch opening and leaned over the handrail around the small platform at the top of the steps. Nicholson and the miners had disengaged the pressure grab from the retracted connecting arm. One of the miners shook a hand ruefully and then examined it. Beckett heard Nicholson tell the man to be more careful and then the three of them, each with a hold on the grab, carried the heavy prize towards the main steps leading below deck.

Nicholson turned and shouted back to the captain. 'I'll be back for the scoop. There's a tube worm. I can see it through the mesh.'

The ship's company was in shock at the second major accident in three days. All navy crew had been summoned to the bridge for a firm pep-talk by the captain; while the miners at their end of the boat grumbled and plotted, fuelled by beer and bourbon.

Nicholson had changed into dry clothes and sat with Dansk in the canteen. They had left Kathy and the doctor alone in the lab and their conversation had turned to practicalities.

'I think the tube worm is more urgent,' Nicholson was saying. 'It was completely unprotected.'

'So what's to be done?' Dansk asked, contemplating his empty bottle of Michelob on the scratched formica tabletop. 'We're not trained for lab work.'

'I agree. It's hopeless.'

'Kathy's the only one left.'

'If you delay dissection for too long, the change in pressure destroys the shape of the organs and decay sets in,' Nicholson explained. 'Maybe the doctor can do something to preserve it,' Dansk suggested.

'Listen, who cares? What's it matter when two people are dead?' Nicholson drained his glass. He shouted to the kitchen hand across the other side of the canteen who was wiping down tables, 'Two more beers, Rico.'

The man nodded, left the plastic bowl with dirty crockery, went to the hatch and shouted, 'Santini, two beers.' He brought the two bottles to the table and uncapped them.

'What a fuck-up,' Nicholson said. 'No, not you, Rico. Thanks.' The kitchen hand went back to his clearing up.

'Do you realize,' Nicholson addressed Dansk, 'the man who used to look after Saturn for the Institute retired in January after seventeen years? Never had a serious accident. The first fatalities in seventeen years and they're on my first trip.' Nicholson snorted his indignation, 'Beckett will blame me, too.'

'Don't let him get to you. He's a bastard.'

'He was right about one thing. There are strange marks around the outside of the hatch.'

'From where he scraped the lava?' Dansk suggested.

'Another thing. How did that hatch open? Saul didn't explode the hinges. Even if he had, it wouldn't have made a damned difference at that depth, and you can't open the hatch manually until pressure inside is roughly the same as outside.'

'Until pressure outside is equal to that inside.'

'Same difference,' Nicholson said. 'Just as impossible six miles down.'

'Except that if Saul didn't explode the hinges, there *is* no way of opening it from inside. Not even for Houdini.'

'I'm beginning to think we're cursed.'

'Ships do get jinxed,' Dansk said. He held up the stub of his left forefinger. 'The day after I lost my finger, a man was killed by a wrench which dropped out of the top of the rig. Another man died of shock the same week after his arm was ripped off in the drill assembly. There were fights, accidents, broken drill bits. Within three weeks, the drill hole was abandoned.'

'Maybe Beckett will see the light and cancel this crazy mission,' Nicholson finished his beer from the bottle. 'Let's get back. There's got to be something we can do.'

'I thought you were a selfish, devious bugger when we set out,' Dansk said.

'And now?'

'Maybe I misjudged you.'

'I'd never have believed you were superstitious,' Nicholson said as the man walked out of the canteen and down the corridor.

'Too damned right I am,' Dansk said. 'Anyone who works long enough in mining or oil gets to be. Disaster or a lucky strike can come at any time. You start by looking for signs. You end up living your life by them.'

The two men walked through the open lab door. Nicholson saw Dr Mendoza in the lab's rest area standing beside the settee. He couldn't see but he assumed Kathy was still stretched out on it.

Dansk walked over to the pressure grab which sat untouched on Herbie's workbench exactly where it had been left.

Nicholson stepped around the empty mesh scoop lying on the floor and looked at the worm which lay in one of the aluminium sinks curled like a bicycle inner tube under water. It was white over its full three-foot length except for a reddish gill-like crown protruding at one end.

Helen Mendoza emerged from the rest area. She joined the two men at the sink.

'How is she?' Dansk asked.

The doctor raised her eyebrows and gave a shrug. 'Alert. She seems calmer – resigned – now it's all over.'

'That's understandable,' Dansk said.

'What are we going to do with this tube worm?' Nicholson asked the doctor.

'Ask it what happened to Saul?'

Mendoza, Dansk and Nicholson were each startled at the sound of Kathy's voice. They turned to see her standing in the doorway between the lab and the rest area. She appeared composed and held a cup and saucer in her hand.

'Are you OK?' Mendoza asked.

'Don't fuss, Helen. There's work to do. There's an insulation jacket and heater that needs fitting to the grab before we start decompression. The sooner we start the sooner we can take a look at the fish.'

'Are you up to this?' Dansk asked.

Kathy nodded. 'Will you stay and help, Helen? You can keep an eye on me at the same time, stop me doing away with myself with a scalpel.'

Helen Mendoza smiled. 'I'll stay,' she said.

'Emptying the pressure grab after decompression is going to be heavy work. Too heavy for us.' Kathy's concerns were fiercely practical. She appeared determined to ignore what had happened.

'I'd be happy to help,' Nicholson said.

'You'd better clear that with the captain,' Dansk said.

'I won't need you till tomorrow, Carl,' Kathy said. 'It will probably take twenty-four hours to decompress the grab.'

'Well I've got to prepare some sort of report on Saturn,' Nicholson said. 'And then I could always fix that extractor fan in here.'

'About time too,' Kathy said. 'Dissecting the tube worm could get smelly. And I'd like to be able to keep the lab door shut – if only to keep the captain out. I'll feel more secure.' Kathy paused, allowing reality to intrude for a moment, and then said quietly, 'It's going to be lonely with Herbie dead and Saul gone. You know, I can't think of him as dead when there's no body.'

14

For a long while there was nothing – just a blackness, a total lack of sensation. Then slowly, fragments of the outside world started to break through. A sliver of sound intruded. A half-formed thought swam closer, lingered, then disappeared.

When Saul first opened his eyes, it took a surge of effort, a mighty concentration, to make sense of what was happening. Bending over him was a young man, with dark hair cut severely short and eyes that bore an Oriental slant.

The man grinned and patted Saul on the shoulder. Saul felt nothing. The man's mouth moved but the words made no sense. Waves of sound washed around inside his head, echoing inchoately. Saul struggled to sit but found he could hardly move. He became aware of pain, of swollen, tender flesh, of a hard mattress. He wondered if his eardrums had burst. The effort of staying awake became too much. The man's face dissolved and darkness descended.

The next time he awoke, the face had changed. This face was older and partly covered by a ginger beard. Once again, the man's speech made no sense.

Saul felt as if something had snapped inside his head. He began to feel afraid. When he tried to speak his lips moved but no sound emerged. His head throbbed and his throat burned. Unconnected images flickered through his mind. He remembered moments from the dive and then the heat – especially the choking heat. The moment he had known he would die caught up with him. He began to feel himself fade away.

The man at his bedside stood and disappeared from Saul's narrow field of vision. He returned seconds later with a hypodermic.

Dimly, Saul felt the needle sink into his arm. There was no further pain. He greeted the tide of blackness like an old friend.

When Saul next awoke, he was alone in darkness. His head was clearer. There was a tightness across his chest and a foul taste, a taste of sickness, in his mouth. He tried to sit up and accomplished the movement. His lungs hurt him and his windpipe burned as he breathed. His body ached. After a few seconds of giddiness, Saul eased himself off the bed and tried to stand. His legs felt like lead balloons. He took his first step and then, more confidently, another. He groped his way around the room until he found the light switch. For a moment or two he was dazzled.

As his eyes adjusted, Saul saw a small cabin, with metal walls and a curved ceiling. There was no porthole. He was not in the *Voyager*. Saul had no idea where he was, or how he had got there. But at least he was alive.

'You made it, you lucky bastard,' he said to himself. 'Escaped from the jaws of death like a bloody comic-strip hero.'

Saul was naked except for his underpants. His skin was bloated and pink. He saw the foil insulation suit he had been wearing in Saturn draped over the back of a metal-framed chair.

The room contained a single bed and a single metal locker. In one corner was a washbasin and a mirror. Saul went to the mirror. He hardly recognized himself. The face which squinted back at him had a light stubble, but what shocked was the red, raw skin. It was sore to the touch. When he looked at his hands, he saw that the fingers were fat and puffy.

Saul was without his watch. He had no idea of the time, whether it was day or night. Because there was no porthole, he assumed he was well below decks. Yet if that was the case, he reasoned, he should feel the vibration of engines. All he could hear was a light, high-pitched hum, a sound totally unfamiliar to him.

Saul became irritated. He crossed to the door. The handle turned but the door was locked. He rapped on the sheet metal panel. The impact hurt his knuckles. There was no response. He walked back to the sink and tried the taps. They worked. He filled the basin and splashed water on to his face. He cupped his hands under the running tap and drank. His parched throat stung.

Pulling out the top drawer of the metal locker, Saul examined its contents. There was a pile of men's underwear, several pairs of white tennis socks and a small framed photograph. This showed a man and a woman and two children. Saul recognized the man as the younger of the two who had sat by his bed. In the photograph he wore a fur hat. The family group was posed stiffly on a porch, the adults leaning against a wooden railing. The woman was well wrapped against the cold. There was snow on the ground and fir trees in the distance. The sky beyond was blue. He checked the clothes in the drawer. They bore no labels. He carried a cardigan with him back to the door and thumped on it again, wincing at the pain in his fist. He felt weak and giddy.

Saul returned to the bed, dropped the cardigan and stretched himself out under the sheet. The exertion had exhausted him. He remained thirsty but he dared not try to reach the sink again. He still did not know the nationality of the vessel but he had begun to feel himself a prisoner. He faded into a deep, dreamless sleep while waiting for the door to open.

15

Nicholson spent Saturday morning examining Saturn. First he drained it of seawater. Then he crossed off on the safety check sheet all instruments which had been damaged by heat, change of pressure or saltwater. The bathysphere appeared watertight, the flotation ring had survived and the two mechanical arms still worked. He disconnected the two arms at the shoulder, removed the wrecked cameras and their gantries and freed the ballast lever which had jammed, probably after impact with the lava or the cliff face.

It was the marks around the outside of the hatch rim

which puzzled Nicholson. They had a symmetry and even-ness which made him doubt that they had been sustained accidentally during Saturn's turbulent time on the seabed. But there was no other explanation available.

It was mid-afternoon before Nicholson delivered his report to the captain on the bridge. Dansk, Bell and Hend-erson were compiling, with the computer's assistance, a map correlating elevations and temperature readings on the seabed, preparatory, Dansk confided, to a descent of Bottom Miner sometime in the next couple of days. The mood of the men seemed sombre; the air charged with tension. Nicholson helped himself to a paper cupful of water from the dispenser but was dismissed with a curt, 'You can go,' from the captain.

The atmosphere in the lab was altogether different. Kathy and the doctor greeted him warmly and bent their heads back over the dissection tray, cutting, scraping, preparing slides, fully absorbed in their work. They hardly spoke. The one constant sound in the room was the regular hum of the equipment servicing the bank of fish tanks which lined the lab's corridor wall. The smell of formal-dehyde was pervasive.

Nicholson took a closer look at the tube worm before settling down to strip the extractor fan. The worm's white casing had been sliced down its full length. The red flesh inside, occupying about half of the tube, lay exposed like a turtle without its shell. Nicholson stared in wonder at the brilliant soft organ. He regarded the innards of the extractor fan more prosaically.

Nicholson left the lab twice, once for some tools and copper wire with which he fashioned a new coil for the extractor's electric motor, and the second time for a meal in the canteen. It took him two hours to mend the fan. When he had finished, he proudly announced, 'Ladies, your attention please.'

Kathy and the doctor looked up from their work. Both peeled off their plastic gloves and pulled down their facemasks.

Nicholson plugged the extractor lead into its socket and smiled broadly when the fan began to spin.

The doctor clapped her hands. 'I'll make some coffee to celebrate,' she said and went through to the rest area.

'What's that you're doing?' Nicholson asked Kathy, coming over to the workbench.

Kathy was preparing several Petri dishes for the lab's incubator. 'This is agar. It's a jelly made from seaweed, rich in minerals. Bacteria grow well in it.' She added the jelly to the flat circular glass dishes with their distinctive raised lip, and then carried a tray of them to the incubator which stood between the entrance to the rest area and the deepfreeze.

'And what about the worm?' Nicholson watched Kathy return to the workbench, enjoying the swing of her hips under the white cotton lab coat. Her face betrayed a legacy of night-time tears but she moved confidently and exuded enthusiasm.

'It's fascinating,' Kathy said. 'The white tube is to protect the body of the worm and anchors it to the rock. The worm can't move. It's got no mouth and no gut.'

'How does it eat?' Nicholson asked.

'I can't pretend we've solved that all by ourselves. But from the descriptions of Barnard and Beainy on *Alvin*,' Kathy pointed to a volume lying on Saul's workbench, 'it seems we've got much the same animal they found in the Galapagos. Their worms absorbed some inorganic food through the red crown at the top of the tube. But they also found that the worm's blood helped to create bacteria inside the worm which in turn provide energy.'

'Is that really blood?'

'Yes, it's bright red because of the haemoglobin molecule – about fifty times larger than in man.'

'Amazing.'

'Here's some coffee,' Mendoza said, returning from the rest area with a tray.

'We can shut that door now the fan's working,' Kathy said. She went and pushed the heavy steel security door closed, checked that the monitor above the door showed the corridor and tested the electronic door release. 'Wonderful,' she said. 'I'm going to sleep in here again tonight, Helen. It's not necessary for you to stay again.'

'Are you sure?'

'You're the other side of the corridor. No way could I face sleeping in my cabin yet. It reminds me of Herbie. His clothes are there. I'll pick up anything I need. I've even got a small kitchen here.'

'And a walk-in freezer,' Nicholson said.

The women laughed.

'I wouldn't want to eat what's in it,' the doctor said.

'You'd be surprised,' Kathy said. 'Saul put in some sourdough bread,' Kathy's voice trailed away. 'And vodka, and some chocolate.' She forced herself to smile. 'I could hole up in here for a week with no trouble.'

'Well I'm hungry right now,' the doctor said. 'We worked through since lunch.'

'You'll miss the fish,' Kathy said.

'I've had enough excitement for one day. I'm pooped.'

'Thanks for everything, Helen.'

'It was fascinating.' The doctor looked at Kathy. 'Make sure you call me if you change your mind about sleeping here alone.' She looked at Nicholson, 'Make sure she does.'

After Mendoza had left, Kathy fetched Nicholson a lab coat and then examined the pressure grab on Herbie's workbench. It was wrapped in a heated insulation jacket. For more than twenty-four hours, since 8 p.m. the previous evening, the pressure inside the metal container had been escaping through a decompression valve attached to one side of the metal grab. According to the dial set in the valve, the grab's contents were now at surface pressure. Whatever was inside could be safely transferred to an open tank.

Under Kathy's direction, Nicholson placed a large empty tank next to the grab on the workbench. He ran a hose from the seawater inlet feed near the bank of fishtanks across the lab to the empty tank and half filled it. He inserted a heating element and thermometer. They waited while the water temperature slowly rose to 40°C.

'That's as hot as it will go. It'll have to do,' Kathy said. 'Now that the moment's come, I don't think I can bear to watch.'

'Why not?' Nicholson tried to unscrew the nuts fixing

the inspection plate to the top of the pressure grab. He put all his strength into the effort but without success.

'The temperature in the grab may have fallen too low. It may have decompressed too fast,' Kathy said. 'The fish could be dead.' Kathy went and sat at the far end of the lab at Saul's workbench, on Saul's stool. She fingered the buttons of his intercom nervously.

Nicholson selected a larger wrench from the toolkit he had used to mend the extractor fan. This time the nuts moved, slowly at first, until he was able to remove them one by one with his fingers.

'We'll know soon enough,' Nicholson loosened the final nut and slid the inspection plate out of position. 'I can't see anything in here.'

'Use a net. There's one on the hook by the freezer.'

Nicholson collected the net and poked it inside the pressure grab. 'My God. Whatever it is, it's alive,' he said.

Kathy sank her head into her hands. 'I can't watch.'

Nicholson swept the pressure grab from one end to the other with the net. He felt weight and then a violent movement inside the net. Warm water splashed out of the grab. Nicholson had grown up with the thrill of fishing for tuna with his father from the back of a motor launch. But his anticipation had never been greater. With both hands gripping the wooden handle, he lifted the net out of the grab.

For a moment, he was unable to see any shape to the weight at the bottom of the net. Then he detected one end twisting – the tail. The fish was about two feet long and resembled a fat eel – a fat, humped eel.

'I've got it, Kathy,' Nicholson said.

Kathy peeked through her fingers. 'Get it in the tank.'

Nicholson swung the net over the half-full tank. The edge of the net caught on one corner. Nicholson changed his grip on the handle and used his right hand to free the netting. As he did so, the fish thrashed, brushing the back of his hand. Nicholson quickly lowered the net into the water and then inverted it. The fish, confined to the lower half of the tank, snaked madly around the glass. Slowly it became calmer until it hovered stationary, tail undulating lazily from side to side.

Kathy could restrain herself no longer. She ran forward to see the fish. She drew in her breath sharply as she gazed at the animal which had lured her husband and her lover six miles down into the deepwater. 'My God, it's got no eyes.'

'Vicious bugger,' Nicholson said, looking at the back of his right hand for the first time. There was a long but bloodless diagonal scratch from the root of his thumb to the base of his little finger.

Kathy stared at the fish. Its eyeless snout featured a small mouth in the centre and pulsing cheeks. About one-third of the way down its body, there was a hollow cavity from which two short stubs protruded. The gills resembled limbs.

'It's almost exactly the same as one of the pictures Herbie built up with the computer. If I can retrieve it,' she was speaking as much to herself as to Nicholson, 'I can get back to Herbie's hypothesis.' Kathy moved to the terminal near Saul's workbench at the far end of the lab. 'Carl, transfer some water from the pressure grab and fill the tank while I do this. Use the siphon. The fish probably prefers its own seawater.'

Kathy switched on the terminal, keyed in the user code and her password – 'Good evening, Mrs Kipling,' appeared on the screen – and began to track down Herbie's fish projection studies based on the tail fragment he had analysed.

'What about the nodules?' Nicholson asked.

'Keep them separate,' Kathy said, her back towards him.

Nicholson peered into the grab through the open inspection cover. On an instinct, he rolled up his sleeve and dipped his hand inside. He had to stand on tiptoe and lean in most of the way up to his shoulder to reach the bottom of the grab. He felt some rough lumps, the size of large pebbles, and withdrew a fistful.

Nicholson stared at the red-black ore in his hand. The

nodules were a different colour to those he was used to. One small lump glinted. The glint held promise.

Kathy was tapping away at the terminal. Nicholson dropped the handful of nodules into the pocket of his lab coat. He slipped his hand into the grab again. The saltwater stung the back of his hand where the fish had scratched him. He dropped the extra nodules straight into the lab coat pocket and took another look at his hand. It was no more than a graze, but it was beaded with blood now in one or two places.

Kathy turned round, saying, 'This is going to take time. I'll have to settle down to it later.' She saw Nicholson inspecting his hand. 'What's that?'

'It's just a nick.'

'You should be wearing gloves. Put some on. There's a pack by the sinks.'

'Too late now,' Nicholson said. He put his hand to his mouth and licked the blood away.

'How did it happen?'

'I think the fish caught me through the net as I tipped it into the tank.'

'Do you want a Bandaid?'

'No, there's not really any blood.'

'Well, you've done a grand job, Carl. Let me help you get that water into the tank.'

Nicholson held one end of the siphon in the grab while Kathy squeezed the suction bladder. A column of water rose through the hose and began to flow freely into the fishtank. The fish puffed its cheeks and pumped its small jaw in the jet of water.

'That'll do,' Kathy said. 'Get an empty tank for the rest.'

The procedure was repeated until the pressure grab was emptied. Only the nodules remained.

Kathy fetched a small canvas bag from a cupboard under the sinks and handed Nicholson a pair of disposable gloves. 'Do you think you can reach the nodules?' she asked.

'Let me try.' Nicholson put the gloves on and then plunged one hand into the grab as he had done a few minutes earlier. 'Yes, here they are,' he said withdrawing a handful.

Kathy looked at the nodules in Nicholson's gloved palm. 'So that's cobalt. Big deal. Put them in this.' She passed Nicholson the canvas bag.

Kathy observed the fish closely while Nicholson filled the bag.

'That's the lot,' he said, feeling around the bottom of the grab. 'What now?'

'It's past 10 p.m.,' Kathy said, looking at the lab clock. 'I'm bushed. The captain can wait for his bits of rock.' She opened the top drawer of Herbie's workbench and said, 'Stick them in here.'

'You want to call it a day?' Nicholson asked, dropping the bag in and pushing the drawer shut.

'I guess I'll stare at the fish for a while longer. And I'll get to grips with the computer. But there's nothing further you can do tonight. I'll do some biopsies and other tests tomorrow – if you're still interested.' Kathy smiled at Nicholson and put an arm on his shoulder, 'I want to thank you for today. Sure you're OK?'

'I'll be back first thing,' Nicholson said. 'What are you going to feed it?' he asked as he walked to the door.

'I've got a multi-nutrient jelly. *Haute cuisine* compared with what it's used to. I must add some hydrogen sulphide to the water. If I need human flesh, I'll be sure and let you know.' She smiled. 'Hey, hang the lab coat in the cupboard.'

Nicholson disengaged the door lock. 'I'll bring it back, don't worry,' he said and turned into the corridor.

Nicholson walked back to his cabin. As soon as he got inside he emptied the coat pocket on to his bed. He switched on the bedside light and held the nodules up one by one under the glare. He was disappointed. He couldn't find the one which had glinted so promisingly at him. Had he mislaid it? He was certain he hadn't.

Nicholson collected the nodules together and dropped them all into the fishtank. They disturbed the moray eel which had been coiled like a snake, head erect. It darted around the glass cage, baring its needle-shaped teeth as Nicholson pushed the nodules into the sand at the bottom of the tank with his net handle. He tapped the glass and pulled a face. 'Gift for you, old buddy.'

He settled back on the bed tired at the end of a long day. He would go to the canteen for a drink in a minute. His hand throbbed. He blinked and flexed his hand. It was sore. He tied a handkerchief around it clumsily, with his good hand. He yawned and wriggled further down the bed until he was stretched out. He let his eyes shut.

16

The moray eel curled and slithered its way around the cramped fishtank while Nicholson lay on the bed, tossing in his sleep. The moon and stars shone white, chill light into the cabin. Nicholson's forehead was beaded in sweat. He began to grind his teeth. Then he bared them, grimaced and woke up.

The nightmare receded as soon as he opened his eyes. He wiped his brow with his hand. It was still tender. He felt sweaty all over. As he raised his head he saw a damp patch on his pillow. The bedcover felt sticky. He swung himself upright and then stood to open the porthole.

There was an open can of beer on the table beside the bed and Nicholson drained it to slake his thirst. He felt feverish. He drew back the covers and undressed before slipping into the bed and pulling the blanket around his shoulders. Determined to break the fever, he turned on his side and waited for sleep to overtake him.

His mind filled with familiar images. He saw the yellow bathysphere resting on its cradle on the deck. He remembered it waterlogged and the shock he had felt at Saul's death. Nicholson had little respect for authority but Saul had been different. What at first he had taken as aloofness, he had grown to regard as thoughtfulness. First Herbie Kipling, then Saul. This was a dangerous trip. He imagined Kathy nestled under a blanket on the settee in the lab.

Nicholson drifted into sleep dreaming of Kathy finding comfort in his arms. Then he saw Bob Wilkins, his best friend among the miners, rush towards him with a wild look in his eyes, holding a box. Silently the miner directed his attention to the box. Nicholson lifted the lid and peered in. Inside was a mound of nodules, among them several with rich veins of precious stone. Nicholson went further into the box and the nodules vanished. He faced a blank wall, turned, saw another and then another. He counted six different walls.

In the sixth, Nicholson caught sight of his own reflection. His head was balding, and his shoulders sagged. On the next wall was the image of his mother, in a picture frame, just as it had always stood on his father's mantelpiece in the wood-framed house that had been home in Coconut Grove, south of Miami.

With horror, Nicholson realized that he was standing on his father's grave. There was one big bunch of flowers and three mourners whom he barely recognized. As he struggled to put names to the long faces, he became elated. For there in the distance was his father. Father put a protective arm round his son. But then from above them came a long shrill whistle. A naval officer was being piped on board. The figure assumed the gaunt shape of Captain Beckett.

The officer removed reflecting sunglasses with slow deliberation. His eyes were hollow. The man separated Nicholson from his father. Nicholson went cold with fear and struggled to intervene. He was unable to move. He watched helplessly as the naval officer brandished a scroll of paper tied with pink ribbon. There was a badge on the man's chest. Nicholson strained to see. It read, 'Retired'. Now the ex-navy officer stood with a foot imperiously placed on the bottom rung of a ladder. At the top Nicholson's father stood, paint can in one hand, brush in the other. The sign above the jetty read '. . . olson's yard'. The letters disappeared one by one as Nicholson saw his father forced to paint himself out of existence. The man at the base of the ladder had stripes of blood on his arm to signify rank and a chestful of medals. He laughed with a deep, hearty roar as the last of the letters disappeared under the paint. He took his foot from the bottom rung and Nicholson, heart tripping, saw the ladder slide, his father fall . . . and then he woke.

The moray eel made another turn in the fishtank. Nicholson's breathing returned to normal. He had not had that dream about his father on the ladder for a long time. At one time it recurred every few weeks. Then the interval had become months. Just as he began to think it was banished forever, it would return.

Nicholson felt his brow with the fingers of his good hand. It was cold and clammy. Yet his pulse beat inside his temples with a terrible ferocity. He looked at his watch and saw it was 2.30 a.m. He threw off the covers. Nicholson knew he needed medical attention. He used the wall to steady himself and shuffled towards the small bathroom by the door. He took a dressing gown from behind the door, slipped it on and left the cabin.

Once in the corridor, Nicholson moved slowly down the passage. He passed the silent canteen, the kitchens and the entrance to the laboratory. He stopped and listened. The ship lay still and quiet. Mendoza's cabin was next to the sickbay. She would be asleep. But Nicholson was beyond caring. He knocked loudly on the doctor's door.

A voice full of sleep replied, 'What? Who is it?'

'Sorry, Nicholson.'

A moment later the door opened and Nicholson almost fell on top of Helen Mendoza in her flannel pyjamas.

'What's up?' she asked. 'Is it Kathy?'

'I'm burning up. Sorry to wake you like this.'

'You look like death, dear boy. Let's get you next door.'

The doctor put on a dressing gown and then steered Nicholson towards the sickbay. Once inside, she turned on the lights and disappeared to her office to collect a thermometer and stethoscope.

Nicholson waited beside one of the three beds in the room. Each could be curtained off separately, but the curtains were open and the beds empty. There was a fourth empty bed in a glassed-in booth which served as an emergency operating theatre. One of two doors on the far side of the room led to the bathroom. The doctor reappeared through the other door from her office, a stethoscope hanging round her neck.

'I'm sure it's just a fever,' Nicholson said. 'Can you give me something to stop this hammer in my head?'

'Tell me from the beginning.'

Nicholson recounted his sudden illness and answered the doctor's questions. No, he hadn't ever felt like this before. Yes, he had eaten dinner. In the canteen, early in the evening before mending the extractor fan. He'd had the chicken. Yes, he'd seen other people eating it too. He'd felt fine in the lab.

'We'll see,' Mendoza said. 'It could be a busy night. Food poisoning can produce a sudden, violent fever. Have you had any cramps? Nausea?'

'I'm hot and cold all over and someone's still quarrying stone in my head.' Nicholson managed a weak smile.

Mendoza produced a thermometer from her dressing gown pocket. She shook it down, examined the mercury and said, 'Put this in and let's see how high it is.'

Nicholson did as he was told and sat mute at the edge of the bed with the thermometer in his mouth.

The doctor took Nicholson's left wrist and felt his pulse. She yawned, apologized and yawned again. After a minute, she removed the thermometer and held it up against the light.

'No wonder you feel dreadful,' she said, 'It's 103°F. Aspirin. Lots of it. Get into bed. You're staying here where I can keep an eye on you. And I'll get you something to help you sleep.'

Nicholson needed little encouragement to lean back on the fluffed pillows.

'What's that?' Mendoza asked, noticing the mark on Nicholson's right hand.

'A scratch,' Nicholson said. 'From the fish.'

'Your moray?'

'No, the fish Saul caught.'

'How on earth . . .? Oh, never mind. It'll get infected

unless you're careful.' The doctor went to the drug cabinet outside her small office. 'What's the fish like?'

'Ugly little monster,' Nicholson said. 'And vicious with it, as you can see. It's not so little really – about two feet. And no eyes. It's weird.'

'Was Kathy all right when you left?'

'Yes. She's incredible, although I don't suppose she's taken it all in yet.'

'That's what worries me,' the doctor said, returning with a tray containing bandage, scissors, antiseptic dab and two types of bubble-packed pill. She put a glass of water on the table at the head of the bed.

'Now give it here.'

Nicholson submitted. The scratch along the top of the hand was puffy but there had been little bleeding. The antiseptic stung. A few moments later his hand was comfortably swathed in bandage.

Mendoza held out the pills. 'With water. All of them.'

When Nicholson woke it was morning. He took in his surroundings. The curtain at the foot of the bed had been drawn closed, cutting him off from the rest of the sickbay. He sat up in the bed, rearranged the pillows and idly scratched an itch on his right arm near the shoulder. He held up his bandaged hand and flexed his fingers. His hand felt no worse.

Nicholson scratched his upper arm again. He turned to examine the itch. What he saw shocked him. The skin had erupted into blisters. Dried blood matted the hairs and there were trickles of fresh blood where he had scratched. He began to itch all over. He inspected his left arm and his chest under the bedclothes. There was nothing unusual he noticed except that the sheets were flecked with blood where he had been lying on his shoulder. His armpit felt swollen and tender. He called out for the doctor.

The office door opened and shut and footsteps crossed the sickbay floor. The curtain was whisked halfway back. Nicholson blinked at the light. Helen Mendoza stood there, dressed in day clothes under a white cotton coat. He remembered the doctor's flannel pyjamas of the night before. The white coat – as he'd already concluded from his weekly visits to the lab for his vitamin B12 injection – lent the doctor her authority.

'Feeling better?'

'Take a look at this.' Nicholson held up his arm.

Mendoza frowned as she inspected the arm. 'That looks painful.' She walked to the other side of the room and filled a small aluminium basin with water.

'How's your head?'

'Better, I think.'

Mendoza returned to the bedside. 'I'll take your temperature in a minute. Let's see what we've got here.'

The doctor arranged a towel under Nicholson's arm. She began to dab at the dried blood with cotton pads. 'This is some reaction. How much does it hurt?'

'It itches something rotten.'

'I'll bet. Keep your arm still.' Mendoza took a pair of tweezers from the trolley. She hooked a corner of a scab and picked it loose. She dabbed a swab on the clear serous fluid underneath, put it into a bottle and screwed on the cap.

'My armpit's also sore.'

The doctor felt. 'Glands,' she pronounced. 'It all points to a toxic reaction of some sort. I still think it's something you ate. But you do have that cut.' Mendoza began to unwrap the dressing she had put on in the middle of the night. 'Tell me some more about this.'

'Nothing to tell really. I was moving the fish from the pressure grab to the tank. It brushed the back of my hand. Just scratched me. It hardly bled.'

'How long before you began to feel ill?'

'Half an hour, maybe less.'

Mendoza was puzzled. 'Well, it's certainly possible.'

'What is?'

'You could be having a toxic reaction to the fish.'

'You mean it poisoned me?'

'In a manner of speaking. Like a jellyfish sting. There are fish – scorpion fish, stingray, that sort of thing – which cause allergic reactions.'

'I suffered from poison ivy pretty badly when I was a kid.'

'Yes, same sort of reaction. Kathy can test the swab I've taken. Toxins can be hard to detect, but she's got all she needs in the lab.' Mendoza wiped some perspiration from her forehead. 'It's hot already.' She looked at her watch. 'Not yet 8 a.m.'

'When can I get out of here?'

'Soon enough, dear boy. Now what did I do with that thermometer? I want to take your temperature.'

Nicholson slipped it under his tongue obediently. Mendoza smiled encouragement and wheeled the trolley back across the room. When she returned, she removed and read the thermometer.

'Still over 100°F. You're staying right here until it's back to normal.'

'Can I get some breakfast?'

'Sure. Breakfast in bed. No Sunday paper, I'm afraid, but I won't let you starve. I want a word with Kathy first, if she's awake. Then I'll call the kitchen.'

Mendoza returned to her small office on the far side of the sickbay and shut the door behind her. She searched in the centre drawer of her desk, found what she was looking for and swallowed two pills with some water from the dispenser just outside the door. She returned to her desk and picked up the phone.

Kathy answered immediately.

'How're you feeling?'

'Not too bad, Helen. I slept. Thought I'd have a shower, maybe we can have breakfast together, and then it's a morning devoted to the fish. It looks exactly the way Herbie thought it might.'

'Make sure you don't touch it.'

'Why ever not?'

'I've got Nicholson here in the sickbay. He came in last night, this morning rather, with a bad fever. He's developed blisters on his arm. He got cut, I gather, by the fish.'

'Not so as you'd notice.'

'You would now. His arm is swollen, blistered, glands

up, temperature still over 100°F. It was 103°F when he woke me.'

'What's he got?'

'Could be toxic. I've taken a swab. Can you check it out?'

'I suppose so. I wanted to get on with the fish. That reminds me, the cultures we took from the tube worm are flourishing.'

'That's good.' Mendoza didn't know at first why the information disturbed her. Then she did. 'Say that again. The bacteria in the incubator are multiplying?'

'Yes, very fast. The change of pressure must agree with them.' Kathy stopped herself. 'Oh, I see what you're getting at.'

'Yes, what if Nicholson's reaction isn't toxic? He probably wasn't infected by the tube worm. But what about the fish?'

Kathy remained silent.

'You're right,' Kathy said. 'The fish could well have the same bacteria.'

'Or other bacteria. Or a virus for that matter. Perhaps you'd better take a look at the fish. Try to grow some cultures. But be careful. I wouldn't wish the sort of reaction Nicholson's had on anyone.'

'Should you impose quarantine?'

'Do you think that's necessary? Even if it is an infection, we've had no indication it's epidemic. You're feeling all right still?'

'Yes, I'm fine,' Kathy said. 'Healthy, at least. I'm still shaken, of course. I keep thinking that without a body, there must be some hope. Then I realize how stupid I'm being. But I can't let go of it.'

'To be expected,' Mendoza said. She had begun to think about Kathy's suggestion. 'Maybe I should start Nicholson on a broad spectrum antibiotic. And you could try some antibiotics on the tube worm bacteria. See what kills them off fastest. It's an extreme precaution but maybe you're right about quarantine – at least until we know more about the swab. We can't be too careful.'

'What's the procedure?'

'I've got the details in my desk somewhere. No breakfast together for sure. We're the ones most at risk.' The doctor let out a sigh of frustration. She leaned across her desk and switched on the tabletop fan. She held her face towards it and closed her eyes. The fan played across her face rippling her hair with its breeze. It felt good. She remembered how it felt to have a man run his fingers through her hair. It was all so many years ago.

While they discussed where to leave the swab and what tests to conduct, the doctor kept her eyes closed and missed what she would otherwise have seen through the glass partition between her office and the sickbay. The outer door to the corridor opened and a miner appeared. It was Bob Wilkins, Nicholson's best friend among the miners. He disappeared out of sight behind the curtain in Nicholson's cubicle.

'Do you have to report this to the captain?' Kathy asked.

'If we move into quarantine, we'll have to do it by the book. I just hope you come up with some sort of toxic finding, and quick. I'll get Nicholson's cabin put out of bounds. We should isolate ourselves for the time being and I'll find out who Nicholson saw after he left you last night.'

'I'll do the chemical analysis first. If I find a toxin, I'll let you know and we can call the whole thing off.'

Mendoza said, 'So I'll put the swab in a quarantine bag outside your door right away.' She put the receiver back on its hook and pulled open the left-hand drawers of the desk one after the other. She reached the bottom drawer, dug under a headscarf, a paperback, some magazines, note-paper and other paraphernalia before she found what she was looking for, a small pamphlet entitled 'Quarantine Regulations'. She skimmed through it.

Once again her attention was not on the sickbay. So she failed to see the miner, Bob Wilkins, return to the door from Nicholson's cubicle, hold a finger to his lips, wink and then disappear into the corridor shutting the door behind him. Had Mendoza seen him, she would regretfully have concluded that sub-section three of paragraph one of the regulations had been breached. A crew member under suspicion of suffering from an unidentified infectious disease of unknown origin had *not* been kept isolated from all except essential medical staff. There had been a breach of the quarantine within minutes of the decision to impose it.

Mendoza left the pamphlet open on her desk. She dropped the swab bottle into a quarantine bag and, after checking that the corridor was empty, deposited it outside the lab. She pressed the buzzer to alert Kathy and slipped back into the sickbay.

'How about breakfast?' Nicholson asked.

'That's next.' Mendoza called the canteen and, offering no explanation, asked for the tray to be left outside the sickbay door.

Nicholson's first reaction to the news of quarantine was an obscenity. His second was to ask, 'How long for?'

'Until Kathy discovers if it's a toxic reaction.'

'How long does that take?'

'A few hours.'

'And if it's not toxic?'

'Then we've got problems.' Mendoza did not elaborate. 'Now, did you see anyone, however briefly, between leaving the lab and knocking on my door?'

'No.' Nicholson answered the question as asked. He did not tell the doctor about Wilkins' lightning visit to his bedside. He did not want to cause trouble for Wilkins and the other miners. Besides, he'd answered the question truthfully.

'Are you allergic to any drugs?'

'I never had anything like this before,' Nicholson said, looking at his upper arm. 'Hey, this is spreading to my neck.' The blisters had advanced across Nicholson's shoulder.

'Don't scratch them. I want you on an antibiotic. Are you allergic to anything?'

'I don't think so. Won't that sort of thing be on my file? I had a big medical when I joined the Institute – because of my surgery.'

'My file gives your birthdate, your blood group and that's about it. Except, of course, that you need a weekly shot of B12.'

'That's all it says?'

'That's all. Just the bare bones. Tell me about that operation. I've asked before but you're not exactly forthcoming.'

'Well, I wouldn't be.'

'I need to know now. It may affect treatment. It may even help to explain what's wrong with you.'

'I had the operation in Mexico.' Nicholson lay propped against the pillows, silent for a moment, remembering. 'A butcher of a surgeon cut out half my stomach, removed huge stomach ulcers and nicked my liver in the process.'

'How on earth did you get into that sort of mess?' Mendoza asked, shocked.

'It began, I suppose, in Florida. My father's business collapsed. It killed my father; I was out of a job. The guy who foreclosed on the boatyard was a retired naval officer. Cold and mean. Just like Beckett.' Nicholson remembered his fevered dream. 'In Florida there's always one way out. Marijuana, cocaine, you name it, I ran it. I used to hang out at the marinas. Someone always needed crew to collect from the motherships. I got paid in dope. I sold some. I did plenty myself. Got kinda strung out. Lost a lot of weight. Got my own boat, my own contracts. When I started carrying a gun I suddenly realized it was getting too heavy. I looked around for something else and I got an offer. A trip to the Yucatan for three months. Good pay – and a bonus if we found treasure.'

'Treasure?'

'Treasure,' Nicholson said. 'Illegal again, but less dangerous. Some millionaire from New Orleans had followed up on an old explorer whose boat sank in a storm off the Mexican coast near Villahermosa. In about seventy feet of water. Near where they're pumping oil now. He'd got hold of a map drawn by one of the survivors.'

'Did you find the treasure?'

Nicholson nodded. 'I was in charge of the engine and the scuba gear. While the divers searched the sand, I sat in the sun on deck and drank – mescal, tequila.'

The doctor wiped her brow, as if feeling the Mexican sun.

'There was plenty of good dope on board too. We found nothing at first. Nothing but a million tons of sand and shit. Then one day, they found the wreck. Just like that. It took only a couple of days to get the crates on board. One contained gold. There was pottery, stone figures, reliefs hacked off temples. We celebrated. You can imagine. That's when I collapsed with hallucinations and gut ache. I got so sick, they landed me in a fly-ridden hospital a couple of days later, half dead. Some surgeon there decided to practise a gasterectomy on me. He hit my liver and nearly killed me. I limped back to the States a couple of months later. Collected my bonus – a hundred thousand bucks – just like the man said.'

There was a knock on the sickbay door. Mendoza crossed the room and called out, 'Yes?'

'Room service!'

Nicholson recognized Rico's voice.

'Leave it there,' Mendoza said.

'Have you got a man in there or something?' Rico asked.

'Just put it down, Rico,' Mendoza snapped. 'Nicholson's ill.'

When Rico had gone, Mendoza collected the breakfast tray.

'Can I get up to eat?' Nicholson asked.

'Sure. Bring a chair over here.' Mendoza put the tray on a small table near the drug cabinet, sat down herself and poured the coffee.

'A hundred thousand bucks is a lot of money,' Mendoza said when they were both seated, eating the scrambled eggs. 'But hardly worth a ruined stomach.'

'I'm not so sure. It cost me twenty thousand bucks in doctors' bills and some more gut ache. But it forced me to clean up my act. I could afford to get out of the dope business and I moved to California.'

'No more trouble with your stomach?' the doctor asked.

'Not if I have jabs every week. And provided I don't overdo the booze. Turned out the Mexican butcher had done a halfway decent job. I'm clear of stomach ulcers. And it's cheaper to get drunk these days – half as much does the trick.'

'You have the B12 on Tuesdays, don't you?'

'Right.'

'It won't do you any harm to have an extra shot. Those blisters have got worse. If this is an infection, the last thing you need are any complications. Let's do it now.'

Mendoza returned from the drug cabinet with a syringe, a vial of the B12 solution and a bottle of tetracycline tablets. Nicholson watched her prepare the injection. Nicholson felt her hand tremble as she pushed the needle home in his left arm.

'Are you all right?' Nicholson asked. 'You don't look very well.' He was feeling worse himself.

Mendoza said, 'Old age. There's no cure for that. I didn't get much sleep last night with you crashing in on me.'

'Of course. I forgot.'

'All part of a doctor's job. Now, take two of these,' Mendoza tipped two of the orange pills from the bottle and passed them to Nicholson. 'I'll want you to take two of these four times today.'

Nicholson swallowed the pills with water from the dispenser. 'I think I'll go back to bed for a bit,' he said. 'I'm not feeling good.'

'I've got things to do in my office. I can open the porthole in there.' Mendoza removed her white coat.

Nicholson stared at the doctor's upper arms. They were swollen. He could see small blisters beginning to rise from the surface.

Mendoza scratched one arm unconsciously, saw Nicholson's face and then stopped. She looked at her arms. 'That's bad news for all of us. It means it *is* an infection. Almost certainly some bug from the bottom of the sea. Kathy must know at once. She's got a lot to do. It's time to inform the captain he's got disease on board.' Mendoza looked at Nicholson and said slowly, 'No confirmed origin, no known cure.'

17

Saul opened his eyes. The only light in the room came from the strip bulb above the washbasin mirror. A man was standing at the metal locker rummaging inside.

'Where am I?' Saul asked.

The man swung round. 'Hey, how're you feeling, buddy?'

Saul struggled to sit up. He got to one elbow and then sank back again on to the single pillow and hard mattress.

'Take it easy. You've had a rough time.' The man approached. 'You in pain?' He placed some folded clothes from the locker on the chair at the foot of the bed.

'I don't think so.' Saul's voice broke as he spoke. 'You're American?' He felt fingers of fire stab the back of his throat.

'And you sound like a limey. Saul Peters, right? Don't speak if it hurts.'

Saul wondered how the man knew his name.

The man squatted by the bed and inspected Saul's face. He turned Saul's head first one way and then the other. 'Not bad. Not bad at all.'

'What happened?' Saul croaked.

'You've had a lucky escape. We were only just in time. Those burn bandages seem to have done the trick.'

Saul remembered the suffocating heat again. 'Who are you?'

'It must be kinda confusing. Don't worry, I'll explain. First, drink some of this.' The young man produced a glass of juice from the table beside the bed.

Saul accepted gratefully. He let the man put the rim of his glass to his thickened lower lip. Much of his mouth was numb but he felt the juice glide across his tongue, cool the back of his throat and, with an effort, he swallowed.

'That's better. Slowly does it.' The man tipped the glass and Saul swallowed once again, feeling the juice begin to lubricate his sore, raw throat. His tongue resembled furred leather and he could feel that his palate was swollen and tender. But the sensations were welcome. They were a confirmation that he had survived the ordeal.

'I'm Dave, Dave Grearson. My commander is Jack Roseman. He said you might be the Englishman. Jack's in charge and I'm the crew.'

'Just two of you?' Saul didn't understand.

'We're on the seabed. In a submersible.'

Saul was amazed. 'You're kidding me.'

Grearson grinned, 'I'll show you around as soon as you're back on your feet.'

Saul remained perplexed. 'An American submersible six miles down? There's no such thing.'

'That's where you're wrong, buddy. You're in one. How come a limey got on board the *Voyager*?'

'We get around,' Saul said drily. He was still trying to accept what Grearson had told him.

'You had bad luck. Your cable snagged on the lava cliff. We didn't have much time.'

Saul didn't understand what Grearson was saying. The pressure and the heat six miles down made it impossible for any rescue from the cliff face. Yet he was alive. And he was in some craft other than the bathysphere. He suddenly thought of Kathy. 'Have you told my ship I'm safe?'

'That's not so easy.'

'Why not? You seem able to perform miracles.' Saul became sensitive to Grearson's hesitation. He grew uneasy.

'Let's just say it's a question of security. Jack's waiting to find out from base what we're to do with you.'

'You are American, aren't you?' Saul had a moment's doubt. He studied Grearson's sallow features and slanted eyes. He remembered the fur hat in the photograph he had found. He was confused.

'As apple pie,' Grearson said. 'I had a great grandfather who came from China to work on the railroads. But that was a long time back. I'm from Detroit. Live in Oregon now.'

'Why was I locked in?' Saul remained suspicious as he remembered the locked door and his effort to attract attention.

'A precaution. I was asleep next door in Jack's cabin – this one is mine – and Jack is on duty. We didn't want you wandering around in God knows what state. I only came in for a change of clothes.'

'And you drugged me – or the other fellow did.' Saul remembered the hypodermic.

Grearson grinned. 'Don't worry. Give yourself a little time. We didn't think you were going to pull through at first. We doped you to keep you asleep and out of pain. You've made a remarkable recovery.'

'How long have I been here? And where's my watch gone?'

'I took it off. The strap was cutting into your wrist.' Grearson looked down at his own watch. 'It's later than I thought – my shift starts at noon.'

'Twenty-four hours!' Saul said, astonished.

Grearson gave another of his wide grins. 'Think again. You've been out for forty-eight hours.'

'You mean it's Sunday?'

'I guess. Days of the week don't mean much down here.'

'I must get a message to my ship. Let them know I'm all right.' Saul thought of Kathy. She and everyone else would be certain he was dead. 'What happened to the bathysphere?'

'Back on *Voyager*. They cleared the snag themselves. Clever. They moved the boat. Changed the direction of pull. We only just had time to disengage before they began to winch her up. Still, you'd have been dead if we'd left you inside. You couldn't take much more. Your lungs were beginning to fill. You were on our respirator for a while.'

Dave Grearson rose and turned for the door. 'I must let Jack know you're back with the living. And I'll bring you more juice and something to eat.'

'Wait, please. A couple of questions first.' Saul was hungrier for answers than for food.

'Fire away.' Grearson returned to the edge of the bed.

'Are you spying on the *Voyager*?'

'We were sent to keep an eye on you, if that's what you mean. Check on progress. We report back regularly. Let me ask you something. What happened on the first descent? Was it you?'

'No, my assistant. The heat killed him.'

'I was on duty but it happened so quickly. We were too far off. It was clear something was wrong when the bell went almost straight back up. I only found that extraordinary heat – the volcanic vent – afterwards when I used the thermopile. We followed the second dive much more closely. Just as well.'

'So you know about the hotspot and what else is down here.'

'The cobalt nodules? Sure. That's why we were sent. Make certain no one else came along uninvited – like the Russians.'

'Have they?' Saul asked, shocked at the thought.

'If they have, they're invisible. And there's not much on the surface. The nearest ships are some stragglers from a Japanese fishing fleet. Nothing else.'

'Is Beckett in on this? Does he know you're here?'

'I'd bet he doesn't.' Grearson seemed quite certain. 'When I say we're secret, I mean it. We operate outside all the usual channels.'

'I thought he did too?'

'There's CIA and CIA. He's in Covert Naval Operations, sure. But we – or I should say, these submersibles – are one hell of a lot more special.'

'So you know about the *Voyager* – that's how you knew my name.'

'Right. We carry information for a mission like this on floppy discs. If there's anything else we need, we get it from our LA desk.'

'How? Not this deep, surely?'

'Laser. The latest. We've only had it the last couple of trips. It's great. First, we lock on to a buoy on the surface. A string of them get dropped by plane along our route. Our messages are compressed and fired from the sub in a laser pulse. It gets to the surface and triggers the buoy. That boosts the signal to a satellite 22,000 miles up. All scrambled, of course. Meaningless to the other side. It's bounced back down on to the LA desk.'

Saul was fascinated. 'How do they contact you?' he asked.

'The buoys are like floating relays. They store incoming information until we bring it down. You can send or receive long messages quickly if they're prerecorded. Same as with punched tape and telex. Or you can keep the line open with an intermittent series of pulses. LA could put you on to Ma Bell if you want to call home.' Grearson laughed. 'Not that it's allowed. I shouldn't be telling you this. No more than a handful of people even know the sub exists.'

'I certainly didn't and I once lectured on the history of diving. I could tell you about Alexander the Great's diving bell or how Phoenician frogmen destroyed the ancient city of Tyre in 332 BC. But I'm clearly not up to date.'

'I don't think you'd be able to find out much about us or the laser,' Grearson said. 'This sub is the sort of thing that affects vital strategic interests, the balance of power.'

'So how come you rescued me?'

'I guess the rulebooks don't take account of human nature. There's a kind of brotherhood of the deep, right?'

Saul nodded cautious agreement.

'Couldn't stand by knowing we might be able to get you out alive. But you're right. The LA desk freaked badly when they heard. You're giving them a headache. We're waiting for orders. Maybe Jack's heard.' Grearson turned towards the door. 'I'll check with him and then I'll fix you something to eat – if you think you can swallow. We'll have plenty of time to talk. That's one thing down here. There's always plenty of time.'

'Can I come?'

'Can you walk?'

Saul rose with care. He steadied himself with a hand on the bed and then against the wall. His body hurt less than when he had hobbled around the room by himself. His hands were still blotchy but less swollen.

Grearson brought some clothes from the locker. 'Try these.' He helped Saul to dress.

Saul sat and pulled on some thick socks. His fingers worked well enough for him to accomplish the task. He had more trouble with the shirt buttons. He took a few tentative steps and followed Grearson into the corridor. The ceiling was low and curved. Within a few feet, the corridor opened into a small galley kitchen. Some dried provisions and a few root vegetables were hung in nets slung from the ceiling. Space was at a premium.

'That's the control room,' Grearson said, crossing towards a door in the far wall beyond a table and benches bolted to the metal floor. He knocked on the door and pulled it open.

Saul saw the commander appear first in profile and then in full face as the padded chair slowly rotated. He recognized the ginger beard at once. The man was older than Grearson, his face lined, his head balding. He looked preoccupied.

As soon as Jack Roseman saw Saul, who stood half-hidden behind Grearson in the narrow doorway, his expression mellowed. He held up a hand in greeting. 'So you're on your feet,' he said.

Grearson spoke before Saul could reply. 'You were right, Jack. It is Peters.'

'Well, good for you, fella. Glad you made it, Saul. Long time since we had a visitor.' Roseman looked genial now. His face creased as he smiled.

'Thank you for all you've done. I appreciate it,' Saul said. He scanned the banks of instruments surrounding the commander. The small control room was like the flight deck of a passenger jet. Except that where the windscreen should have been, there were a half-dozen monitors and display screens.

'It's only when I see all this that I begin to believe you did get me out of Saturn.'

'What did you call it?'

'Sorry, the bathysphere. I'd love to know how you did it.'

'Dave will oblige, won't you?'

'Sure. I was going to fix some food as well. Want some?' Roseman looked back at his banked console for a moment. 'I'll join you in a few minutes. I've been trying to hook the buoy up with the satellite. The bitch hasn't been accepting a signal. But there's something incoming to collect. Might be what we're waiting for.' Roseman raised his eyebrows at Grearson. 'They haven't been too sure back on land what's to be done with you,' Roseman said, turning a broad smile on Saul.

Saul moved aside as Grearson backed out of the control room, closed the door and crossed to the kitchen.

From a wall unit in the back of the galley, Grearson pulled three frozen packs in aluminium foil. He opened the infrared cooker, put the containers in, dialled a time, shut the door and pushed Start.

Saul saw a digital clock on the cooker.

'Are you on Pacific Standard or Hawaii time?'

'Hawaii.'

'Same as *Voyager*.' Saul coughed and then winced as he felt a stab of pain deep in his throat.

'Some ice cream might help,' Grearson said, opening the freezer again. 'Here, have an Eskimo pie.'

Saul took the ice cream gratefully and began to unwrap it. His legs felt weak but he wasn't prepared to surrender to tiredness.

'You want the tour?'

'Please.'

'It doesn't take long. We can do it while the food cooks. The sub is eighty feet long,' Grearson began, 'average twelve feet across. Propulsion rotors stick out wider. We also carry a pantry box and some other tricks outside. But the basic shape is a cigar tube.'

Grearson enjoyed Saul's undivided attention. 'Inside we have six main areas. The control room, the kitchen and the cabins – you've already seen.' He led the way past the cabins and into a small room with an incubator, a foldaway work surface and a light microscope which was secured on its rack along with other scientific paraphernalia. 'This is the experiment control centre. We also have some of the cold water tanks up there,' Grearson pointed to four circular drums fixed to the ceiling. 'And there's a carbon dioxide scrubber, access to ballast and batteries over there.'

'What's that?' Saul asked pointing at a small cubicle. He took a bite of his ice cream.

'Shower and lavatory,' Grearson said. 'This way.' He

entered a narrow corridor through a door on the far side
of the room. The light high-pitched hum, which Saul had
first heard in the cabin, grew much louder.

Grearson tapped the solid steel wall. 'This houses the
engine – nuclear-powered. Has its own water-cooling
system. Totally self-contained. Never have to touch it.' The
men moved on to the end of the corridor, through yet
another door and stopped outside an airlock set in the tail
of the submersible. 'This is the entrance to the rescue
chamber.'

'That's where you brought me in?' Saul asked.

'Yes, there're another two airlocks inside which we can't
see without going through. We check pressure before ever
opening up.'

'You really wouldn't know you were underwater,' Saul
said. 'Could be a space station.'

'Those who know say there are similarities.'

'Astronauts in outer space and you guys in inner space.'

Saul followed Grearson back to the galley, nibbling at
his ice cream as if on a museum outing. 'You still haven't
told me how you rescued me,' he said between mouthfuls.

'Not difficult. Much as you'd expect. We backed in. The
nozzle of the rescue tube – it's a real neat design – hooked
itself on to the bell enclosing your hatch and made a seal
between the two vessels. The nozzle has electromagnetic
clamps. We pulled your bell away from the worst of the
heat – to get us both out of the main blast. After balancing
the pressures, I went through the first airlock which was
closed behind me and then through the other two. I spun
the hatch wheel and dragged you out. It's the deepest I've
ever done it. But it worked.'

'Thank goodness.' It was all Saul could think of to say.
He crumpled the empty ice-cream wrapper into a ball.

'How was the ice cream?' Grearson asked. The infrared
oven pinged to indicate the food was ready. 'I hope you
can swallow this. It's stew with mashed potato.'

Saul nodded. He felt pangs of hunger as well as tiredness
run through him.

Grearson put some slices of a hard, wholemeal bread on
the table. 'I wouldn't try that. It might be a bit rough on

your throat. And wait for the food to cool. Your mouth is going to be sensitive.' Grearson removed three containers from the oven and put them on trays. He removed the foil from two.

Saul eyed the food greedily. 'That looks good. You seem well organized. How long have you been out?'

'Couple of weeks, that's all. We can stay underwater up to six months. The longest Jack and I ever spent was four months. Helping you folks out in the Falklands.'

'You what?' Saul was surprised, and not for the first time since he had found himself alive in the submersible. 'What on earth were you doing?'

'Picked up some interesting information: core samples for oil and gas studies, the black box of a Harrier that didn't make it, an unexploded Exocet missile.'

'Are you armed?'

'Nothing fancy – not sea-to-air. But some torpedoes, sure. They're slung either side of the conning tower above the control room and there are a couple right underneath us.'

Saul looked at the floor under his feet. He saw handles inset in two floor panels.

'Never had to use them,' Grearson was saying. 'But Jack did one time – on a freighter full of stolen guns. He picked his moment well. He sank them in the Bermuda triangle. The government was happy to see it put down as a mystery disappearance.'

'Do you two usually work together?'

'For a couple of years now. Not that we see much of each other. We each do twelve hours on, twelve hours off. One of us is asleep most of the time the other's on duty.'

Saul could wait no longer. He took a forkful of his meal. The heat stung his palate and he couldn't taste the food. But he didn't care. His stomach needed filling.

The two men ate in silence until Grearson pushed his meal away half finished and lit a hand-rolled cigarette he produced from his shirt pocket. Saul recognized the acrid smell of marijuana.

Grearson inhaled deeply and then slowly let the smoke out. 'No booze allowed on board,' Grearson said by way of explanation. 'We do have a couple of bottles of bourbon Jack brought on for special occasions – birthdays and the like. But grass is easier – less bulky. No empties.' Grearson laughed. 'We smoke now and then to cool out.' He offered the joint to Saul.

Saul shook his head. 'No thanks. Tell you what, if you've finished with your meal . . . .'

'Of course, should have thought.' Grearson pushed the tray across to Saul, then frowned. 'Sure you don't want a fresh one? You can have Jack's and I'll start him another.'

'No, that'll do just fine.'

The door from the bridge opened and Roseman appeared. He was taller than Saul had expected and his bushy ginger beard gave him the appearance of an old-fashioned sea captain. Grearson, by comparison, looked a product of astronaut training, clean cut and a bit wet behind the ears.

'You know you've made one hell of a recovery,' Roseman said to Saul sitting down on the bench beside Grearson. 'When we got you on board, I thought you weren't going to make it.'

'I told him,' Grearson said.

'I haven't thanked you enough for what you did,' Saul said. 'I gather you bent the rules a bit.'

'You'd have done the same,' Roseman said, holding up his hands as if to shield off Saul's gratitude. 'We had no choice. I'm just glad you didn't die on us.'

'Would you think it rude of me to go lie down again? Now that I've eaten, I feel terribly tired. And I still ache all over.'

'Fine with me,' Roseman said. 'You need plenty of rest.'

'Use my bunk again,' Grearson said. 'I'm due on duty in a few minutes. You know where to find it.'

'I think I'd better do just that before I pass out on you.' Saul rose a little unsteadily to his feet and walked the few steps to the cabin. The bed was inviting. He fell asleep almost as his head touched the pillow. He slept the sleep of a contented child, at peace with himself, secure in his safety and completely unaware of the consternation in the galley.

Roseman rejected the relit joint which Grearson offered him, saying, 'I'm still on duty.'

'Only for a few minutes,' Grearson said. 'What's eating you?'

'Be prepared for trouble. Washington could come on line any time.'

'I thought maybe they already had.' Grearson took one further puff before stubbing the joint in the ashtray between them.

'No, it was the goddamned LA chief.' Roseman snorted his contempt. 'He's chewed us out real good. You can read the hard copy. I left it in there.'

'For what we've done, for saving a guy's life?'

'That's what it amounts to. Can't have helped interrupting the bastard's weekend, I'm certain. He was woken in the middle of the night somewhere in Santa Barbara. The deskman tracked him down.'

'Why didn't the desk go straight through to Washington as we asked?'

'Exhaust local procedures where life is not at risk. That's the rule. The LA deskman must have applied it for once. Anyway the chief is hopping mad. He's thrown the book at us – the jerk. It reads like a charge sheet. Cites every order we've violated. Goes on about compromising the security of the sub by taking a foreign national on board.'

'No shit!' Grearson said. 'How were we supposed to tell he was English?'

'Keep the volume down, Dave. In case he's still awake. I'm fuming too but I think we should keep problems with base to ourselves from now on.'

'Agreed. So what now?' Grearson had dropped his voice to a conspiratorial whisper.

'They claim they are now consulting Washington and will pass on instructions in due course.'

'In other words, he's passed the buck to HQ.'

'It's not just the Englishman, I guess. The trouble *Voyager*'s got with the cobalt must be worrying them too.'

'Well, at least they can't ask us to mine it.'

'If they could, they would,' Roseman said with emphasis. 'In the meantime, while Washington deliberates – and you're not going to like this one little bit – the LA chief has taken it on himself to order an EVA.'

'What! Hell, no.' Grearson's voice was indignant, no longer a whisper.

'The chief's revenge. His instructions are to take a closer look at the source of the heat – in the mermaid suits. Photographs, a few samples, that sort of thing.'

'Christ, that limey was practically cooked when we got him out of his bell.'

'They're checking temperature specifications of the mermaid suits.'

'They want their heads examining,' Grearson said. 'Or I do for taking orders from such creeps. This trip has stopped being fun.'

'You said it.' Roseman reached for the joint-end in the ashtray. 'What the hell, I'll have a puff before turning in. Don't wake me unless it's the Coordinator in person on the line. It won't be, of course. It's Sunday, if you didn't know. He's probably on some golf course. Check on the hotspot's heat distribution – make sure it doesn't vary. That won't take long. Chances are you'll have a quiet shift to play chess with yourself.'

'I'm going to choose a lower level of play. I need a win to cheer myself up.'

18

Saul was all the better for another long sleep. He had taken a tepid shower in the cramped cubicle after waking, re-dressed in his borrowed clothes, still without shoes, and was seated opposite Roseman at the galley table. Saul's body had responded to rest. The puffed and swollen flesh had retreated. His face now felt mildly sunburned and the inside of his mouth as though he had recently gulped down a spoonful of boiling soup.

Saul had been explaining the origin of hotspots and the

possibility of life sustained exclusively through microorganisms generated by the earth's heat.

Roseman listened attentively, then said, 'Oh, that's enough science for one day. Tell me something about you. What part of the country are you from?'

'I grew up in Kent, near Canterbury. You ever visited England?'

'Once. Spent most of my time on a NATO course at Chatham. But I got to drive along your south coast. Stayed in Brighton.'

'I own a cottage near there. In South Dean, on the edge of the Downs, just a couple of miles from the sea. Never really lived there though. I've spent too long abroad.'

'Where?'

'Oh, all over. I joined a big marine project in the Indian Ocean straight from college. Then did some graduate work in British Columbia. I went back to teach at Sussex University – before I had the cottage. I missed the survey work. And I loved India. So I went back to the Indian Ocean project.' Saul thought wistfully of the beautiful Soomintra and what might have been. 'After three years, I returned with a girl in tow, bought myself the cottage with plans to settle down at last. But it didn't work out.'

Roseman displayed interest. 'Any children?'

'We never made it to first base. We never married. She left, tugged back to India by her family. The cottage sort of lost its magic.'

'You kept it?'

'It was convenient. My father had retired. He had taught at a minor public school – that's a private school to you. He was alone. My mother had died while I was still a student. My sister was married. It seemed a good idea for him to move into the cottage. I still pay the mortgage, but I took off to seek solace – and my fortune – in the States.'

'I've been married twice,' Roseman said. 'Divorced twice. This sort of life doesn't mix well with a wife and kids. I've got five in all – three boys, two girls. They know their daddy does something important for the government. And that's what they tell their friends. For months at a time I don't even see them at weekends.'

'That's a shame,' Saul said.

The door from the control room opened and Grearson appeared with a mug in one hand and some papers in the other. He leaned against the door to shut it.

'Here's the heat map you wanted, Jack. And the specifications from the LA desk.' Grearson put the papers in front of Roseman and moved into the galley where he poured himself coffee. 'No message from Washington. What do you think they're playing at?'

Roseman looked at his watch. 'It's past 10 p.m., that's 3 a.m. Washington. We won't hear tonight. More like the end of my shift.'

'If you want EVA first thing tomorrow, would you check out my mermaid for me?'

'Sure,' Roseman said.

'I've beaten the computer three times in a row. I'm feeling strong enough to go back up a level.' Grearson opened the door and disappeared back inside the control room.

Saul was left bewildered. 'What does he mean, "beat the computer"?'

'They play chess.'

'Oh, I see. And what was that about mermaids and EVA? Does that mean what I think it does?'

'Extra Vehicular Activity.'

'Down here? How?'

'Mermaids,' Roseman said. 'The official term is SCUV–7s – Self-Contained Underwater Vessel, mark seven. Built by Natcom Marine. Cost about ten million dollars each. Nothing else like them in the world. We have two.'

'Where do you hide them?'

Roseman pointed above his head. 'Attached. At the back, above the rescue hatch.'

'And you propose to take them to the hotspot. What are they? Some kind of mini-sub?'

Roseman nodded and corrected Saul. 'One of them. Only Dave is going.'

'I've heard of the Pisces, which is British, the West German Manta, the Canadian Hyco, and there's an American one called Beaver. Used for pipeline maintenance, cable burying, that sort of thing. I've never heard of mermaids – or SCUV–7s.'

'They're a bit special, as you might imagine, and top-secret. We're not trying to sell them to anyone else, for a start. They're fish-shaped – you lie flat in them. And they're built to take over 1000 atmospheres of pressure.'

'What about the heat?'

Roseman picked up the top sheet of paper Grearson had left. 'LA has been hard at work. They say no problems up to 350°C.' He scanned the sheet of paper and then turned it around to let Saul see.

Saul studied it. He was not convinced.

Roseman chewed on some candy. His ginger beard bobbed as he munched and then swallowed. 'Point is, the mermaid was specifically developed for deepwater salvage – radioactive materials, missiles, crashed satellites, nuclear waste . . . . It's a titanium and ceramic compound that can stand just about any amount of heat. Inside there's a cooling system that could keep a snowball frozen in the middle of a furnace.'

'It'll need to,' Saul said. 'I know. I've been there.'

Roseman suddenly stood. 'You want to see one? I've got to check power levels and air supplies. You might as well join me.'

Saul accepted with alacrity. He followed Roseman down the narrow corridor past the cabins, across the sample room, back into the corridor past the insistent hum of the engine until they stood in front of the airlock which led to the rescue chamber.

Roseman slid back a panel in the wall, revealing several switches and dials.

'We show normal pressure in the chamber, but we have a fail-safe just in case a dial is faulty. I can't open the airlock until the control room confirms a normal reading.' A green light came on. 'He has and he's thrown his release switch.' Roseman flicked a switch and the airlock slid open.

Saul stepped on to rubber matting which covered the narrow floor laid along the tubular chamber. It looked like the inside of a squat, black, metal drum. The drum was about ten feet long, a little less in diameter, with an identical airlock to the one he had just passed through at the far end. He started when the airlock behind him slid closed.

Roseman stood himself in front of more dials, lights and switches on a console protruding from the curved wall. A second console, symmetrically positioned, stood near the far airlock. 'Look above your head,' he told Saul.

Saul watched one of two oval hatches on the roof slide back.

When the hatch had fully retracted, Roseman reached inside the cavity and pulled down a lightweight ladder. 'I'm going inside to read power and air levels. I'll only be a moment.'

Saul watched Roseman disappear into the belly of the mermaid. A dim yellow light emanated from the cavity but Saul could see only Roseman's trousered thighs lying horizontally across the entrance. Saul marvelled at the technology which allowed atmospheric pressure to be maintained with such apparent ease in the submersible, the rescue chamber and the mermaid. He went and studied the control console by the entry airlock and was beginning to make some sense of the knobs and dials when he heard Roseman on the ladder.

'The mermaid needs some air,' Roseman said. 'The valve has a very slow leak. Nothing serious. It'll only take a few minutes.'

Roseman bent to lift a panel of flooring. It revealed a sausage-shaped contraption which to Saul bore a passing resemblance to a domestic vacuum cleaner. Roseman remounted the ladder with a hose in his hand unreeling from the machine under the floor, reached inside the mermaid and attached the nozzle. 'Push that white button on top,' he asked Saul.

Saul did so and the tube stiffened. 'Clever machine,' he said to Roseman who returned to floor level.

'It's very convenient. Other hoses transfer current to the sixty and thirty volt batteries. We recharge after docking and check levels within twenty-four hours of taking a mermaid out.'

'A real space-age gadget,' Saul said. 'It's strange to think that the first man to find nodules – only 100 years ago –

fished them up completely by chance while dragging a net across the seabed.'

'Sir John Murray on *Challenger*, wasn't it? One of your compatriots.'

Saul was impressed by Roseman's knowledge. 'I used to quote Jacques Piccard to my students. "Early oceanographic work is like a blind man making a butterfly collection".'

'We've come a long way quickly in the past few years,' Roseman said. 'Remember *Thresher*?'

'Yes,' Saul said. 'She was the sub which sank off Cape Cod.'

'In just 8000 feet of water. That was 1963. Piccard had already gone 36,000 feet to the bottom of the Marianas Trench but there was no submarine rescue vessel that could go lower than 1500 feet. That's when the US navy finally got their finger out.'

'*Thresher* was the turning point, I know. And that's when military developments start getting hard to follow.'

'There were six rescue submersibles built after *Thresher*. They could go 5000 feet. Just in time for the Palomares accident.'

Saul remembered the outcry when an American bomber had dropped a hydrogen bomb by accident into the Mediterranean off the coast of Spain. He had been a student at Bristol at the time. The incident had fuelled protests in British universities against American involvement in Vietnam and raised student consciousness.

'The Palomares operation,' Roseman said, 'was so successful that the navy, with CIA funds, decided to maintain development. This is one of the third generation. First they tripled the depth by going from steel hulls to titanium and then they doubled the range again by increasing the thickness.'

'But you don't lose hydrogen bombs very often, do you?'

Roseman pushed the white button on top of the machine in the floor. The hose into the mermaid went limp. He studied a gauge for a moment and then restarted the pump. The hose jerked and stiffened again.

'All sorts of embarrassing things happen,' Roseman said.

'We're starting to get bad radiation spills from old canisters dropped in the sixties. And you don't find us getting a bad press like the Russians had when *Whiskey 137* got stuck in a Swedish archipelago. That's not because we don't have submarines run aground. We pull ours off.'

'I remember that Russian sub. It was a farce – the Swedes dropping depth charges all over the place.'

'That's why there are three submersibles like this one. The mermaids are even tougher, even more versatile. They need the mothership of course. But they store three hours of independent power and air at a time. That's enough. They can go places we're too big to go. They can go deeper than we can. They allow direct vision through a canopy viewport. It's like being one of the fishes. It's wonderful.'

'Could I have a look?' Saul asked.

'Sure,' Roseman said. 'Wait till I unhook the hose.' When Roseman was satisfied with the pressure, he unclipped the nozzle and let the hose rewind.

Saul climbed the ladder, poked his head into the cavity beyond the top rung, and got a dim view of the interior.

'More light on your right,' Roseman shouted up. 'Turn the key.'

Saul found the key, turned it and the inside of the mermaid grew brighter. It resembled an over-sized diving suit which he had entered through a hatch in the stomach region. He pulled himself in on two handles set either side of a lit dashboard of instruments and then tucked his legs backwards until he was fully horizontal. The mermaid was well padded and Saul felt no claustrophobia in the small, snug compartment.

The controls were all hand-operated and looked no more difficult to master than those of an automobile. Above his head, Saul felt the smooth finish of what he was certain was the transparent viewport. It stretched in a curve towards the mermaid's nose. It was cold to the touch and incredible to contemplate that the black world outside was bearing down with over 6 tons of pressure on every square inch.

Saul was a sucker for adventure. He knew what he

wanted to do. He turned the interior lights off and climbed back down the ladder to rejoin Roseman.

'Impressed?'

Saul nodded vigorously.

'Let's get back,' Roseman said.

'One thing first,' Saul said. He pointed to the closed hatch on the other side of the rescue chamber ceiling. 'Is that the second mermaid?'

Roseman nodded and said, 'That's right.'

'I've got a request.'

'Well, make it. I don't promise to grant it.'

'You're staying in the submersible while Dave goes to the hotspot?'

'Yes.'

'You know I'm fascinated by the hotspot. And I can contribute a lot.'

'I know you've been half boiled in one,' Roseman said, smiling.

'Let me go with Dave. In the second mermaid. The controls don't look anything I couldn't learn to handle. I could be useful out there, I'm sure.'

Roseman said nothing.

'Look at it this way. Even if I came a cropper, I'd be no worse off than before you rescued me. And your problem with base would be over.'

'We'd have a new one. Those mermaids cost ten million dollars.'

19

Grearson grunted with effort as he held a length of steel rod at arm's length. His face contorted as the effort became too much for his muscles and he began to tremble. The submersible's copilot was stripped to his shorts performing his daily exercises between the cabin corridor and the galley.

Saul sat at the table studying Grearson with a mixture

of admiration and amusement. A manual lay open, face down, on the table. The cover read:

'SCUV–7. OPERATING INSTRUCTIONS. RETAIN FOR REFERENCE.'

Grearson slotted the steel bar back into clips beside the door frame. He spread a mat over the riveted metal floor and sat on it. He hooked the index finger of his right hand around his right big toe and stretched the foot straight up away from his body. He spoke while he held the pose.

'I spend so much time underwater, I feel weird on the surface. Like I don't really belong there. They've got these things called day and night and rain and fog. Down here it's all the same.' Grearson let his leg bend back down and switched to left hand and left foot.

'It would drive me barmy before long,' Saul said. 'You must lose all track of time and season just for starters.'

'Sure. It can feel like a few days since you left base. But the log tells you it's been as many weeks. That's why you've got to look after yourself. Exercise, regular exercise, helps.' Grearson stretched both legs straight in front of him and sat up squarely. He patted his flat, muscle-ridged stomach. 'You have to learn to live by the clock.'

Grearson interlaced his fingers, inverted his hands and then raised and straightened his arms above his head. He held the pose for several seconds before relaxing. 'The first time I spent a long spell underwater – not this sub, it was an old Polaris – my body rhythms went completely. You're supposed to go to bed at the same time every day, eat your meals at the same time every day, shit at the same time. I didn't bother with any of that. Ended up falling asleep on duty. Jack thinks I overdo the exercises. But believe you me, get a routine and stick to it.' Grearson rolled over on to his stomach and extended his arms and legs as far as he could before beginning to raise them and arch his back. As he held the position, a trickle of sweat dropped off his nose.

The door from the control room opened and Roseman appeared in the doorway. 'How much longer you going to be, Dave?'

'Just finishing up.'

'It's 8.30 a.m. already.'

'I know.' Grearson picked himself up off the floor. 'What about Washington?'

'Still nothing.' Roseman turned to Saul. 'Which is good news for you. If asked, you can be sure they'd flip at the idea. As it is they'll probably court martial me if they ever find out. Any questions, any problems?'

Saul shook his head. 'None.'

Roseman addressed Grearson, 'How'd the run-through go?'

'He learns fast. Can't say I did my first practice at 30,000 feet. Still,' Grearson smiled at Saul, 'he's keen for sure. And he knows the theory.'

'Not more than ninety minutes, right.' Roseman looked at both men and got affirmative nods. 'You can always go out a second time. I want a big safety margin. Did you look at the air pressure again, Dave?'

'Yes,' Grearson said. 'I topped it up a bit. There's still a very slow leak.'

'You're carrying both flares, right?'

'Yes,' Grearson said. 'Come on, Saul, Jack's making me nervous. Strip off to your shorts – *my* shorts, I should say.'

Saul turned to Roseman. 'Thanks for letting me go. I appreciate it.'

'Ah, what the hell. Get going both of you.'

'Don't move off, Jack, before we're back,' Grearson said, 'Whatever Washington tells you.'

Roseman smiled tolerantly, retreated a step into the control room and pulled the door shut.

Grearson addressed Saul. 'Leave the clothes in my cabin and make sure you stop off at the john. That's one thing missing in a mermaid. I'll see you down there. I'll open up.'

When Saul reached the chamber, Grearson was dressed in a loose white one-piece suit. The mermaid hatches were already open, the two ladders in position. Saul climbed into the suit which Grearson handed him. Only his head and his hands were left unenclosed by the white silky material.

'Remember to plug in,' Grearson said.

'Yes.'

'OK. Let's go.'

The men climbed into their respective mermaids.

Saul was nervous with excitement as he pulled himself flat, plugged in the suit, switched on power, put on the headset and wriggled to get comfortable.

'You reading me?' Grearson's voice came through the headset.

Saul pressed the speak button. 'Yes, Dave, I hear you.'

'Good. Close both pressure seals.'

Saul pressed the two glowing red buttons on his right. The double gate of rescue chamber hatch and mermaid belly began to slide closed. For a moment Saul experienced panic. The trapped feeling slowly dissipated as Grearson conducted the pre-departure checks. The instructions were delivered simply and slowly.

Saul had practised with Grearson's guidance earlier that morning until both men were confident that Saul would be able to manoeuvre the mermaid safely. Saul took a final look round the dashboard display, felt the weight of the steering stick and rested his finger on top of the inset throttle.

'Lights on.'

Saul clicked the floodlight switches and the blackness outside the viewport was replaced with the eerie shape of Grearson's bullet-nosed mermaid, its spotlights forging into the water, its outline illuminated by the light reflected from the submersible's outer skin. He heard Grearson say over his headphones, 'Jack, we're ready to cast off.'

Roseman replied, 'Saul, keep your distance. I don't want any collisions.'

Saul pushed his speak button, 'Understood.'

'In your own time, Saul.' It was Grearson again.

Saul switched off the magnetic clamps which still held the mermaid to the submersible. The mermaid slipped free. Practice was over; Saul's mermaid adventure had begun.

No amount of rehearsal could have prepared Saul for the sensation. It felt a little like being in a glider at the moment when the launching aircraft dropped its towrope. Saul remembered how the earth had slid away, silence descended, and the plane had become a creature of the wind, moving with it, not through it. Without use of the throttle, the mermaid would be carried and turned by the currents drifting up from the ocean floor.

Saul travelled head first on his stomach. There was nothing to be seen any longer through the viewport. Two tiny video screens no more than six inches across showed the view from two cameras set in the underside of the mermaid. He could adjust their direction and also record up to half an hour of what either screen showed.

Saul had already lost his bearings. He lay pressed against the roof padding, disoriented. Then he saw Grearson's mermaid straight above him. Grearson appeared to be travelling upside down.

'You've turned on your back,' Grearson said. 'Rotate, slowly, and then lose some height.' Grearson's voice was gentle but firm across the void between them.

Saul realized that it was he and not Grearson who was upside down. He adjusted the steering stick as he had learned and fired a short burst of throttle. Slowly, he turned, until Grearson's mermaid appeared on the screen below him. Saul dipped the mermaid's nose and touched the throttle again. He saw the seabed approach head-on through the viewport and, when he judged himself at twenty feet, he levelled off and looked at the screens to confirm that the sea floor was beneath him.

'That was good.' Grearson's voice was reassuring. 'Hang about while I move in front. Then follow.'

Saul saw the ghostly mermaid, lights ablaze, move into direct view. Then, keeping close to the reddish mud sea floor, he set off behind Grearson in the direction of the hotspot.

The mermaids approached from the east, as Saul had done in the bathysphere. They stirred a swirling sediment which began to obscure Saul's vision. He adjusted the steering stick to bring himself a few feet higher. The view ahead cleared; the detail on the screens became sharper.

Some isolated slabs of volcanic rock appeared; then pockets of rounded pillow lava, evidence of earlier vents and fissures in the ocean floor. Each hotspot lasted ten, perhaps twenty years, before the magma pumped from the earth's core found fresh veins in which to rise through the shifting crustal plates. The old sites became underwater cemeteries. Spores and eggs, pushed by the seabed currents, colonized new hotspots nearby.

A large empty clam shell lay on the lava ahead of Saul. The falling figures on the depth indicator showed that he was now moving up a steep incline. Water temperature was also rising. Saul began to see movement on the seabed. Spaghetti-like acorn worms swayed in the draught of Grearson's mermaid. There were limpets and crustaceans lining hollows in the lava floor. The temperature had reached 80°C and Saul's mermaid was at a depth of 30,890 feet.

Saul followed the incline and the rising heat towards the spot some forty feet higher where he had come to grief. He saw small piles of nodules, the size of pebbles, coating depressions in the lava. He saw once again the huge red-crowned worms attached in their white tubes to the rock. A white crab wandered over a limpet-encrusted rock. The edge of the cliff loomed up. Saul searched for and then located the fractured lip of lava on which he had dangled.

'Over here,' Saul said in as calm a fashion as he could muster.

Grearson's lights added definition to the view.

'That's where I was.'

'That's it, all right. You were resting on a spur of lava and it just snapped. You dropped like a stone until the cable snagged.'

'Good thing you were around.'

'We needed the company,' Grearson said. 'You've done well so far. Here's what we do now. As soon as we're over the edge, I'll drop the first flare bomb. If all goes as it should, we'll get a real floodlit eyeful of everything within about 150 feet. If it looks safe, we'll go closer. Remember, let's keep the right side of 300°C.'

'I'd just as soon not push it to the limit,' Saul agreed.

'Watch out for convection currents as we go down. They could be powerful. If you start to spin, just back off. Ready?'

136

'Yes.' Saul was nervous with anticipation.

'Stay above and behind me. The flare will detonate on anything it hits.'

Saul followed Grearson out over the edge of the cliff without fear. He concentrated on the screens showing the view below him. Both screens darkened as the spotlights sank into the abyss.

'Flare away.' Grearson's announcement was followed by silence.

Then, a few seconds later, there was a burst of brilliant white light which rippled outwards and illuminated the scene.

Saul held his breath in wonder. At the foot of the cliff, more than 200 feet below, he could see a long, curling snake of smoke which oozed from what might have been the mouth of a cave. Smaller chimneys close by added coils of their own.

'It's like some smoggy industrial landscape,' Saul said.

'Or a vision of hell,' Grearson said. He sounded overawed.

'Those chimneys are spewing out minerals.' Saul knew that as the earth's heat met the ice-cold seawater, sulphides of copper, iron, zinc and other metals formed fine dusty plumes. The accumulated mineral mounds on the sea floor had layers of dark green, yellow, orange, red and brown. 'No one's ever seen anything like it before. Dave, you're watching the birth of the earth's mineral wealth.'

'And there are the nodules – a whole carpet of them.'

Saul saw the dense clusters of nodules scattered along the seabed stretching away from the hotspot. It was on this lower tectonic plate that Herbie had lost his life. Where the light from the flare was nearly swallowed by the dark void of the sea, Saul saw a thin shadow of a line – the Bottom Miner track. The mining head had just skirted disaster. Herbie had come too close, attracted towards the heat by the thick mounds of nodules.

The panorama was without parallel in Saul's experience. He dipped the mermaid's nose and sank lower towards the seabed. Life prospered in this bizarre environment. On the outer edges of the nodule carpet, towards the Bottom Miner track, there were fields of swaying weeds and sea cucumbers. Worms poked out from crevices. The lava rocks were encrusted with molluscs of all shapes and sizes at the top of the cliff. This was a flourishing oasis in the underwater desert.

Saul turned his mermaid back towards the cliff face where he had so nearly lost his life. It was bathed in light. This edge of the tectonic plate had come out on top. He stared into the swaying dandelion plants anchored to the cliff face by thin threads. Weaving in and out was one of the eel-like fish which Saul had captured in the bathysphere's pressure grab.

Saul saw Grearson's mermaid below him. He followed, dropping to within fifty feet of the sea floor. He could now see the main conical chimney which emerged from near the foot of the cliff in much greater detail. A fountain of smoke and glitter poured from the orifice, tumbling and swirling upwards.

Saul could see a cloudy blue colour among the precipitating sulphides. It was not one of the fine sulphur powders, but a living soup thick with bacteria. This was the organic life generated by the earth's heat. This was the base of the food chain so many miles from sun and photosynthesis.

The first flare began to fade slowly and blackness began to return like some fast falling night. Within seconds, the hotspot was in darkness. The mermaid spotlights stretched into the surrounding veil for only a few yards.

'I'm dropping the second,' Grearson said. 'Keep well away.'

An instant later the flare burst forth radiating light. The cascade of glitter returned. Saul caught sight of several more of the eel-like fish. There was a shoal of twenty or thirty swimming in and out of a pile of nodules.

'How do they stand the heat?' Grearson asked.

'Incredible, isn't it?' Saul saw from the dashboard dial that the temperature outside was 230°C. It was pleasantly cool at 17°C inside the mermaid.

'What do they live on?' Grearson asked.

'There'll be some organic matter falling from the sea overhead,' Saul replied. 'But see that bluish cloud near the mouth of the big chimney? That's bacteria – easily the most important food source down here. That'll get recycled around the whole ecosystem. The bacteria must be the primary food source for the whole community. Somehow it thrives on the hydrogen sulphide coming through the hotspot straight from the earth's core. It's the origin of life.'

'Holy cow,' Grearson said.

Saul began to descend even further to get a better view of the fish. Within twenty-five feet of the bottom, he was caught by a sudden surge. It tossed the mermaid up like a tin can and then pulled it back down. Saul was buffeted by the convection current swirling around him.

Grearson was having the same trouble. He waited until the mermaid was at the highest point from the seabed and then gave the craft full throttle. He broke clear of the current's circular tugging.

Saul was still rising and falling like a yo-yo. He was rattling around inside the mermaid like a pea in a pod.

From a safer height, Grearson instructed Saul how to break free. At the second attempt, as he reached the top of the vicious circle, Saul used full throttle and broke the current's grip.

'Well done,' Grearson said.

'You've got company,' Saul said, surprised. A shoal of the blind hotspot fish were clustered around Grearson's mermaid. 'You look like the Pied Piper. Turn the other way.'

With the fish following, Grearson moved past Saul.

'No, turn round.'

'I can't.' Grearson's voice was measured but there was no disguising the note of alarm. 'I've got trouble with the steering. The jets don't seem to respond.'

'Let me take a look.'

'For God's sake be careful.'

Saul approached Grearson's mermaid with great caution, only too aware of his inexperience in handling the mermaid. He edged closer and directed his spotlights at the small turbine. This rotated in a socket to give the mermaid its manoeuvrability.

'Turn the jet left,' Saul said. 'Without power.'

Grearson did as he was told. Any movement was imperceptible to Saul.

'Now right.'

The jet once again failed to swivel more than a fraction.

Saul explained the position, 'I think one of those fish has swum straight up your ass and got mangled.'

'Let me see if I can clear it with the throttle,' Grearson said. A moment later the mermaid shot away from Saul in a slight arc. 'I'm stuck like some satellite in orbit. I don't see the way out of this. If you get above the top of the cliff, you can raise Jack on the radio. Ask him if we might be able to get the whole mermaid in through the airlock.'

As Grearson spoke, the second flare faded. The smoke and glitter of the hotspot billowed below the mermaids, unlit and unseen.

'Why don't I try to clear the blockage with a sampler arm?' Saul asked.

'You'll never do it. It's like threading a needle at the best of times.'

'You forget,' Saul said, 'I've had practice with the bathysphere.'

'Well, try then. But don't for Christ's sake hit me. You could cripple us both.'

Gently, like a surgeon wielding a knife, Saul brought the mermaid's sampler arm up level with the other mermaid's turbine. He opened and shut the three-fingered claw at the end of the mechanical arm. The top two fingers were thinner than the lower wedge-shaped thumb and they could be operated individually. By trial and error, Saul arranged the fingers so that one of the top two fingers pointed horizontally straight ahead, with the others tucked in a folded position.

'Here goes,' Saul said. He moved in towards the other mermaid as if performing a midair refuelling procedure. The finger found its target and Saul worked the gap between motor and socket. Bits of flesh fell from the hole as Saul kept working the finger in a semicircular direction up first one side and then the other side of the socket.

'Try that,' he announced after a couple of minutes.

Grearson's mermaid once again shot forward, this time in a tight arc, first one way and then the other.

'You pass the exam,' Grearson said. 'With flying colours. I've got control through about forty-five degrees each way. That's enough. Let's head for home before there's any further trouble. I'm out of film – and the samples will have to wait. Our time's up anyway.'

'That's fine with me,' Saul said.

'Lead on. I'll shout if I have trouble.'

The journey back proved without further incident. After docking like parasites rejoining their host, Saul entered the body of the sub.

Grearson followed a moment later through the other hatch. 'That was quite something. Thanks. It could easily have ended in disaster. I owe you.'

'We're even,' Saul said.

Grearson hung his suit on the wall of the rescue chamber. 'Put Jack's next to mine,' he said.

While Saul removed his suit, Grearson contacted Roseman.

'You won't believe it,' Grearson said. 'This man's a genius.'

'How come?'

'He may have saved my life out there. The propulsion jet got jammed. Jammed solid. No directional control.'

'Dave, I've got to talk to you.'

'Go ahead, I'm listening.'

'No.' There was a pause. 'On the bridge.'

'What's the problem? Lost your chewing gum?' Grearson winked at Saul.

'Do it.' Roseman sounded tense.

Grearson stared at the intercom on the wall. 'Right, I'll be with you as soon as I've hooked up the rechargers.' He scratched his head and frowned. 'It's not like Jack to get uptight.' He connected air and battery connections inside each mermaid and then said, 'I'd better get on through and see what's eating him. Speaking of which,' Grearson said as the two men passed through the airlock back into the main body of the submersible, 'I'm hungry. Make us both some sandwiches if you feel like doing me another favour.'

Grearson left Saul in the cramped galley and disappeared through the control room door, shutting it behind him.

Saul switched on the coffee pot and examined the fridge for sandwich makings. He pulled out a plate of pre-sliced ham and beef. It looked unappetizing. He put the plate on the workspace beside the fridge and found a knife to butter some of the hard wholemeal bread. He made himself a beef sandwich using a liberal amount of mustard to give the sandwich some bite. He looked at the intercom, studied it without becoming any the wiser – the keys were numbered – and took pot luck. He pressed one button and then another until he heard Grearson and Roseman in the control room.

Saul interrupted. 'Sorry to bother you. Ham or beef, Dave? And do you want anything, Jack?'

The two men carried on their conversation without heeding the question.

Saul tried once more. 'Can you hear me?'

There was no answer. The intercom was functioning one-way only. He could hear them but they couldn't hear him. He didn't know which button to press. Saul was about to go and knock on the door when he heard his name mentioned. For the first time, he listened to the conversation.

'. . . and that's a direct order from the top,' Roseman said.

There was a pause. Grearson said, 'I don't believe it. It's the sickest thing I've ever heard. The man saved my life out there.'

'It's crazy, but the whole world's crazy. People like the Coordinator are even crazier than the rest of us. But he gives the orders.'

Saul furrowed his brow. The Coordinator? Beckett had mentioned the Coordinator at that first briefing after he'd arrived on the *Voyager*. Saul wondered whether the submersible crew was working in cahoots with Beckett.

'It still hasn't really sunk in,' Roseman said.

Saul heard Roseman exhale with frustration, then say, 'It came nearly an hour ago. You'd not been gone long. Here, read it.'

There was another silence. Then Grearson said, 'To kill him, just like that? And then dump him out the rescue hatch.'

Saul still held the knife with which he had been preparing the sandwiches. He gripped the handle harder, listening intently.

Roseman said, 'I went back to the LA desk on direct voice transmission. The deskman eventually connected me with Washington. The Coordinator was angry I'd dared to question the order. He just went straight in – absolutely ape shit. Said I'd committed a gross error of judgment which I was compounding. Said I broke the cardinal rule. Said I should never have taken an outsider on board. No matter what circumstances. It jeopardized the whole submersible programme.'

'Holy shit! That's over the top. We've rescued mini-sub crews before.'

'There's a difference. They were American – special services at that. He said Peters was a foreign national over whom they had absolutely no control. They couldn't pay him off and by rights he should have died three days ago. Everyone would be better off. That's what he said.'

'Better off? Not Saul, that's for sure.'

'You know what makes me mad?' Roseman said. 'If we'd rescued a Russian down here, someone spying on the cobalt operation, they'd have been over the moon with joy. We'd be getting herograms. Commended for our service to the country.'

'They'd have milked him of everything he knew,' Grearson said. 'And then what? What do you suppose happens to all those guys we lift – and the defectors?'

'If they fall into the clutches of that bastard back in Washington, they probably end up in the Potomac. It really wouldn't surprise me, after this.'

Saul was having trouble believing his ears. He hardly dared breathe in case the crew members closeted in the control room just a few feet away should suddenly hear his end of the intercom. He put the knife down slowly on the table.

'I owe him,' Grearson said slowly. 'Besides I like him.'

'What happened out there?'

'Some fish committed suicide in my propulsion socket. Attracted by the heat, so Saul thought. I lost all direction. He cleared the jet socket, very skilfully.'

'Well, we've been ordered to conduct major surgery,' Roseman said, 'and make sure the patient doesn't survive.'

There was a long silence. Saul backed into the mess table and sat back on it, in shock.

'What are we going to do?' Saul heard Grearson ask.

'That's up to us. The longer we wait the harder it will be.'

'Yes, but . . . .'

Roseman interrupted Grearson, 'I've already decided. I'm going to give it twenty-four hours. Let matters cool down, let them develop a perspective. Tonight, I'll go back through to the LA desk to seek clarification of something or other. Like as not, they'll have changed their minds.'

'If not?'

'If not, we toss a coin. But it won't get to that.'

Saul, hanging on every word, was less optimistic. By his reckoning, he could now count on only twenty-four hours to live.

20

The strain grew slowly through the day. At first Saul tried to dismiss as ridiculous the idea that Roseman and Grearson would kill him. People did not go around killing other people – especially those they had taken great risks to rescue. But Saul could not escape the certainty that assassination and murder were part of the CIA's stock in trade.

He felt in no immediate danger while Roseman slept and Grearson was in the control room working his noon to midnight shift. He used the time to think out a plan of action. There was no way he could remain on the sub and survive against two fit men. Not for any length of time. If he took refuge in a cabin, they could either starve him out or break the door down. There was little point in trying to overpower the two men and take control of a submersible he couldn't operate. His only advantage was that he was forewarned; but it was a fast-wasting asset.

Roseman had appeared, yawning, at 8 p.m. After a shower, he invited Saul to talk him through the video of the hotspot taken by Grearson on the mermaid trip. Saul spent a joyless half-hour describing the amazing world he had witnessed such a short time before.

'You look tuckered out,' Roseman said. 'Maybe the mermaid trip was too much, too soon.'

'It's this underwater lifestyle – day and night running into one another.'

'Be patient. It won't be long. It's a big mistake to go short of sleep. We've got Valium and Mogadon if you need a little help.'

Saul smiled a wan smile. 'Thanks,' he said.

'Let's get some food,' Roseman said. 'I bet Dave's ready for a break.'

By the time the three men sat together in the galley, the digital clock in the infrared cooker read 9.34 p.m. Saul pushed the food around his tray. Roseman and Grearson sat opposite. There had been no overt change in either man's attitude towards him. Neither revealed any hint of what lay in store. This was the first occasion Roseman had been with Grearson since the change of shift at noon.

'Dave, did you check on that monitor?' Roseman asked.

'What monitor?' Grearson said, before adding unconvincingly, 'Oh, that monitor. No, I forgot.'

'Let's take a look then,' Roseman said.

'Sure,' Grearson said. 'Now?'

'Couple of minutes. It won't go away. Finish your food first.'

'I'm finished,' Grearson said, forking in the last mouthful and standing up.

Roseman rose, poured coffee and moved through to the

small control room with Grearson, saying, 'We'll be a little while.'

Saul managed, 'OK, fellers, see you later.' He watched the two men disappear into the hub of the submersible's brain.

Like any condemned man facing his last night on death row, Saul had no particular confidence that he would win a reprieve. He also realized that there might not be another occasion when both men would be closeted away together in the control room. He was tempted to eavesdrop on the crewmen's conversation over the intercom, but was also afraid of giving himself away. He knew there was no sensible course other than immediate action.

Rifling through the kitchen drawer, he selected a sharp knife and hurried from the galley into the corridor leading towards the back of the submersible. He had another thought and returned to the doorway and found what he wanted clipped safely where Grearson had put it that morning after his workout. Saul slipped the weightlifting bar out of its clips and, mindful of its awkward shape, crossed the galley towards the control room door.

Saul moved quietly across the metal floor. He jammed one end of the bar against a leg of the galley table which was bolted to the floor and the other against the control room door. It might give him a few extra minutes. He scampered back to the corridor and into the small lab. He searched the drawers beside the foldaway table and found wire, a screwdriver and paperclips.

Saul's electrical ability was limited to changing fuses or plugs but he knew enough to work out what he had to do to gain access to the mermaids. The light hum from the engine rose in volume and then subsided as Saul passed through the final short corridor and faced the airlock which stood between him and escape.

He slid back the wall panel and stared at the switches. The dial indicating pressure in the chamber read normal, but he couldn't open the airlock until the control room had confirmed the reading and thrown the master release switch. The system, however, was designed as a safety double-check, not as an anti-sabotage measure. Saul had somehow to bypass the control room switch.

He unscrewed the two small bolts holding the airlock switch to the console. The wire ran through the switch and on behind the console. He pulled a few inches of the wire out of its duct and cut through it with the knife. He stripped away the plastic insulation covering and then wound the naked wire tightly round a paperclip. He turned his attention to the light which he had seen turn green when he had first been shown the rescue chamber by Roseman. He worked quickly, unsure how much time he had.

Using the screwdriver, Saul dismantled the light socket casing until he could see wire. His intention was to short-circuit the system. Taking the paperclip he pushed it on to the contact. He turned the airlock switch from Off to On. The light remained off; the airlock remained firmly sealed.

Saul didn't understand where he had gone wrong. With his thumb, he wiggled the paperclip. Then everything happened at once. The green light flickered, the airlock creaked briefly to life and Saul felt a massive punch in the armpit. Turning, surprised that one of the crew had arrived unheard, Saul was puzzled to find himself alone. He could smell singed flesh and then realized it came from his thumb. The punch in the armpit had been the result of an electric shock as he pushed the paperclip on to a live connection. Saul had succeeded in bypassing the control room's switching mechanism.

The wire, ending in the paperclip, now hung loose. Saul turned off the airlock switch and attached the clip firmly, without receiving a further shock. When he tried the switch again, this time the green light stayed on and the metal barrier began to slide open.

Saul stepped on to the rubber-matted floor of the stark, barrel-shaped chamber which housed the mermaids in its roof. He stared at the console which controlled the oval hatches. Both had been open when he had arrived for his mermaid trip with Grearson. He tried to remember how Roseman had released the hatch on his first visit. He took a deep breath and pushed what he hoped were the right buttons.

First the airlock slid closed. Then one of the hatches opened – it was to Grearson's mermaid, but Saul was not fussy about which one he stole. He reached inside for the ladder, once again beginning to feel that escape might be possible, and collected the headless white one-piece suit from the hook where he had left it earlier in the day. The suit had been on the large side and Saul did not take the time to strip to his shorts before clambering into it. His fingers fumbled with the fastening. Then he adjusted the tight collar around his neck so that it was more comfortable.

'Saul! Don't be foolish.' The urgent voice on the intercom belonged to Roseman. 'Saul. Report to the control room. Immediately.'

Saul realized that the switches controlling the mermaid hatches must also have registered on the bridge. It had taken Roseman only a moment to work out what was happening. Saul climbed the ladder, poked his head inside the mermaid and pulled himself in on the two handles set either side. of the main dashboard. He turned on the internal lights, plugged in his suit and switched on power.

The intercom in the rescue chamber was instructing him to return to the main body of the ship. Saul could also hear pounding noises across the intercom. It was followed by a shout, from Grearson, of 'I'm out.'

Saul quickly pressed the two glowing red buttons on his right. The double gate of the rescue chamber hatch and mermaid belly began to slide closed. He was now connected to the submersible only by magnetic clamps. Saul confidently donned the headphones. He pushed his speak button, 'It's too late, Jack.'

'Why are you doing this, Saul?' Roseman replied.

'I know your orders,' Saul said. 'It's easier this way, for both of us.'

'I can't let you go,' Roseman said.

'You must.'

'Grearson will come after you. And he'll catch you.'

'If you don't stop him, I'll depressurize the chamber. I'll open the hatch before leaving.'

There was silence. Then Saul heard Roseman tannoying his copilot, 'Dave, don't enter the rescue chamber. Repeat, do *not* enter the rescue chamber.' Roseman returned to Saul, 'You heard?'

'I heard. Wish me luck.'

'I wish you luck,' Roseman said, sounding resigned. 'You're going to need it. You're in Dave's machine – with the air leak.'

Saul turned the outside lights of the mermaid on and the magnetic clamps holding him to the submersible off. He gunned the throttle with his finger. On the video screens showing the view beneath him, he saw the misty pewter of the submersible's outer skin slip into the distance. Saul dipped the nose of the mermaid, went down towards the seabed and levelled off as it came into view.

His plan was to follow the same route as the day before to the hotspot. Then he would ascend vertically and, if all went well, he should break surface close to the *Voyager* about one and a half hours later. With relief, Saul saw the outcropping of volcanic rock appear on the seabed below. A few minutes later, the temperature began to rise. Tempting though it was to return to explore the hotspot, Saul hardly gave the acorn worms and molluscs a second glance as he climbed the incline towards the cliff edge. When the edge loomed, he pulled back on the steering stick until the mermaid was travelling straight up towards the surface. The depth gauge began to spiral backwards. It fell by about 1000 feet every three minutes. He was heading for the surface at nearly 6 feet a second.

Saul peered into the narrow beam of light through the transparent viewport. Direct vision was a luxury not available in Saturn. In any case the bathysphere's lights and cameras were usually reserved for the thinly populated ocean floor. Saul began to see occasional bright flashes, like lightning, on his ascent. They came from creatures with skin glands and organs capable of producing light in this black world – fish with exotic names like von Simson's gulper and Leifer's eel. They used their lights to lure prey, to frighten off enemies, even to find a mate.

He saw some devil fishes with phosphorescent throats and little lights swinging above them like lanterns. In the spotlight they looked like miniature grotesque monsters, as broad and as tall as they were long, each no bigger than a man's fist. An appendage hung from the mouth, crescent-shaped and branched, a sensory organ which helped the fish to gauge the size of its victims. Then he passed through a shoal of high-backed, three-inch-long hatchet fish, their many lights giving a metallic gleam to their scales as if they were crumpled tinfoil.

Saul's concentration had remained unbroken for more than an hour when it happened. He had only seconds to take evasive action. The screen filled with a dark, solid object. Saul pulled back sharply on the steering stick and released the throttle. He slowed and tried to regain his bearings. The depth gauge read 10,850 feet, two-thirds of the way to the surface. It was not the whale or shark which Saul had instinctively feared. The outline of the drooping snout told him it was Bottom Miner.

Saul completed a backward loop, dropping 50 feet, and tried to locate Bottom Miner once more at a slower speed. He proposed to convert a near miss to his advantage. The pipe could lead him straight back to the ship. If he followed it up, he would emerge right in the horseshoe harbour at the stern of the *Voyager*.

With relief, he saw the mining head reappear through the gloom. It looked like some prehistoric animal. As he approached – from below and to one side – he saw the huge caterpillar tracks underneath and then the patches of red oxide paint on the side which always suggested that the machine was in need of a respray. One thing above all puzzled Saul. Bottom Miner was not moving. It lay, suspended like bait on a fishing line, dangling from the end of the pipeline.

Saul could understand that Beckett might have become so obsessed by the cobalt that he would order Dansk to send the machine down. But, short of mechanical failure, Saul could think of no good reason to stop the mining head in mid-descent. Saul could see the pipe stretching upwards into darkness. He began to circle the mining head slowly. Then he frowned. As he watched, Bottom Miner changed shape before his eyes. He blinked. Perhaps his tired eyes were playing tricks on him. He looked again.

What Saul saw shocked him. Two yellow eyes with thick, black horizontal pupils across the centre stared back in at him. They belonged to a giant octopus. Saul guessed that the body alone might be 12 feet across. He reversed until he was some 25 feet clear but still able to see the beast.

Both deep-sea octopus and squid were molluscs – descended from the lowly clam. Outsize examples had long figured in seafaring legend. Fishermen handed down tales, father to son, relating heroic battles with seething 60-foot tentacles and ships lost in mysterious capsizes. Only in the 1950s had such stories taken on new meaning. The evidence was washed ashore on the Oregon coast. A series of photographs and measurements were taken proving the existence of squid with a span – tentacle tip to tentacle tip – of more than 100 feet.

The octopus Saul stared at was not that big. He guessed its span at forty to fifty feet. The octopus was an intelligent creature. Its brain was a five-lobed ring of nerve cells set around the oesophagus. Three separate pumps pushed a green copper blood around its body. The animal could change colour, shape, form and surface texture. It ate crab by first cracking the shell between abdomen and tail and then inserting its tentacles to pull out the meat. The tentacle tips could reach the furthest recess of a lobster's legs and claws and carried the meat from sucker to sucker all the way back to the mouth.

Saul saw a tentacle snaking towards him. It flashed across the video screen before striking the mermaid some-where towards the tail. Saul had miscalculated the animal's size and reach. He was well within range. He saw another tentacle through the viewport. There was no time to lose. The second tentacle struck home. With one hand Saul gunned the throttle, with the other he activated one of the mermaid's mechanical arms and used it to slice through the water. Saul could feel the mechanical arm strike its target and the mermaid begin to pull clear.

The fight was not yet over. Roused by the sudden assault which had met its probing tentacles, the octopus tried to remove the main cause of its irritation. Saul felt the mechanical arm seized. He could see on the video screen a second tentacle join the first and wrap itself tightly around the thin metal arm.

The octopus began to pull in its catch. Saul saw other tentacles approaching and knew that within seconds he would be totally encompassed in their grip. He felt underneath the dashboard and grabbed hold of a handle which he knew he should find there. He twisted it and gunned hard on the throttle again. The mechanical arm separated from the mermaid at the shoulder. Saul was happy with the exchange. The octopus now had one of the mermaid's limbs; Saul had his freedom. He climbed until he was certain he was out of the octopus's reach, thankful he had studied the mermaid instruction manual on board the submersible.

Saul searched for and found the pipeline which would lead him back to the *Voyager*. He kept within about fifteen feet of the pipe and steered himself parallel to it. The depth gauge once again started to drop steadily but Saul soon became aware of a new problem. He began to snatch at breaths. His air supply was slowly failing. He clenched his fist around the steering stick and returned to full throttle.

The mermaid was scarcely larger than a coffin and Saul was panicking. He forced himself to relax and breathe slowly, practising the techniques he used in meditation. He stared at the depth gauge willing it down – 6000, 5000, 4000, 3000 feet. It all seemed to be happening in slow motion.

He had only a few hundred feet to go when suffocation began to grip his chest. Cramps swept over his body. He heard a change in the note of his engine. It sounded so far away. He realized with a start that his finger had slipped from the throttle. He tightened his grip and the jet whine climbed once more.

Now Saul could feel the veil of unconsciousness

approach. He thought of Kathy and fought the temptation to go under. He had not come through such bizarre adventures to fail within a few hundred feet of the surface. He struggled to focus on the depth gauge and saw it move from three to two figures. He swallowed another empty mouthful of stale air, practically bereft of oxygen. He had lost sight of the pipeline. It no longer mattered. He would hit the surface within seconds. The most important thing was to stay conscious until he could get the hatch open.

The mermaid burst through the divide between water and air, leaping like some spent ballistic missile. The screens went white and Saul felt the mermaid belly-flop on the swell and begin to roll.

When Saul pressed the hatch button, he heard it unclick and then air rushed in. He managed two joyful gulps before the water followed. He struggled to slide the hatch open and get clear. He clawed at it with failing fingers. Water now filled the mermaid. The hatch moved. Suddenly he was out, in cold saltwater, gasping and choking as he bobbed under a bright, star-filled sky. He trod water, gaining strength with every breath of air. He could see the lights of the *Voyager* twinkling ahead of him, a couple of hundred yards away. The mermaid filled with water and sank with a last glug of air rising to the surface. He let out several yells.

Saul wanted to attract the attention of the sailor on duty. But he also wanted to hear his own voice. He had made it.

He yelled once more, with pleasure, and promptly swallowed a mouthful of seawater. He turned and floated on his back. The moon was bright and beautiful. There was the most gentle of swells. Saul was glad to be back on the surface of planet earth. He breathed deeply savouring warm, fresh air and then began to swim once more. The *Voyager* seemed further away than before.

Saul was only a moderately strong swimmer. All of a sudden the two hundred yards to safety seemed a long, long way. He swam steadily for five minutes against a current, thankful that the white suit he wore assisted his buoyancy. He switched to his back, counting each stroke and concentrated on establishing a steady rhythm. When he reached one hundred, he changed back to breaststroke. Saul was relieved to see the *Voyager* gradually loom larger on his horizon.

There were lights on the bridge but Saul was approaching the darkened stern, lit only by navigation markers. He started to swim for the opening to the horseshoe harbour. He knew there was an inspection ladder in the centre of the horseshoe next to the Bottom Miner pipe which curled out over a large roller into the water.

Saul's arms were aching and his lips were sore with salt when he finally grabbed hold of the ladder. He waited a moment and then wearily pulled himself clear of the sea. Hand over hand, rung by rung, he climbed towards the deck until he flopped forward over the gangrail and fell heavily to the deck, gasping and dripping like a landed fish.

It was a minute or more before Saul lifted his head and looked around. When he did, his eyes met an empty moonlit scene. The pipe snaked past him rising towards the first level of the mining rig which towered above the deck casting shadows of its steel ribcage out over the gangrail and across the water. The only sound he could hear or movement he could see came from a huge hook hanging from a derrick. It swayed slightly with a creak of its chain.

Then somewhere in the mid-distance, Saul heard a few notes of a tuneless whistle. He couldn't see beyond the pipe-stack ahead of him. He dragged himself to his feet and worked his way along the harbour rail. When he felt confident enough he took a few unsupported steps. He moved to one corner of the mining rig, then forward to the next. Now the pipe-stack no longer obscured his view. He could see across the mid-decks towards the bathysphere which sat on its cradle, a long bulbous shadow stretching across the deck.

Saul heard the whistling once again. He smiled to himself. Only Nicholson could whistle as tunelessly. He saw Nicholson appear from round the blind side of the bathysphere, walking, head bowed in shadow, one hand dragging on the flotation ring.

Saul watched him walk round again before calling out, 'Carl! Over here.'

Nicholson lifted his head, looked around him and then disappeared on yet another circuit of the bathysphere.

'Carl!' Saul waited until Nicholson reappeared. 'It's Saul. Over here.'

Nicholson looked up and leaned back against the bathysphere cradle, muttering to himself.

Saul took a few paces forward, puzzled at Nicholson's behaviour, and stopped by a bulkhead, illuminated by the pool of light from a safety fitting. 'Carl, don't be frightened. It's Saul.'

Nicholson didn't move. 'Saul's dead.' He stared at the man in the white suit across a forty-foot divide.

'I was rescued,' Saul said. He hadn't thought how his reappearance would affect the *Voyager*'s crew. 'If you come closer, you can see I'm no ghost.'

'I can't,' Nicholson said.

'I need your help. Don't back off.'

'You don't understand.' Nicholson shrank further to the side of the bathysphere and into the full light of the moon. And Saul saw the engineer's ravaged features for the first time. Nicholson's face was swollen and covered in scabs and scars, his cheeks hollow, his eyes haunted and desperate.

'My God,' Saul said. 'What happened to you?'

'Plague. The doctor's dead. Half the ship's got it.'

'I don't understand.'

'I've been going crazy in the sickbay. A corpse, four men screaming at me. I came out on deck and you're back from the dead in a shining white suit!'

'I was rescued – by a submersible. What's been happening here, for God's sake?'

'I told you. Plague. Disease. From that goddamned fish. The doctor died this evening. There'll be more by morning.'

'How's Kathy?' Saul was alarmed.

'Safe. She's in the lab, working on it.'

'Tell me what happened.'

'I got sick – on Saturday,' Nicholson said. 'Then the

doctor, then Wilkins. Then Butcher, Rico and Larkin. God knows who else by now. Maybe I'm recovering, maybe not. The others are going downhill fast.'

'Here's what you do,' Saul said. 'You go back to the sickbay. I'll follow, at a distance, to the lab. Once I've seen Kathy, we'll speak – on the intercom. It's going to be all right. We can turn this thing round. Trust me.'

'I can't go back.'

'There must be somewhere I can reach you on the intercom. The sickbay's best. Don't mention to anyone I'm on board. There's time enough to explain all that.'

'Yes, but . . . .'

'No buts. Come on.'

Nicholson turned and made his way towards the steps leading below deck. Saul followed about ten yards behind. He noticed the flaked and bubbled yellow paint of the bathysphere as he passed. No wonder Nicholson found it hard to believe he had escaped the inferno below.

As Saul rounded the steps into the corridor below deck, Nicholson was halfway to the sickbay, standing in the middle of the corridor. He turned and moved on, apparently satisfied that Saul was not just a moonlit illusion. Saul paused before crossing the entrance to the canteen and to the kitchens. He listened for any sound. There was none. Nicholson reached the sickbay, turned, wagged an admonishing finger at Saul and disappeared inside.

Saul reached the lab door a few moments later. He tapped out his pass code on the display.

The sound of the lock disengaging startled Kathy. She had been dozing in a chair in the rest area, her head slumped to one side. Instantly, she was awake and on her feet.

'Don't come in!' Kathy screamed as the door swung open. 'Whoever you are.'

For a split second, Saul thought that Kathy was going to throw the coffee pot. But she went as rigid as a statue and it dropped to the floor. Her eyes grew wide and a disbelieving smile appeared.

Before he could stop her she had rushed forward and thrown her arms round him. Her hand moved to caress his hair, wet and matted from the sea. Her lips found his. Passion and relief mingled.

Kathy took a sudden step backwards. 'Your suit! There's plague . . . contamination . . . .'

'Don't worry. I've not been within thirty feet of anyone. There's no danger. But let's do it right all the same. Open the freezer.'

Kathy did so without question.

'Now move away.' Saul walked through the open door and unzipped his suit. It fell to the floor and he stepped out of it. He walked from the freezer still in Grearson's borrowed clothes.

'I don't understand,' Kathy said, confused. She stared at Saul who moved towards her. They fell joyfully into a long embrace.

Kathy sobbed. 'I knew you'd make it. I really did.'

'You knew more than I did.'

As he held her, cradling her head against his chest, Saul heard the background gurgle of water aeration in the fishtanks. It was a reassuring sound. The creatures in the glass bank of fishtanks along the corridor wall provided the final proof he needed to convince himself he was back. Then he caught sight of the solitary fishtank on Herbie's desk. He thought of the shoals he had seen from the mermaid. The blind, hotspot fish was six miles from home.

21

Saul woke with a start. He was lying on the settee in the lab's rest area under a light blanket. Kathy sat, legs bent, enveloped in one of the two armchairs, head resting against its back, smiling at him.

'How long have I been asleep?'

Kathy looked at her watch. 'Nearly three hours. You conked out on me in mid-sentence.'

'What time is it? I feel rough.' Saul swung himself to a sitting position.

'Nearly 4 a.m. You lasted half an hour and passed out.'

'And you've been sitting there staring at me since then?'

'Guess so. I don't want to let you out of my sight. I got hold of Nicholson on the intercom and told him what you'd said. He said he'd dope himself as well as the others and try to get some sleep. Haven't heard a word since. You hungry?'

'Not particularly. They did feed me.'

'I still can't believe you're back. Not really.' Kathy rose from her chair and went to sit beside Saul. She held his hand.

'You've really maintained isolation?' he asked.

'Yes, on a diet of chocolate, vodka and your sour-dough bread. It was all in the freezer. There was a bowl of fruit and some cookies in here with the coffee. It could be worse. I only ran out of milk yesterday.'

Saul stood, stretched and walked through to the lab. Kathy followed.

Saul could see boxes of slides and jars of stain around the light microscope on Kathy's workbench. He looked into the incubator and checked the temperature. Most of the cultures sat in small Petri dishes on agar jelly nutrients. Saul paid special attention to a few enclosed in cylinders.

'You've tried them anaerobically.'

'Yes. Once I'd found most of the bacteria in the fish were sulphur oxidizing, I thought they'd do better without oxygen in a hydrogen atmosphere.'

'And?'

'They do better. But tetracycline still wipes them out. That's why I put everyone on the antibiotic – a prophylactic measure. Boost the body's defences to kill the bacteria at the moment of infection. That was the idea. I arranged for the miners and the navy crew to get their pills from the kitchens when they collected food.'

'What dose?'

'Two 250 mg., four times a day. I've kept back about a hundred, that's all.'

Saul approached the fishtank. He fingered the pack of soluble hydrogen sulphide pellets standing beside the tank. 'The fish seems in good shape.' He put his arm around

Kathy's waist when she came up beside him. Together they studied the two-foot-long fish with its small head, hollowed underside, stubby protruding fins and eel-like tail.

'I saw dozens of these around the hotspot,' Saul said. 'The sub crew weren't really that interested.'

'Can we contact the sub?' Kathy asked.

'Only if Beckett radioes ashore first. I'm not sure what use they'd be.' Saul paused. 'Christ, they were going to kill me!'

'Maybe you should speak to Beckett?'

'Not yet. It could be he knows all about the sub. They both seem to work for the same outfit.' Saul paused. 'I think it's best if as few people as possible know I'm here. I'll have to tackle Beckett sometime. I must find a way of getting him to radio. But if he hasn't sent an SOS when he's got plague on board, my turning up won't change his mind. I'm certainly not going to tangle with him till you've told me, slowly, from the beginning again, what happened.'

Kathy stared at the fish. 'It's hopeless. I've taken biopsies and excreta. I've scraped inside its ugly little mouth. I've grown cultures. The tetracycline wipes out all the bacteria I can find. But Helen's dead and people still keep falling sick.'

'What makes you so sure the infection comes from the fish?'

'Nicholson got cut by it. Even if it had been the tube worm, the range of bacteria I've found is identical.'

'So how did it spread?'

Kathy described the progression of the disease from Nicholson to Helen Mendoza on Sunday morning and how the first miner had been infected while visiting the sickbay. 'Nicholson was a complete idiot,' she said. 'He didn't tell Helen about Bob Wilkins until it was too late. He's been trying to make up for it since. Been very cooperative. Can't be fun in there.'

'Why did Wilkins go to the sickbay?'

'Nothing important. He and Nicholson were supposed to have breakfast together and spend the morning fishing over the side. When Nicholson was a no-show, Wilkins searched the boat. He went straight to the canteen from the sickbay. The disease took off from there. As soon as I knew about Wilkins, I shut down the kitchens; Beckett imposed quarantine areas. But by then the damage was done. Wilkins obviously infected Ted Butcher. Rico, the kitchen hand, had a fever and blisters by Monday morning. Then at noon another miner reported sick. They're all in the sickbay.'

'And the sailors?'

'Don't know for sure. Henderson wore a fire-fighting suit for protection when he went to collect food and antibiotics for the bridge. I said he could take unopened packets and food straight from the freezer. One of the ratings, Able, had a temperature last night.'

'Let's find out. Learn any bad news straight away. There'll be someone on duty who can tell us. How's Bertil by the way?'

'Still OK, last night.'

'That's good.'

'I wouldn't count on it,' Kathy said, crossing to the intercom on Saul's workbench. 'He's isolated himself, but it may be too late. Larkin was lowering Bottom Miner when he collapsed. Beckett ordered it down. The other miners stopped work. Refused to continue the assembly. Beckett ordered Bertil to sort it out. Bertil remonstrated with the remaining miners – without success – and ended up carrying Larkin off to the sickbay.'

'Let's hope he's lucky. Anyone else you know about?'

'Six is enough. It's a third of the goddamned crew.'

Kathy lifted the intercom receiver. 'As far as the bridge is concerned, you don't exist?'

'That's right.'

Kathy press-dialled the bridge.

Bell answered.

'Mark, how's Able?'

'Not so good. He's got swellings around his neck and shoulders. He's feverish, itching and frightened. Are we all going to catch it?'

'I don't know. Has anyone else got symptoms?'

'No, not yet. Should we be isolated from him?'

'Honestly, there's not much point. You've all been working together. Just keep trying to get Beckett to radio.'

'I have been.' Bell sounded peeved. 'Even if I jumped him, I don't know where he hid the key. Without it, no circuit.'

'I know. Keep trying.' Kathy put the phone down.

'Able's now confirmed?' Saul asked.

'Afraid so,' Kathy said. 'He asked about isolating Able.'

'There's no point. Any damage is already done. Besides Able will need help.' Saul sighed. 'Tell me where you've got to with the lab tests?'

'I've been going round in circles.'

'Try me.'

'In the beginning, when only Nicholson had symptoms, it was easy. I thought it was a toxic reaction. Helen thought it might be food poisoning. But then she went down with the same symptoms and she'd eaten completely different meals, I checked.'

Saul nodded.

'So, virus or bacteria? The electron microscope takes so long to prepare and I'm not good on the microtome. I started looking for bacteria. I had serous swabs from the blisters. I got Nicholson to organize sputum and stool samples – as well as blood.'

'Nicholson took blood?'

'Yes. He surprised me. Knows all about syringes. He's been working hard – preparing samples, labelling them, pushing them across the corridor in quarantine bags. He arranged distribution of the antibiotic with Rico. Maybe that's how Rico caught it – though I tried to make sure they both knew what to do.'

'Don't blame yourself.'

'Nothing obvious stands out. Nothing at all. The bacteria I've grown – from the fish and from the tube worm – are knocked out by the mildest doses of antibiotic. The only unusual organism I found was in the serum from the blister. It wouldn't culture and didn't take a stain.'

'Have you still got those slides?'

'Yes, I think so.'

'I should take a look at them. Anything else?'

'I did a blood count just in case I was ignoring a virus. But the count clinched it. Nicholson and Mendoza were both high in polymorphs and low in lymphocytes. Wilkins too. I haven't tested the others.'

'Excellent. So it is a bacteria. We've got a better chance than with a virus.'

'It may sound silly,' Kathy said 'but I don't think it's the infection which killed Helen. I think there's something else going on.'

'How do you mean?'

'The antibiotic doesn't knock out the infection – despite the lab results – but it does seem to bring it under some sort of control. As the worst of the feverish symptoms moderate, they're replaced by respiratory problems.'

'Pneumonia?'

'There were none of the usual signs. No cough, no phlegm. Helen hardly responded to the oxygen cylinder. But don't forget I've been working through Nicholson.'

'Are you saying you think that something's interfering with oxygen absorption?'

'That's my hunch.'

'But Nicholson is different.'

'Yes. Which is strange. You'd think if anyone was going to have trouble, what with his stomach operation, it would be him.'

'Now you could just have something there,' Saul said. 'Nicholson has been having those massive B12 jabs every week. I wonder if the vitamin could make a difference.' Saul stared hard into the fishtank on Herbie's old bench. 'Is that the same water the fish came up in?'

'Yes. I've added hydrogen sulphide pellets.'

'There'll be free-floating bacteria in there as well as the bugs you scraped off the fish. We should take a look see.' Saul collected a pipette from a drying rack by the sinks. 'We'll let Nicholson sleep.'

Nicholson was not asleep; but he was hardly awake either. He sat, deeply doped, in the one comfortable chair in Dr Mendoza's small office staring vacantly into the sickbay.

The background noise of groaning came from the prone figures twisting in tortured sleep and painful consciousness.

The blisters seemed to have stopped spreading over Wilkins and Butcher. They lay in adjacent cubicles, curtains drawn back, either side of an oxygen cylinder. As with Nicholson himself, the visible ravages of the infection seemed to have been finally contained. But, in exactly the same fashion as the doctor, both Wilkins and Butcher now had considerable breathing difficulty. They went through phases of heaving for air followed by semi-consciousness. The oxygen facemask hung between them unused. It brought little apparent relief.

Larkin and Rico were still at the earlier stage of the disease. They lay sharing the third cubicle, Larkin on the operating table which Nicholson had wheeled out of the glassed-in operating booth. Each man had been alternately hot and cold, complained of thirst, and scratched at his itching until the blisters were raw and open, the skin torn bloody. When ignored for too long, they directed abuse at Nicholson, blaming him for their predicament. Nicholson's efforts to calm them by demonstrating the extent of his own recovery failed to convince. Only the sedatives which Kathy had told him to hand out had brought a modicum of peace to the sickbay.

There was one person present who gave no trouble. Her disfigured body lay under a sheet on the floor of the operating booth. Nicholson had watched the doctor transformed into an aged, wrinkled hag as lumps swelled and blisters leaked serous fluid and pus. On Monday there had been the agony of watching her struggle for air for hours, knowing there was only one likely outcome. It had arrived at 7 p.m.

Nicholson's foray on deck had been a necessary escape from the horrors of the sickbay and the doctor's death. Since then he had begun to think about escaping from the boat altogether. He had a stockpile of food which Rico, and then Santini, had brought to the sickbay door. He would go with his stolen nodule collection in one of the lifeboats. The sick could swallow their antibiotics without him. He tapped out the last Marlboro in the pack and lit it. It was Saul's problem, he argued to himself, remaining unconvinced. The cigarette hung limply from his lips.

He stared unblinking into the sickbay. What he saw made him hoist himself out of the chair. Wilkins was half out of bed, struggling for air. Nicholson hurried as fast as heavy legs allowed to his friend's side. Wilkins was flailing, searching for the facemask which provided pure oxygen from the cylinder standing near the head of the bed.

'Here,' Nicholson said, placing the facemask over Wilkins' nose and mouth. Nicholson twisted the flow-control knob on the cylinder from demand-only to open. He heard the oxygen hiss into the facemask.

Wilkins breathed in uneven short gasps. Nicholson opened the oxygen tap further. He might as well have been pumping poison through the facemask for all the good it did. The fight for air was almost over. Wilkins lost consciousness, the sleep of death upon him, his body composed and relaxed as he drifted away.

Nicholson did not recognize the moment of death. But there came a moment when he knew that Wilkins was dead. The oxygen continued to hiss fiercely into the facemask. Nicholson let it drop, moved the cylinder closer to Butcher's bed and dragged himself wearily back to Dr Mendoza's office and the intercom.

'Yes?' The voice was Kathy's.

'Wilkins is dead; Butcher not far behind. What the hell now?'

'Let me give you Saul.'

Nicholson heard Kathy explain the latest disaster to Saul. His first words to Saul were, 'Don't soft soap me.' He felt at the end of his tether. 'Christ, I signed on as an engineer. Not a goddamned nurse.'

'I know, Carl.' Saul was soothing. 'We're working on it.'

'This isn't a sickbay any longer. It's a mortuary.'

'What can I say? I don't know I can do anything about it. Depends how lucky we are. Let's hope it's not as hard to isolate as Legionnaire's disease.'

'That supposed to be encouraging?'

'No.'

'Because it damn well isn't.'

'Hold it, Carl. I do have a suggestion. You know where the B12 is you get for your injections?'

'Yes.'

'You had one last week, as usual, if I remember right.'

'Sure. And the doctor gave me another on Sunday morning.'

'She did!' Saul sounded surprised, almost excited.

Nicholson explained, 'She said she didn't want me to risk anaemia. Said an extra shot couldn't do any harm.'

'That really could be it,' Saul said softly. 'You're the only one among six people to have caught this disease who's making a recovery. The B12 could be protecting you. How many vials are left? Go count them. I'll wait.'

Nicholson walked round to the drug cabinet and returned a moment later with the carton in his hand. 'Eight.'

'That's not much to play with.'

'Hell, no. My weekly jab is due today, by the way.'

'It'll be my pleasure to give it to you,' Saul said. 'I'm coming through. I'll be a while. I have to rig up some sort of headpiece to fit over that white protective suit.' Saul broke off conversation and Nicholson heard him say to Kathy, 'Have we got charcoal filters?' Then Saul said, 'Carl, you'd better prepare Butcher and Larkin, and Rico. I'll be a strange sight.'

'I can give the injections.' Nicholson was agitated.

'I want to see this disease for myself close up. I've got an unpleasant procedure to perform on the bodies. From the rest of you, I want some blood for tests and then it's B12 shots all round. I'll see you as soon as I can – ten or twenty minutes, no more.'

Nicholson put the receiver down and got to his feet. He shook his head, trying to clear the hangover effect of the sleeping pills he had taken just a few hours before. He now had plenty to do and not much time. Saul's talk of the B12 had decided him.

First he emptied a holdall he found behind the office door, shaking the bag upside down. A towel, tee shirt, pants, bra, shoes, socks and shorts tumbled out in a heap on the floor. It was the doctor's running kit. He dropped the carton of B12 into the bottom of the holdall. Then he went back to the drug cabinet in the sickbay and grabbed a handful of disposable syringes from a box. Each was individually sealed in a sterile polythene pack. He dropped them into the holdall.

Butcher lay on the cubicle bed diagonally opposite. He had propped himself on one arm with the oxygen mask in the other hand. He stared at Nicholson. 'What . . . are you doing?' he asked weakly.

'You'll see. All in good time.'

'I don't think I have much left.' Ted Butcher sounded beaten. 'Can't you do something?'

'Don't worry. Help's on the way. Saul turned up alive in the night.'

'You're kidding me! He's dead!' Butcher delivered his reaction in short bursts between several quickly taken breaths.

'He'll be here shortly, looking like a spaceman, no doubt, but he'll be here.' Nicholson took the holdall with him into the doctor's office. He took a tray stacked with provisions, inserted the edge in the holdall and tipped in sliced loaves, a smoke-cured ham, chicken drumsticks and cans of beer. He hung the bag on his shoulder and swung out of the office with a sudden display of determination.

'Where are you going?' Butcher was alarmed.

'I'll be back,' Nicholson said. He felt in the holdall. 'Here, catch.' Nicholson threw Butcher a can of Budweiser. It landed beside him on the bed.

'Hey, thanks,' Butcher was distracted for a moment. 'It's cold, too.'

Nicholson thought of the B12 at the bottom of the holdall. They were his shots and there simply weren't enough for him to go handing them out. He needed a regular weekly jab. He had no good idea how long it would take him to reach land once he'd jumped ship.

'What about Mike and Rico?'

'Saul will see to you. He'll be here. I promise.' Nicholson was having trouble maintaining his composure. If he waited any longer, he would weaken. 'OK then, buddy, farewell.' Nicholson turned for the door, unlocked it, opened it, looked both ways and then stepped out into the corridor. He shut the door behind him, locked it again and left the key for Saul to find.

Relief far outweighed guilt. He felt like a man released from jail. The corridor was quiet and the only sound was from his own footsteps as he hurried towards his cabin. He slowed as he approached the kitchens. The door was slightly ajar. He heard no sound within. Nicholson moved quietly past and finally reached his own door. A moment later, Nicholson was bolted safely inside.

The moray eel swam languidly around its fishtank, still protecting Nicholson's store of stolen nodules. Nicholson looked into the mirror. His hair was matted and greasy, his face pockmarked and ravaged. His eyes bore the stare of a wounded, cornered animal. His pulse still raced and there was a pounding in his temples.

He sat on the bed and let his breathing return to normal. The *Voyager* was not a floating Alcatraz from which escape was impossible. Nicholson intended to get off the plague-ridden tub as soon as possible. He looked out of the port-hole at the first light of morning. The sea was as flat as a millpond. It would be hot and sunny. He grabbed a heavy pullover from a drawer and pushed it into the top of the holdall. There was no time to lose.

Ten minutes later, with the holdall hanging from its strap around his shoulder and carrying another bag in his hand, Nicholson left the cabin, careful to make no noise. He climbed the mid-decks stairway, almost opposite his cabin, out on to open deck. The sun was still low in the sky. He waited in the shadows of the bathysphere crane listening and watching for any noise or movement, wondering how to reach the closest lifeboat without being spotted by whoever was standing watch on the bridge. He would need to make a couple of trips to the kitchens to find water containers he could fill and take with him. He felt more confident of survival on the open sea than on the doom-laden *Voyager*.

22

Saul shut the lab door behind him. He wore the white protective suit taken from the submersible, white rubber lab boots, plastic disposable gloves and, most extraordinary of all, a heavy duty, clear plastic hood, taped to his suit, with two air filter tubes emerging at mouth level and curving over his shoulders like a pair of distorted tusks.

He crossed the corridor, a metal tray in his hands. One compartment was packed with ice. There were several sterile containers as well as syringes of different sizes. Puzzled by the key in the sickbay door, Saul was shocked by what awaited him within.

A corpse, covered with a filthy sheet, was on the bed nearest the door. Saul put his tray down on a trolley standing at the foot of the bed. His eyes swept the room looking for Nicholson.

Saul saw Ted Butcher in the next cubicle under bed-clothes soiled by sweat, streaks of blood and pus. He held a mask, attached to the oxygen cylinder, unused in his hand. The man gasped noisily for air and groaned out his exhalations. He seemed unaware of Saul's presence.

In the far corner, sharing the third uncurtained cubicle were two men wracked with pain. Their faces were so swollen and blistered that Saul had trouble at first distinguishing them. He identified Rico who moaned, unseeing, consumed by his battle with the fever. The other man had to be Larkin. He thrashed about, the bed coverings thrown clear, revealing a bloodstained torso.

Larkin stopped his twisting and turning when he saw Saul. He struggled to one elbow and stared, quite blankly, eyes dulled by exhaustion, at the mysterious hooded figure.

Saul turned away for a moment towards the rooms leading off the sickbay opposite the cubicles. He quickly checked Dr Mendoza's office and then the bathroom. There was no sign of Nicholson. Then he entered the operating booth and saw a covered heap in the corner. He knelt beside it, awkward in his suit, and pulled back the sheet. Dr Mendoza looked at him – a hideous, bloated, waxwork mask. The eyes were glassy and she lay crumpled like a discarded cloth doll. There was no semblance of dignity about her death and the smell of putrefaction was already rising from her pores. Saul closed the eyelids, stood and returned to the open sickbay.

'Where's Nicholson?' he demanded roughly of Larkin. Saul's voice was muffled by the hood, conveying a cryptic message.

Larkin looked first afraid, then resigned. 'Take me,' he said hoarsely.

'It's me – Saul. Where's Nicholson?' Saul spoke clearly, slowly and intelligibly.

'Take me. Now,' Larkin said. His gaze was fixed on Saul who assumed Larkin to be hallucinating, mistaking him for the devil or some other supernatural spirit who might deliver him from his pain. Rico's fight with fever continued unabated in the neighbouring bed.

Saul gave up hope of sense from either man and moved to Butcher's side.

Butcher squinted and then blinked. 'Saul?' he asked. He panted with the effort of a single word.

Saul nodded. 'Try to answer. Where's Nicholson?'

Butcher understood. 'Back. Coming back.' He sucked painfully at the oxygen mask which Saul helped him hold in place.

Saul tried to take stock of the grotesque symptoms of the plague. It was as if each victim had been stung by a swarm of bees and then punched out by a heavyweight champion before, in the terminal stages, experiencing the agonies of oxygen starvation. Saul managed a smile for Butcher in an attempt to reassure him. 'You'll make it. Don't talk anymore, I'll bring something to help.'

Saul moved quickly to the drug cabinet outside the doctor's small office. The doors were open and Saul scanned the shelves for the vitamin supplement. He reached the bottom shelf and started again at the top, pulling out cartons to double check their contents. He saw a gap in the neat rows and began to wonder. No Nicholson, no B12. It might be more than coincidence. The tortured noises from Butcher, Larkin and Rico compelled him to do something – but what? In desperation, he took a large vial of liquid Valium and prepared a hypodermic.

He shook the bottle, broke off its glass top and inserted the needle. He pulled back on the handle and the liquid was sucked inside. He held the syringe up against the light now streaming through the portholes and squeezed until he saw a fine spray shoot from the needle, sparkling like champagne in the bright rays of sunlight.

Each man in turn received a shot of the tranquillizer. The effects were rapid as the Valium coursed through veins depressing nerve centres. Larkin fell back and began to rock his head gently from side to side. Rico's battle with his fever became less anguished. Butcher's struggle for air eased slightly.

Saul thought of asking Kathy on the intercom to report Nicholson missing. Even without letting the bridge know of his own return to the boat, she could get them to tannoy Nicholson to report to the sickbay. He dismissed the idea. Nicholson would either return of his own accord or not. The tannoy announcement would not sway him. Saul's samples would take only a few minutes to collect. He could then set out to track Nicholson down personally.

His first task was to collect blood from the living so that he could conduct a biochemical analysis. A high lactic acid level in Butcher, for instance, would confirm that the normal oxygen-providing chemical pathways were being interfered with and that the second stage of the plague, characterized by increasing respiratory difficulty, was not due just to impaired lung function. He took a syringe from the metal tray which he had left on the trolley near the door. He took the samples without trouble from the sedated patients. Only with Rico did he at first have difficulty finding a vein. He labelled each bottle of blood, marking it with the matching initials of its donor.

Then Saul pushed the metal trolley into the glassed-in operating booth. He returned to the bed nearest the door where Wilkins lay under a sheet. He released the brake which held the wheels firm, and then pushed the bed across the centre of the sickbay into the glass booth.

Saul first stripped the sheet off Wilkins. Barely glancing at the bloodied body, he shifted it to one side of the bed. He bent to lift the doctor's corpse and laid it head-to-toe beside Wilkins. He swallowed hard.

An autopsy would be messy. Saul did not have the experience or the time. He proposed to conduct a rough and ready postmortem procedure revealing information about the way the bacteria promoted respiratory failure. Without cutting open either body, Saul could obtain secretion specimens. Thick needles inserted through the neck into the trachea and through the chest into the lung cavity would collect the necessary fluids.

Saul prepared the first syringe with an eight-inch needle from a selection which, for size, would not have looked out of place in a knitting basket. He felt Wilkins' ribs beneath swollen lumps of flesh and chose the gap. Exerting considerable force, he leaned on the needle and felt it disappear into the chest cavity.

Kathy tried to dismiss from her mind the gory means by which Saul was obtaining samples. She had brought tweezers, beakers, a rack of test tubes, pipettes, slides, Petri dishes and agar jelly to her workbench ready to receive the tracheal and lung secretions. She had also found PCA acid and enzymes required in the lactic acid tests. These stood beside the centrifuge on the work surface near the electron microscope. The presence and amount of lactic acid would finally be revealed by the degree of colour change read in the spectro-photometer which stood next to the centrifuge.

When the buzzer sounded, Kathy went to the answer-phone at the steel security door and turned on the overhead monitor.

'Who is it?' she asked.

'Daniels. Come for the nodules.'

The monitor screen brightened and Kathy saw the miner, Sam Daniels, head enlarged by the camera angle, moving nervously from foot to foot. Kathy had forgotten all about the nodules. She had been instructed two days ago by Beckett to get them to Dansk who had the equipment to grade and analyse the ore content. But as she herself had no intention of moving from the lab, she had asked Dansk to send someone to collect them.

'Does he still want them?' Kathy asked Daniels. She was surprised that Dansk would send for the nodules after all prospect of lifting cobalt during the mission had disappeared.

'Those are my instructions.' There was a wheedling quality to Daniels' voice.

'It's a bit early, isn't it?' Kathy looked at her watch. It was just 6 a.m. 'Is he unwell?' she asked, suddenly concerned.

'I don't think so, Ma'am. We're doing just fine down there.' Daniels added, 'Could use more of that antibiotic. It seems to work.'

'You should have enough for another two days.' Kathy noticed at Daniels' feet a cardboard box reduced by the perspective of the camera but clearly visible in the corner of the monitor. 'What's in that box?'

'Food – from the kitchens. We're running short.'

'Only unopened packets, remember. Is Santini all right?'

'The kitchens were empty. No sign of him. You have got more of those pills, haven't you?'

'Only an emergency supply,' Kathy said. 'You'll be all right if you reduce the dose by half.'

'We'll settle for the nodules.'

'Oh yes, I was forgetting.' Kathy went to Herbie's workbench where the hotspot fish continued to patrol the heated tank. Kathy found the bag of nodules in the top drawer where Nicholson had dropped them. She wondered whether she should keep some for Saul to examine. She returned to the security door. 'I think I should . . . .' She hesitated, not wanting to mention Saul. Not that Daniels would believe anyway that Saul had returned from the bottom of the sea in the middle of the night. Dansk had the best equipment to analyse the nodules. She made her decision.

'I can't let you in. Back off – a good distance – and I'll slip the bag out the door.'

'As you say. Ready any time you are.' The miner spoke more eagerly than might reasonably be expected from the menial nature of his errand.

'Move well away.' Kathy checked the monitor. She put her hand on the door release button and watched Daniels back out of range of the camera. As he did, she saw a strange nod of his head. Was there someone else out there with him in the corridor? Why hadn't he said? Or had he? Kathy dismissed the nod and depressed the release button. The electric lock would deactivate in precisely ten seconds.

Nicholson was on his second trip to the kitchens for water. He had found several two-gallon plastic containers there. He had filled two with water and deposited them in his chosen lifeboat. If he could manage another two, he would feel happier about facing the open sea for what might be a number of weeks rather than days. He moved stealthily down the steps from the deck and turned into the corridor.

What Nicholson saw astonished him. Beyond the kitchens, on either side of the laboratory door, two miners were pressed flat against the wall. The man closer to him, Paul Gerinsky, held a knife gleaming in his right hand. Sam Daniels stood on the far side of the lab door. He too held a long-bladed knife.

The noise of the security door lock dropping was audible down the corridor. If Kathy was alone inside, she would be overpowered or dead in moments. Nicholson had no idea what was going on but his reaction was straightforward and instantaneous. He yelled, 'Kathy, no,' and hurtled towards the men outside the laboratory.

It would have taken an Olympic athlete three seconds to cover the distance. It took Nicholson four seconds at most. In that time, the door had begun to surrender to the combined weight of the miners.

Kathy, on the other side of the door, realized as soon as she heard Nicholson's shout that she was under attack. She tried to wedge herself at an angle between door and floor to resist the push which came from the corridor. The outcome hardly seemed in doubt. She could not hold back two men. She did not even have anything to hand to use as a weapon.

Nicholson crashed into Gerinsky with a body tackle from the side, sweeping him off balance. He careered with the miner beyond the lab and on to the other side of the corridor.

Daniels, still pushing against the heavy door, said, 'Nicholson, keep out of this.'

Nicholson kept a tight hold of Gerinsky's knife hand at the wrist.

Gerinsky struggled. 'Let go of me, you bastard. Let go!'

Daniels said, 'You're making a mistake, Nicholson. We don't want the woman. It's the antibiotic.'

'So why knives?' Nicholson screamed at Daniels. He swung Gerinsky in front of him, still firmly holding on to the knife hand, so that the miner would make some sort of shield should Daniels decide to attack.

'To kill that fish,' Daniels shouted back. He maintained enough weight against the door to prevent Kathy from pushing it shut.

Gerinsky, gaining strength from fear, suddenly broke free of Nicholson.

Nicholson expected the worst. But instead of a kitchen knife between the ribs, he saw Gerinsky retreat a few yards down the corridor towards the stern, shouting, 'Keep away from me, you diseased bastard. I'm warning you.'

Nicholson now realized that his role in spreading the plague from the fish to the crew had one unexpected advantage. So far he had experienced only the ostracism of a leper. Now he could exercise the power this created. If he invaded a healthy miner's space, it was the miner who would turn and run. Nicholson took a half step towards Daniels with more confidence.

Gerinsky shouted to Daniels, 'Come on, Sam. Miller's waiting. What's it matter about the fucking fish?'

'We need the pills, you jerk. She's got them. You heard her.'

Nicholson saw Daniels' jaw drop suddenly and then his whole body freeze. The miner looked as if he had been turned into ice sculpture. He gaped past Nicholson at the sickbay door.

As soon as Nicholson glanced behind him and saw the mysterious, hooded figure in the doorway, he knew it had to be Saul.

Daniels seemed to recognize the face beneath the plastic hood despite the charcoal filter tubes. 'What kind of trick is this?' he demanded uncertainly.

Nicholson moved towards Daniels, staying just out of arm's reach. The two men glowered at one another without speaking. Nicholson left Daniels an escape route to allow him to join Gerinsky.

'Go on, get moving,' Nicholson snarled.

'Keep your distance,' Daniels said. He lunged with the knife. But as he did so he moved sideways. The knife thrust was little more than a diversion. Daniels was intent on escaping from Nicholson and the mysterious hooded figure who seemed resurrected from a watery grave.

Nicholson watched Daniels join Gerinsky down the corridor. Gerinsky pointed back towards the lab saying to Daniels, 'The food.' Nicholson heard Daniels say, 'We've got enough. Let's get out of here,' and then the two miners left the corridor by the stern stairway to the deck.

Nicholson, pausing only to collect the box of food in his arms, made his way back towards the main mid-deck stairs. He was halted by a bellow from Saul who stood astride the corridor like some medieval jousting knight.

'Where the hell have you been?' Saul untaped the front of his hood and lifted it like a visor. 'Where's the B12?'

'Don't talk to me like that,' Nicholson said. 'It's mine. I've paid my dues. Kathy's safe. If you know what's best, you'll stay with her.' He strode away down the corridor, more worried about what the miners were up to than whether Saul chose to follow him.

23

Saul watched Nicholson turn out of the corridor and up towards the mid-decks. He remained rooted to the spot, torn three ways – between the men in the sickbay, Kathy in the lab and Nicholson.

Kathy peered from behind the heavy, steel security door. She still held the bag of cobalt nodules in her hand.

Saul turned to her. 'If you start on the samples, I can go after Nicholson. I'll fetch them.'

He disappeared into the sickbay and, a moment later, wheeled out the trolley with its metal tray of containers, some on a bed of melting ice. He locked the sickbay door behind him and pushed the trolley across the corridor against the wall abutting the lab door.

'Gown, gloves and facemask before you touch them,' Saul said to Kathy. He put the trolley brake on with his booted foot. 'I'll be back as soon as I've got the B12 off Nicholson. It's the best chance we've got to save the men in there.'

'Wait, I think you should . . . .' Kathy's voice trailed away. She stood holding out the bag of nodules. Saul was already striding off down the corridor.

Saul approached the deck with caution. He wanted to track Nicholson down without, if possible, running into either Beckett or the navy crew. They were still ignorant of his safe return. He stood in shadow scanning the mid-deck area before him. Saturn sat on her cradle, still attached to the crane. The bathysphere was in a sorry state. There was no sign of anyone, but Saul needed a better observation point.

He looked at the rig which towered above the deck at the stern. The second platform offered the best view of the boat's decks but he was unlikely to reach it without being spotted from the bridge. He had another idea – bold, perhaps, but none the worse for that.

Saul edged steadily round the corner into a covered passageway and moved closer to the captain's cabin and the flight of steps to the bridge. The doors to the conference room and to Beckett's cabin were shut. There was no one in sight. As quickly as he could, he climbed the metal steps until he reached the open gangway which ran around the outside of the bridge. Bent almost double, he pressed himself against the circular shell of the bridge – careful to stay below window level.

Saul squatted beside the sliding door which faced the stairs he had just climbed. It was slightly open and he could hear an argument in progress between Beckett and Bell.

'We have to hang on for three days – that's all,' Beckett was saying. 'Surely even Able can hold out that long.'

'Able will be dead inside twenty-four hours and you know it,' Bell said. 'The second kitchen hand, Santini, has taken to his bed. Henderson here's got a fever – he'll have blisters and lumps before the day is out. This is plague. We need outside help. We need it now.'

'The cargo ships will be here in three days.' Beckett seemed not to have heard Bell. 'It's important to get the rig working. I want Bottom Miner pumping cobalt by then.'

'Forget the fucking cobalt! Get the ships here now, get the sick taken off by chopper. Maybe there's a sub that could be sent to help. Use the radio for Christ's sake!'

'A sub? Near here? Not unless it's Russian,' Beckett said. 'And to use that radio would be like taking prime time on television. We cannot advertise our presence or our problems.'

It certainly didn't sound to Saul as if Beckett was aware of the American sub below them. He tried to calculate the impact of making an entrance at this juncture but quickly rejected the notion. He couldn't improve on Bell's performance. And it would not help him to reach Nicholson or the B12. Those were his priorities.

Saul searched the bow from where he crouched, straining for a sight of Nicholson. The empty helicopter circle looked forlorn. The lifeboats were tightly covered by tarpaulin.

There was no movement. To see the mid-decks and stern, Saul had to get past the open doorway.

As he crossed into the rear semicircle of safety, he caught a glimpse of the scene on the bridge. Mark Bell was pacing nervously. Jennings sat in front of the radar controls at one end of the chart table. Someone else was on the floor half-covered by a blanket. The figure with his back to the sliding door was dressed in the *Voyager*'s single, non-inflammable, red fire-fighting suit. Saul noticed he wore a pistol in a holster on the waistband. It could only belong to Beckett.

Saul settled himself in the centre of the semicircle between the sliding doors on either side of the bridge. He faced aft concealed by the housing for the klaxon and tannoy speaker. He had a good chance of remaining undetected even if someone came out on to the open gangway. He could keep himself well tucked away and screened from sight. One of the tinted bridge windows was wound partly down and Saul could hear the heated bridge discussion continue unabated.

'The sickbay is isolated,' Beckett said. 'So is mining. We've plenty of food and drink. There's antibiotic . . . .'

One of the sailors – it was Henderson – tried to say something.

Beckett would not give way. 'Listen, Henderson, and listen good. You're going to be sweating a lot harder than you are right now before I excuse you from a work detail. We're going to get that machine moving down. I don't give up on missions. And nor will you.'

Saul was horrified. The man was mad. But Saul's immediate concern remained Nicholson. He surveyed the deck carefully – the area around the pipe-stack, the mining rig and the horseshoe harbour behind. A loose tarpaulin on the furthest starboard lifeboat flapped. There was no wind. Then Saul realized that there was a man inside the white dinghy. For a moment, he felt certain he had found Nicholson. Then he saw it was the miner, Sam Daniels, who was busily unstrapping the tarpaulin. From the door leading down to the miners' quarters, Saul saw two other men emerge heavily laden.

Miller was struggling under the weight of the glass container which usually dispensed fresh spring water into small paper cups just inside the entrance to the miners' quarters. The five-gallon jar was obviously almost full. Miller made slow progress towards the lifeboat. Gerinsky carried two cardboard boxes, one stacked on top of the other. With Daniels' help, the provisions were loaded and the men climbed into the boat. Daniels began to wind out the lifeboat until it hung over the water.

Saul watched, fascinated but also alarmed. Anyone escaping the *Voyager* might carry plague with him. The possible consequences were awesome.

'Hey, what's going on out there?'

Beckett's raised voice cut sharply into Saul's thoughts. He shrank inside his shelter, fearful for a moment that he had been detected. Beckett sounded very close – just the other side of the window. The tannoy speaker above Saul's head crackled an assault on his eardrums. Saul bumped his head in fright. Beckett's voice blared from the speaker across the *Voyager*.

The miners had lowered the boat halfway to the water when they heard Beckett order their return.

'Only one thing for it,' Daniels shouted. 'Hold tight!'

Gerinsky and Miller flattened themselves in the belly of the boat. Daniels pulled the emergency release. The lifeboat dropped clear of its ropes and hit the water with a bone-rattling crack. It lurched to one side and cold seawater slopped in soaking the men.

Gerinsky stood, lost his balance, fell, half rose again and got himself to the engine controls. He pulled at the starter. The engine turned but failed to catch. Daniels and Miller were struggling to unclip the oars. They pulled on the rough, round handles and opened up clear water. Gerinsky pointed towards the rear of the *Voyager*. Daniels nodded.

None of the men was prepared for what followed. Gerinsky was still trying to start the engine; Daniels and Miller were heaving away at the oars trying to put distance between themselves and the *Voyager*. Suddenly a splinter of wood flew from the oar in Daniels' hands.

'Someone's shooting,' Daniels shouted at his colleagues. He stared up towards the bridge where he saw a figure wearing the red fire-fighting suit holding a rifle levelled straight at them. Daniels, shocked, held his oar limply out of the water. Miller pulled hard on his oar at the thought of bullets. The boat swung lopsidedly round to present the widest possible target to the bridge sharpshooter.

Miller let out a gasp. He took his hands off his oar and clutched his chest. He removed a hand and looked at his palm. There was a wet beetroot-red stain. With horror glazing his face, he toppled backwards off the bench. His head hit the deck. It did not hurt. He was already dead.

Daniels knew that he and Gerinsky could be easily picked off in the open boat. 'Over the side. Swim for the ship or we're dead,' he shouted to his friend.

Gerinsky sat tight staring at the prone Miller.

'Come on, idiot.' Daniels grabbed Gerinsky and, catching him by surprise, pushed him over the side of the lifeboat. He followed with a lunging dive and the two men hit out in a clumsy crawl for the horseshoe harbour.

It took only a couple of minutes to cover the short distance to the boat. But neither man could get back on board until he had swum into the horseshoe. It took another minute or two for them to reach the ladder which dipped into the water next to the pipe trailing the mining head somewhere below them.

Daniels was first out of the water and over the gangrail. He helped Gerinsky up after him.

'Was that Beckett?' Gerinsky asked.

'I think so,' Daniels said. 'Who else?'

'The bastard,' Gerinsky said.

'You're dead unless you follow orders.' The voice came from above. Both men, dripping wet, lifted their heads to find Beckett in his red fire-fighting armour, standing on top of the pipe-stack, a rifle in his hands and a pistol at his waist.

'There's no need for that,' Gerinsky said, shivering. 'Why did you kill my friend?'

'Desertion,' Beckett said. 'I'll kill you, too, if you're not up this rig working the pipe assembly within ten minutes.'

'You must be joking,' Daniels said.

Beckett removed the safety-catch and, holding the rifle at his waist, pointed it at Daniels. 'Try me.'

Daniels had heard the click of the safety-catch. 'You can put it away. We're coming.'

The miners climbed the metal ladderway to the first platform on the rig. They stepped over the pipe in the automatic feed and glanced at Beckett just a little below them on the pipe-stack. They climbed the second ladder to the platform where pipe assembly took place.

Daniels stepped inside the control booth and checked the instruments.

Gerinsky stared after the lifeboat, several hundred yards away. He looked at Daniels, questioningly.

'Not a chance. We'd drown, get shot or break our necks. Let's do as the man says.'

Gerinsky examined the heat seal equipment. The last length of pipe to have been joined stretched down below him towards the rollers and into the water; the next pipe awaiting moulding hung above him suspended from the top of the 120-foot mining rig.

'Here we go,' Daniels said.

Gerinsky gave a thumbs up.

The machinery began to clank to life, the sixty-foot length of new pipe descended slowly into the top of the assembly clamp. Daniels watched the temperature rise on the heat seal gauge. The clamp squeezed, released, the length of pipe began to move downwards and, as it did, the hoist raised the next length from the automatic feed until it hung from the top of the rig, ready to be joined and take its place as another link in the chain which would be six miles long by the time the mining head reached the bottom of the ocean.

Saul watched the proceedings from his hideaway on the bridge gangway. He couldn't hear what was said but he understood what was happening. He was even more amazed by the orders Beckett had left the sailors.

Henderson looked flushed with fever when he left the bridge with Newman. They were each armed with a fire axe. Jennings accompanied them carrying a rifle, as instructed. Bell remained on the bridge trying to comfort Able who now groaned almost continuously.

There were five remaining lifeboats hanging from davits – two in the bows, two in mid-deck and one on the port side towards the stern. The sailors lowered the stern lifeboat first and let fly with their axes. The sound of splintering wood was painful to Saul. The sailors worked in a clockwise rotation, moving next to the port mid-deck lifeboat and then to the bow, rendering each boat useless in turn. En route, they collected inflatable dinghies stored near the emergency generator in mid-deck. They threw them overboard and the heavy, black rubber packs floated away from the *Voyager* like jetsam.

Saul saw the consternation on the second level of the mining rig. He shared the miners' concern at the destruction of the lifeboats. Daniels emerged from the control booth and had a hurried consultation with Gerinsky. Gerinsky then climbed halfway down the ladder to the first level. Beckett became agitated and ordered the miner to stop. While Gerinsky was diverting Beckett's attention, Saul saw Daniels take a spanner to the assembly clamp and begin to loosen it. A safety mechanism tripped and the automatic assembly feed stopped.

Saul approved of Daniels's bloody-mindedness. The miner continued to work with the spanner on the assembly clamp. Beckett looked around him uncertain what had caused the interruption. Gerinsky stood his ground on the ladder. Saul saw Daniels on the second platform swing his arm. An object flew through the air, falling quickly in an arc towards the sea. It hardly made a splash as it entered the water but Saul knew that Daniels had most effectively sabotaged the pipe assembly. He felt like applauding. 'No lifeboats, no mining,' he said to himself.

The axe team of Henderson and Newman reached the last of the lifeboats with Jennings still standing guard over them to deter interference from any quarter. Henderson and Newman lowered the mid-deck starboard lifeboat and lifted their axes. The bite of axehead on wood resounded once again. The lifeboat quickly splintered and split. Henderson suddenly stopped chopping. Newman did too. Henderson put his axe down and took a look through the hole in the bottom of the boat. He removed first one and then a second large container of water. Jennings put his rifle on the deck and went to join Henderson and Newman in their search. They removed the tarpaulin and triumphantly pulled out two bags which they put on deck before returning to hunt further inside the lifeboat.

The next moment, Nicholson broke cover. He had been hidden for all this time under the cradle of the bathysphere. Saul saw Nicholson run towards the lifeboat and reach his bags before any sailor realized what was happening. Jennings had to cover several yards to retrieve his weapon. By the time he had done so, Nicholson was at the top of the main stairs heading below deck. He held a bag in each hand, lifted from under the sailors' noses. It was a scene straight out of a silent comedy.

Beckett saw the last part of the incident, raised his rifle, fired at Nicholson and missed. Nicholson disappeared below. Beckett summoned the sailors to the pipe-stack and Saul took the opportunity to make his own move. He edged around the gangway, down the steps back to the deck, through the covered passageway and below deck in pursuit of Nicholson and the B12.

The corridor was empty when Saul reached the foot of the stairs. He looked in both directions hoping for inspiration. He studied the row of doors facing him. It was unlikely that Nicholson had returned to his cabin but Saul could not ignore the possibility. He turned the handle on Nicholson's cabin door and walked in. The room was a mess. There were clothes pulled out of the cupboard and strewn over the floor. There was water lying in pools between Nicholson's fishtank and the bed. There was no sign of Nicholson.

Saul gasped when he saw the moray eel. It had died struggling on the bed. The grey corpse lay on damp and twisted sheets like some exhibit in a surreal art show. The creature's skin was thick and scaleless, its dorsal fin leathery and its evil teeth bared. What had possessed Nicholson? He had lavished attention on the young and dangerous predator. Then Saul saw a nodule lying on the floor. He stooped and picked it up in his gloved hand.

24

Nicholson leaned, breathing heavily, against the inside of the security storeroom door, dropped the canvas bag to the floor, and slipped off the shoulder bag.

Gut instinct determined the choice of Nicholson's bolt hole. He had run the full length of the corridor from mid-deck to stern and climbed from the miners' quarters past the pump room to his place of refuge without being seen. Normally he came to the storeroom to steal. This time he had come to hide while he determined a new escape plan.

Nicholson felt for the light switch, turned it on briefly – nothing seemed to have changed since his last visit – and then plunged his metal-walled sanctuary back into darkness in case Beckett had sent a search party after him. He bent over the canvas bag at his feet, felt for the side pocket and replaced the narrow steel picks he had used on the lock. He rummaged in the pocket and withdrew a pencil torch.

Shining the thin beam along the open storage shelf, Nicholson followed it slowly past leaded containers of radioactive isotopes and machine spares until he reached his immediate goal, Dansk's personal booze supply. He pulled a bottle from the cardboard crate, broke the seal, unscrewed the cap and put the bottle to his lips. The whiskey burned his throat as he swallowed. He took another slug and replaced the cap.

Nicholson returned to the door and searched the shoulder bag to satisfy himself that the B12 vitamin shots were still there. He derived great pleasure – as well as considerable relief – from having retrieved the bags. He played the thin torch beam around the walls once more and on to the storage cabinet. He had had no thought of stealing further precious stones when he sought refuge in the strongroom. But now that he was here, he was loath to pass up the opportunity.

He examined the trays of pearls and irregularly sized stones, some still encrusted in nodule fragments, brought over the shoulder bag and tipped into it the contents of the top tray. He pulled out the second tray but then stopped himself. The bag was quite heavy enough with his stolen hoard of precious stones and cobalt nodules. What he needed was fresh supplies of water and, most important, some new means of getting free of the *Voyager*.

The destruction of the lifeboats had been precipitated by the miners' failed escape effort. Nicholson speculated that one of the miners must have seen him loading his boat and, in concert with the others, had decided to jump ship first. He was still shocked at the sight of the holed lifeboats, torn from their housings, lying splintered on the deck. They would not be easily repaired. The miners' lifeboat was adrift and quite unreachable. He turned his thoughts to the inflatables. Perhaps the crew had missed one or two or kept some back. But where? He didn't even know where they were all stored.

Then Nicholson had a brainwave. The ship's inventory would tell him. He congratulated himself with a further shot of Dansk's whiskey.

Nicholson took his torch and lock picks with him but left the two bags in the storeroom. He retraced his steps past the pump room, through the deserted miners' quarters, along the ship's central corridor and up the mid-deck stairway. He paused and took stock. There was no longer any sign of Beckett on the pipe-stack. But Jennings, still armed, had taken his place. He held a weapon on Daniels and Gerinsky while Newman examined the pipe assembly machinery and controls on the second platform. The mining rig was silent with Bottom Miner dangling like a useless umbilical beneath the ship.

Nicholson moved stealthily along the covered passageway which led to the bridge steps. When he reached the gangway at the top, he looked on the bridge through the open sliding door. What he saw shocked him.

Able lay under a blanket, head propped against the chart

table. He was easy to identify by his red hair but his features were disfigured by the dreadful ravages of the plague. The man was groaning, his face swollen and streaked with blood and burst blisters, eyes open but unseeing. Henderson lay beside him: the navigation officer's eyes were hollow and he shivered. Bell stood staring at the radio equipment on the far side of the bridge. There was no sign of the captain.

Nicholson called through the door, 'Mark, over here.'

Bell turned at the sound of his name. 'Good God,' he said seeing Nicholson. He wiped his forehead which was beaded with a light sweat. 'Where did you spring from?'

'Never mind. I need information.'

'Are you better?'

'Maybe,' Nicholson said. 'Where's Beckett?'

Bell pointed at the closed hatchway between the Bottom Miner and bathysphere consoles at the rear of the bridge.

'Downstairs. Running scared. Doesn't want to stay up here with plague-ridden sailors. The bastard still won't break radio silence.'

'You know Saul is on board?'

'What!'

'Saul is on board.'

'Alive?'

'Yes.'

'I don't believe it,' Bell said flatly. 'Since when?'

'Last night. Speak to him. He'll be in the lab unless he's still after me.'

'He can't be alive. I spoke to Kathy a while ago. She said nothing.'

'Believe me. Don't believe me. What do I care? I thought you'd like to know, that's all.'

The idea of asking Kathy whether Saul had returned from the dead did not appeal to Bell. 'Is anyone else recovering?' he asked. He was encouraged by Nicholson's appearance. Although the engineer's face looked blistered with some large scabs, he had no fever and breathed without difficulty.

'Wilkins is dead – probably Butcher by now.' Nicholson

nodded at Henderson and Able. 'You're running a sickbay in here by the look of it.'

'Can you do anything for his breathing?' Bell asked.

'Nothing. The antibiotic seems to make it worse, not better.' Nicholson changed the subject. 'Mark, I need a look at the ship's inventory. Can you get it for me?' Nicholson took a step inside the bridge.

Henderson recoiled on the floor at Nicholson's approach.

'Keep your distance,' Bell said. He went to a cupboard near the wheel and, a moment later, pushed across the chart table a loose-leaf folder which Nicholson picked up eagerly. 'What the hell do you want it for?' Bell asked.

Able's short and rapid inhalations were suddenly interrupted by a spasm which shook his whole body.

'What do I do?' Bell asked.

Nicholson shrugged.

'You must have some idea. How come you recovered?' Bell went to get the sailor water from the dispenser.

Nicholson avidly scanned the inventory section headed SAFETY. It listed the location of every fire extinguisher and medical first-aid kit. He ran his finger on to Lifeboats and then Inflatables. One entry leapt out at him. At last he knew how he was going to escape.

'What are you looking for?' Bell asked.

Nicholson ignored the question. 'Do you still want to radio?' he asked.

'Sure. But Beckett's got the key. I don't even know where he put it.'

'I do,' Nicholson said. 'Dansk saw it. Get me the master key to the captain's cabin – you have one, don't you? – and I'll get it for you.'

'He's got a gun. He'll kill you.'

'Not if you help,' Nicholson said.

Bell returned with the cabin master key. He handed it to Nicholson. 'I've got nothing more to lose,' he said. 'I've got a raging fever. I try to kid myself I haven't, but before long I'll be like Able and Henderson.'

'If you radio, there might be time.'

'That's what I've been trying to tell him.'

'This is what we do. I wait on deck by Beckett's door.

You make a lot of noise at the hatch over there. Make him think you're coming through. Use Henderson's fire axe to smash the hatch. Freak him out. Your job is to get him out of his cabin and into the conference room. I'll do the rest.' Nicholson was still unsure of Bell. 'You've got a duty to do it,' he said. 'There's higher laws than navy regulations.'

The intercom on the chart table rang.

'If it's Saul,' Nicholson said, 'tell him I'll be over. Soon as we get the radio key.'

Bell answered. It was Kathy.

'Have you seen Nicholson?' she asked.

'He's right here on the bridge.'

'He should be down here. He's running around with a drug we need.'

'What do you mean, "we"?' Bell asked slowly. There was silence. 'Are you holding out on me? Nicholson says Saul is alive and on board. Is he?'

The next voice that Bell heard stunned him. It was Saul, saying, 'There's no time to explain. Not now, Mark.' Bell went wide-eyed in amazement as Saul continued, 'We're getting on top of this bug but we need Nicholson and the drugs he took from the sickbay.'

'They need the drugs you took,' Bell said to Nicholson who stood facing him on the other side of the chart table.

'As soon as we've got the radio key.'

Bell passed the message back to Saul who asked, 'How's he going to get it?'

'He says he knows where it is.'

'Look, tell him to get down here as soon as possible.'

'After he gets the key?'

There was a pause. 'I suppose so,' Saul said. 'But hurry it up.'

Nicholson was outside Beckett's cabin door when Bell started to smash an axe against the hatch. The noise had its desired effect.

'Keep out,' Beckett yelled from his cabin. Nicholson heard him push open the dividing doors which separated cabin from conference room.

This was Nicholson's moment. Now or never. He slipped

key into keyhole. The shaft sank home. Nicholson twisted. Nothing happened. The key was jammed. He tried in the other direction. This time the key turned smoothly.

Nicholson opened the door a crack. He could see Beckett standing, back towards him, framed in the double doorway between conference room and cabin. The sound of axe on wood continued to come from the hatch at the top of the ladderway leading up from the conference room to the bridge.

Beckett shouted, 'No more warnings.' He wore the red fire-fighting suit but without its headpiece.

Bell's response was to shout, 'Give me the radio key.'

As Beckett drew his pistol and took a step into the conference room, Nicholson made his move. He would have only one chance.

The gap was five yards. Nicholson had covered half the distance before Beckett realized where the new noise was coming from. He was close enough to launch himself at Beckett.

The captain's pistol hand was rising as he turned to face the threat behind him. But he was not fast enough. Nicholson tackled Beckett high around both arms, trapping the gun hand firmly against the captain's stomach. The force of Nicholson's tackle carried both men into the conference table off which they bounced. Nicholson held on grimly and, as the two men crashed to the floor, the gun went off. The sound of the shot was muffled by the men's bodies. Beckett stopped struggling in Nicholson's arms.

There was silence on the other side of the hatch at the top of the ladderway.

Nicholson rolled Beckett's body on its back. The gun was still clasped in the man's right hand. There was a puncture mark on the fire-fighting suit where the bullet had entered. It had travelled upwards through the abdomen rupturing the heart. Nicholson uncurled Beckett's finger from the trigger and pocketed the pistol.

He climbed the ladderway, eased the bolts and opened the hatch.

Bell was relieved to see Nicholson. 'What happened?' He followed him halfway down the steps, stopping as soon as he saw Beckett's spread-eagled form on the floor. 'Is he dead?'

'I hope so.' Nicholson walked back to the body. 'He shot himself.' Nicholson unzipped the fire-fighting suit and examined the corpse. 'No sign of the disease,' he said looking up at Bell.

'What about the radio key?' Bell remained on the ladderway, sounding feverish and slightly pathetic.

Nicholson bent back over the body. He opened the top button of Beckett's shirt. 'He showed it to Dansk – up on the rig – last week. And here it is, round the bastard's neck, just like Dansk said.' Nicholson gave the chain a vicious tug and it broke, but not before cutting into Beckett's neck. 'Dead horsemeat,' Nicholson said contemptuously. 'Here, Mark. Happier now? Put out your SOS. You're in charge again.'

'Shall I call the lab and tell them you're on your way?'

'No point,' Nicholson said edgily. 'I'll be there in a few minutes. You concentrate on that SOS.'

'This is fantastic,' Bell said, staring at the radio key in his palm. 'The nightmare is nearly over.' He turned back to the bridge, leaving Nicholson by Beckett's body in the conference room.

Nicholson left by the captain's cabin. But first he knelt and felt under the bed. He caught hold of a rope and pulled out a black rubber pack. He used the fastening rope to carry it over his right shoulder. Nicholson had a lot to do and not much time.

25

The cobalt nodules lay in an aluminium bowl beside a tray of instruments, a rack of test tubes, some bottles, a bunsen burner and the empty quarantine bag. Saul, wearing disposable lab gloves, had split two of the cobalt nodules and prepared a solution of scrapings from the muddy ore.

Interrupted only by the conversation with Bell on the

intercom, he had transfered drops of the solution on to glass slides with a small, looped, metal wire. These he had passed over the bunsen burner to fix the bacteria, then flooded the glass with crystal violet solution, added a few drops from another bottle, washed off the crystal violet with iodine, run acetone–alcohol solution over the slides, washed them again and dipped them briefly in a solution of safranin.

While waiting for the slides to dry, Saul had inspected Kathy's work. The high lactic acid level in Butcher's blood confirmed that the lethal second stage of the disease was blocking cellular use of oxygen. The free-floating bacteria from the fishtank, cultured during the night had, like the bacteria from the fish and tube worm, been destroyed by antibiotic. The tracheal and lung secretions collected from the corpses in the sickbay were now on Petri dishes in the incubator but had not yet had time to grow.

Kathy appeared from the rest area carrying a makeshift breathing hood like Saul's.

'Well, what do you think? Two charcoal filter tubes – see – and the same heavy duty polythene.'

Saul allowed himself a smile. 'Great, Kathy. You should patent the design.'

Kathy laughed and put the helmet down on Herbie's workbench beside the heated tank in which the hotspot fish swam languidly.

Saul returned to Kathy's workbench from the incubator. He was certain that the nodule slides held the secret of the plague. He placed the first slide under the microscope, gazed through the eyepiece and adjusted the focus.

'Spores,' he said. 'Dormant spores. Like the bacteria in Nicholson's swab, they don't take the stain. But you can make them out.' He stood aside to let Kathy look.

'They're like ghost cells – all wall.'

'In the right conditions they'll turn back into active bacteria. A little heat would trigger them. Under normal atmospheric pressure, they'll go ape. Millions of them a day.'

'So I went down a blind alley,' Kathy said. 'Nicholson

was cut by the fish but he was infected by a bug on the cobalt nodules.'

'I'd bet my life on it. The bacteria were still alive because they came up under pressure in the grab. You carefully decompressed the fish and, with it, the bacteria. They also need heat – otherwise they turn into dormant spores. But the nodules were in warm water. If Nicholson was in contact with them after cutting himself on the fish, the bacteria could have swum into a warm bloodstream and begun to multiply.'

'I forgot all about the nodules until the miners attacked.'

'I should have listened to you before rushing off after Nicholson. I only remembered when I saw the nodule on his cabin floor.' Saul looked at the lab clock. 'Where the hell *is* Nicholson? It's been half an hour.'

'At least with the lifeboats smashed, he can't get far.'

'I hope you're right. I'm getting suspicious.' Saul went and picked up the nodule he'd removed from Nicholson's cabin. It was predominantly manganese except for a large pearl which studded it. 'This certainly didn't come up with the cobalt nodules. More the sort of stone Bertil would lock in the storeroom. I wonder how many more are missing?'

'Why would he bother with cobalt nodules?'

'Maybe he just handled them, maybe he took a few out of curiosity. If he'd only show up, we could ask him.'

'How come the plague bacteria weren't on the tube worm, the fish or in the water?'

'They must need something found only on the cobalt nodule,' Saul said. 'My guess is it's some kind of cobalt salt which helps the bacteria to extract oxygen from the water.'

'Haemoglobin is cobalt-based . . .' Kathy said slowly.

'Quite right. It's a cobalt protein that normally combines with the oxygen you breathe. It delivers that oxygen to body tissue for cellular respiration. It's no coincidence that everyone – except Nicholson – develops respiratory problems.'

'You mean the cobalt salt somehow prevents the haemoglobin doing its job,' Kathy said, understanding where Saul's argument led.

'Yes. The cobalt salt normally extracts oxygen under huge pressure. At surface pressure, it would find it dead easy to grab all the oxygen going. The haemoglobin simply couldn't compete effectively. If body tissue doesn't get its oxygen, it starts using other sources of energy – like an athlete in oxygen debt. After a while, lactic acid levels build, the lungs start working overtime and the body's cells start to die. Eventually circulation collapses.'

'Why didn't the extra oxygen from the cylinder help Helen or Wilkins?'

'The cobalt salt mopped it up. It might be different if we could put the oxygen in under pressure, but we don't have the equipment.'

'So the bacteria caused the swelling and fever and the cobalt salt bound in with it stops the haemoglobin delivering oxygen around the body.'

Saul nodded.

'So why should B12 help Nicholson to recover?'

'That's the right question. First, let's find Nicholson and the B12.'

A muffled announcement began to issue from the tannoy in the corridor outside.

'Who is it?' Saul asked.

'Can't make it out. I can't hear what he's saying.'

'Me neither,' Saul said. He crossed to the security door, turned on the corridor camera and watched the monitor as it brightened. The corridor seemed empty. He pressed the lock release.

'Be careful,' Kathy pleaded. 'It could be another trap.'

As Saul pulled the door open, the tannoy became more distinct. It was Mark Bell's voice.

'. . . and I'll keep you informed of developments.' The tannoy went silent.

'What developments, for Christ's sake?' Saul grimaced. 'Try to reach Mark on the intercom . . . .'

Before Kathy could move, the tannoy crackled back into life.

'This is Lt Bell speaking. To repeat, Captain Beckett is dead and I have taken over command. An all-stations distress call went out at 07.35 hours. The lead cargo carrier has responded. They've informed San Diego of our problem. They estimate arrival in thirty-six hours – well ahead of schedule. I want to know everyone's condition, but don't break quarantine – especially those without symptoms. Use the intercom. I'll keep you informed of developments.' The tannoy clicked off.

'I wonder what happened to Beckett,' Saul said.

'Do you think Nicholson killed him?' Kathy asked.

The intercom buzzed. Kathy answered, switching the call through the desk speaker so that Saul could listen.

It was Bell. 'Did you hear?'

'Yes, what happened to Beckett?' Kathy asked.

'Hasn't Nicholson told you?' Bell asked.

Saul and Kathy exchanged puzzled looks.

'He's not here. We've been waiting for him,' Saul said.

'Strange. He said he was going to you – half an hour ago. I was calling about that drug you asked him for. Able's in a bad way.'

'We haven't got it,' Saul said. 'I'll have to search the ship for him – at once. I'll get back to you.' Saul leaned across his bench and cut the intercom off. 'What's Nicholson playing at?' he asked rhetorically. 'I must get kitted up.'

'Not again. Don't leave me alone.'

'It shouldn't take long.'

'I've got a breathing mask, the same as yours.'

'It's too risky. You need a suit as well.' Saul moved towards the freezer for his protective white suit and then stopped. 'I know. You could wear Herbie's foil diving suit. I hid it in the bottom drawer of his workbench – under some things.'

'You hid it?'

'At the time, I thought it might upset you.'

'Not at a time like this.' Kathy crossed to Herbie's workbench and pulled open the bottom drawer.

'Hurry,' Saul said, disappearing into the freezer.

Kathy found the foil suit. As she pulled it out from under the lab coats, one of the notebooks on top fell to the floor. An envelope spilled from inside the cover and scattered photographs across the floor.

Kathy had the suit in her hands and glanced with irritation at the mess she had made. Her heart skipped a beat. She found herself looking at a photograph of herself on skis, taken in the Rockies. She remembered the vacation well. The picture was Herbie's favourite snap of her. Beside it lay a beach shot of them both, taken on honeymoon at Monterey. There was one of Herbie with bushy beard and long hair, wearing a backpack and hiking boots, leaning against a redwood. She had taken that picture shortly after they met. Then there was Herbie with his mother, Herbie looking uncomfortable in suit and tie, and one of both his parents. A tear ran down Kathy's cheek.

Saul stepped from the freezer, fully dressed in his protective outfit, saying, 'You'll need gloves and lab boots . . . .' He stopped when he saw Kathy kneeling on the floor by Herbie's workbench.

'What's wrong?'

'Some pictures of Herbie. They took me by surprise. I'll be OK. You go on. I'll hold you up.'

'Sure? I'll be back for you as soon as I've checked on deck – to make sure he hasn't built himself a raft or repaired one of the lifeboats. Then we can search the ship thoroughly together.'

Kathy wiped away her tears. She moved towards Saul who raised his arm like a patrolman stopping cars at an intersection.

'Get your suit on. I'll be back shortly.' Saul pressed the electric lock, waited ten seconds for it to release and left Kathy clutching her small, worn bundle of memories.

26

Saul took a quick look in the sickbay. Butcher lay still – clearly dead. Rico and Larkin groaned through their sedation. He shut the door on their suffering, hurried up the stairs into the open air and past the lifeboat in which Nicholson had planned to escape. He noticed the two water containers standing among splinters of wood from the holed lifeboat. Saul leaned out over the port rail in case Nicholson was in the shadow of the boat. Nothing. He crossed to the starboard side and then, as his horizon widened, he saw a figure in a small craft a long way off.

Saul scoured the nearby locker for a loudhailer. It was buried under several life jackets. Saul lifted his protective helmet and put the loudhailer to his mouth.

'Come back!' The words were swallowed by the ether. Saul waved the loudhailer from side to side. He knew that Nicholson, if he survived to reach land, could spread the seeds of disease whose ravages might compare with the Black Death. Nicholson had to be stopped at all costs.

Saul headed for the bridge. On his way, through the captain's open cabin door, he saw a body. He diverted from steps to doorway. The corpse lay spread-eagled, as if in semaphore code, staring at the ceiling. Beckett's life had drained away just beyond the double doors which connected cabin with conference room. The fire-fighting suit was stained a darker shade of red around the stomach. Saul turned his back with a sense of shock, but he was unable to summon regret. He climbed the metal steps which led to the bridge.

Able, the first of the sailors to fall victim to the plague, was gasping from behind grossly disfigured features which left him recognizable only by his red hair. Henderson lay beside him, his face also now pockmarked by scabs and blisters. Bell was in obvious distress. His face and neck were swollen. He sat, shirt damp with sweat, staring at the navigation terminal, seated between Jennings and Newman. The trio had a feverish faraway look in their eyes.

There was recognition and disbelief in Bell's eyes when he saw the white-suited Saul with breathing tubes emerging at the mouth of a makeshift helmet.

'Saul!' Bell exclaimed. 'I can't believe it's you.'

'Start up the engines, Mark.' Saul was appalled by the state of the bridge.

'I've been plotting a course to the cargo ships.'

'First, Nicholson,' Saul said. 'He's got something which

might help you all. He's out there, a mile or more. There at ten o'clock.' Saul pointed beyond the port bow.

Bell, Jennings and Newman all turned to stare through the tinted glass where Saul was pointing.

'West, west southwest,' Bell said. 'Newman,' he ordered, 'Take the wheel.'

Bell went through the engine start-up procedure. He cut the stabilizing thrusters keeping the *Voyager* from rolling and drifting. The big diesels fired first time and the water behind the screw propellers was soon foaming white.

Saul felt his right leg gripped. He looked to find Able clutching him.

'Please,' the sailor begged.

Saul remembered the sailor's turn of speed in the weekly basketball games played on the helicopter deck. Now the man was begging to be put out of his wretchedness. 'Hold out. You'll be all right. Try.' Saul extricated his booted foot from Able's grasp. Turning to Bell, he said, 'Mark, I must use the radio to make sure we get B12 flown out from San Diego. That's what saved Nicholson.'

'You want to do it now?' Bell asked.

'Let's not hang about.' Saul and Bell moved from the central chart desk towards the radio. As Saul passed the end of the desk he saw a recurring blip on the screen next to the radar. It indicated something rising from the deep.

As he stared at the screen, Saul realized the blip had to be the submersible. With each sweep of the arm, Grearson and Roseman came a fraction closer. But Saul was puzzled. How could they help? Would they reveal themselves or stay below surface awaiting the cargo ships and helicopters?

'What is that?' Bell asked, worried.

'The submersible which rescued me,' Saul said. He thought of the Coordinator's instructions to the sub crew and wondered whether he had discovered the outcome of this disastrous mission. The sub carried torpedoes and he was certain that Roseman would be prepared to use them. The Coordinator's need to preserve secrecy was as great over a bungled mining mission as it was if the *Voyager* had successfully raised the cobalt – possibly greater. America would want a second, exclusive crack at recovering the cobalt.

Saul had to act fast. The sub was now about five miles from the surface. He had no idea of the range of the torpedoes and no intention of hanging around to find out if his cynical assessment was correct. He punched the buttons of the intercom.

'Kathy, do exactly as I say.'

'What's up? I've been waiting.'

'No questions. Get suited up. Grab any food that's left. Bring as big a container of water as you can manage. Meet me by Saturn. I'll be there as soon as I've checked on Dansk.'

'Be careful. The miners . . . .'

'Two minutes, no more.' Saul put the receiver down.

'What's going on?' Bell asked. He lifted his shirt to dry his perspiring face.

'Mark, I'm sorry. There isn't time. SOS immediately about Nicholson to the cargo ships. In case you run into problems picking him up,' he explained lamely. 'And tell them B12 vitamin may help with the plague. I'm sorry, I must go.'

Saul's mind was racing. He moved as fast as his protective suit would allow. He stumbled at the foot of the metal steps from the bridge, recovered and set off with long, loping strides across the deck to the entrance to the miners' quarters. It was not much of a chance but Saul would not forgive himself if he left without checking on Dansk.

As Saul moved into the mining quarters, he could hear a commotion from below. Gerinsky's voice reached him up the stairwell.

'Let me in, Daniels, you bastard,' Gerinsky shouted. Gerinsky was infected. Daniels might be the last healthy miner left but there was no easy way Saul could find out and extricate him to safety.

Saul turned the handle of Dansk's door. It opened – a bad sign. But from the small bedroom came sounds that gave Saul sudden hope. Dansk was watching his video, out of harm's way, passing the time with his cowboy films. He called out, 'Bertil, it's Saul.'

'*You've got till sundown to get out of this town. If you show your face here again, it'll be the last time you draw breath . . . .*' The music welled over John Wayne's drawl. There was no reply from Dansk.

Saul lifted the curtain which covered the entrance. The blue light of the television screen lit the small room with a ghostly flicker. On the screen the camera panned over John Wayne's shoulder following the baddie to his horse. Dansk lay on the bed in front of the screen wearing a sweat shirt and a baggy pair of shorts.

'Bertil, it's . . .' Saul dried up. There was no point. He had seen the evidence as damning as the mark of Cain. Red weals rose from the side of Dansk's neck. Saul took a step to one side. Dansk was propped against pillows, jaw dropped, eyes white, dead.

The sound of guns blazing came from the television screen. The cowboy had turned, firing from the hip. But John Wayne was faster. The cowboy collapsed in a heap. Saul, hopes dashed, hurried back to the corridor and out on to deck.

Saul could see Kathy looking around anxiously. He hurried towards her. She even managed to look elegant in the foil diving suit and makeshift hood – carrying the outfit as though it were a Paco Rabanne designer item. The bathysphere sat on its cradle, paint blistered, stripped of its mechanical arms, camera gantries and ballast weights.

'I want you inside,' Saul said, reaching Kathy.

'Dansk?'

'Dead. Within the past couple of hours. The video was still playing.'

Saul collected Nicholson's toolbox from the locker near the base of the crane.

'Take your suit off,' he called up to Kathy on the plat-form by the hatch. 'Gloves last, before you get in.'

Saul knocked out the pins securing the bathysphere to its cradle.

'Christ, it's a wreck.' Kathy was looking through the open hatch. 'Is this thing going to work?'

'It has to,' Saul said. 'Our only chance before the sub sinks us.'

'What!' Kathy exclaimed. She asked no questions but quickly loaded into Saturn the plastic water container and bag of food which she had brought on deck.

Saul threw up to her a rubber-covered torch from Nicholson's toolbox and then ran to the two water containers which stood on deck beside the shattered lifeboat. There was a slight risk that the containers were contaminated by being filled and handled by Nicholson. Saul used cutters on a length of rope from the tarpaulin lifeboat cover. He would take no chances and planned to take the containers as emergency supplies only.

Saul struggled the few yards back to the bathysphere and lashed the two containers firmly to a solid mooring above the flotation ring. He still had to disengage power and communication cables so that the bathysphere would be able to float free of *Voyager*. He set to work with wrench and cutters, nervous that the ship might explode at any moment.

The submersible was less than four miles from the surface. Roseman sat at the controls. He didn't like his orders – but they made sense. Plague! Roseman needed no further reason to arm the tubes with the heat-seeking torpedoes.

Grearson stood behind him in the doorway. 'We'll only have to explain away a lost mermaid,' he said. 'Think they'll forgive us?'

'No way,' Roseman said. 'We'll be out. Lose our pensions, no doubt. I'll get to see my kids a bit more if they don't lock us up.'

'Would they do that?' Grearson asked.

'We're well within range. Let's get this over.' Roseman looked behind him at Grearson standing in the doorway before swivelling back in the padded chair towards a panel of yellow and red buttons set under a perspex frame.

Roseman pressed the small keyboard in the arm of his chair. He lifted the perspex cover on the console and entered the day's code. He began the firing sequence. He reached the final instruction. The torpedoes left their tubes coursing towards their target.

Saul wrestled the cutters backwards and forwards biting deep into the cables. Finally he severed the last one. Only the winch chain remained linking bathysphere to boat. He ran to the winch and pushed the starter button set in the main shaft. The winch whirred into life. When Saul swung the lever, Saturn began to rise slowly from the cradle. He moved it sideways across the deck to the starboard side of the ship and then lowered it once more until it was parallel with the deck on the far side of the gangrail, suspended above the water.

He left the winch and clambered over the gangrail. It was only eight hours since Saul had climbed back on board the *Voyager*. He waited for the hatch to reach its closest point to the ship and leapt. His fingers caught the inside of the hatch lip and locked on. He felt with his feet for a firm purchase on the flotation ring.

'You OK?' Kathy called anxiously.

'So far, so good.' Saul removed his white protective suit and helmet and let them drop to the water twenty feet below. He saw Bell, Newman and Jennings staring silently down at him from the open, circular gangway around the bridge. He averted his eyes, condemned by their silence. Although feverish with plague, they knew he was abandoning them even though they did not yet understand why. Saul entered the cramped and gutted bathysphere. Half of the dashboard of dials and instruments had been marked in tape the last time he had dived in Saturn. It was as nothing to the devastation which met him. It was as if a hurricane had raged. Kathy stood amidst the debris looking frightened.

Saul pulled the hatch down behind him and the interior was plunged into darkness. His foot slipped on the ladder rungs and he bumped into Kathy. 'Sorry. Where's the torch?' Saul once again caught Kathy, this time with an arm.

'Here.' Kathy pointed the beam at Saul who took the torch from her. Saturn looked even more wretched by torchlight.

'I hope to God the hoist release works.' Saul prepared

to release Saturn from its crane. 'There'll be a bump. If it works. Hold on to something.'

Saul pulled the hoist release lever sharply towards him and the bathysphere immediately fell free. It hit the water a moment later with a splash. Saul and Kathy collapsed together on to the floor under the impact. The bathysphere began to sink.

'It worked,' Kathy whispered in Saul's ear. 'Well done.'

'Not so fast,' Saul said. He heard a steady trickle of water leaking through the hatch. 'The hoist release worked. But God knows whether there's enough gas in the flotation ring to lift us back to the surface.' He played the torch across the dome of the bathysphere.

Kathy gasped when she saw the small waterfall coming through the hatch cover.

'It can only be sealed from outside,' Saul said. 'By spinning the wheel. The problem is that the heavier we get, the less likely we are to bob back up.'

In the inflatable, Nicholson was growing concerned. He pulled grimly at his oars aware that the *Voyager* would overtake him. It seemed futile to continue. The gap was about a mile and a half when he saw the first explosion.

The second torpedo hit its target within a few seconds of the first, precisely six minutes after it had been fired from the sub. The boat become a fireball as fuel tanks ruptured and exploded. A sheet of flame spread across the water. The *Voyager* tipped towards the stern. The mining rig leaned sharply, its weight bringing the bow of the boat clear of the water. The rig broke loose from the deck and slowly toppled.

Nicholson watched, incredulous. A pall of black smoke rose above the flames. Nicholson rested on his oars – the solitary eyewitness. The *Voyager* rapidly sank lower in the water, on its way to the other hotspot at the bottom of the sea.

27

Saul and Kathy were ankle deep in water when the shock wave struck, rocking Saturn like a church bell. They cannoned into the side of the sphere where the chemical fire extinguisher and bank of three emergency power batteries were usually housed. Saul grasped the hatch ladder to steady himself as they tipped back the other way. Kathy was thrown across the bathysphere. She anchored herself to the ladder in time for the second shockwave.

'What was that?' Kathy asked, shocked.

'*Voyager*, I reckon.' Saul recovered the torch from the cavity in the console where it had lodged. 'Let's hope she doesn't drag us down.' He played the torch around the hatch through which the waterfall cascaded. 'Maybe we're rising. The pressure seems to be easing off.'

The waterfall slowly eased to a trickle. Then it stopped. Saul climbed the metal ladder steps. He unclipped the hatch cover and pushed it open. Light burst in. Beyond the hatch was a dome of bright blue sky. The only sound was the gentle slap of a light swell against the side of the bathysphere. The flotation ring had done its job and brought them back to the surface.

Saul poked his head through the hatch. There was no sign of the *Voyager*. A few yards away a splintered beam floated surrounded by half a dozen empty, red-and-white lifesaving rings, stencilled VOYAGER and US NAVY. There was no one to make use of them. The men had gone down with the ship. Further away, an iridescent film of oil formed an oval slick.

Kathy said from below, 'Move over. Let me see.'

She got head and shoulders out of the hatch. Saul helped her squeeze beside him. 'Isn't it weird?' she said. 'Why? Why did they do it?'

'It's their way of dealing with one hell of a problem. If

we're lucky, the sub won't spot us with all this debris around.'

'But it's monstrous.'

'That's right. But there is a sort of logic to it.'

'No evidence,' Kathy said.

'Except for us.'

'And Nicholson.'

'Yes, Nicholson. I wonder if Bell got that message of mine out. He has to be stopped.' Saul climbed higher out of the bathysphere until he stood on the top rung of the ladder and surveyed the ocean. 'That might be Nicholson over there,' he said pointing. 'Perhaps I could rig up a sail.'

'Not a chance,' Kathy laughed.

'You're right. We go where the current goes.'

'Saul, why did the B12 help Nicholson recover? It was the B12 that made the difference for him, wasn't it?'

'I think so. Nicholson was saved by a lucky coincidence. He's been getting a weekly B12 shot to reduce the risk of anaemia ever since his stomach operation.'

'But why should it help . . .? Did it neutralize the killer cobalt salt?'

'B12 is cobalt-based. To be precise 4.3 per cent. It's the only vitamin with a heavy metal in it. There'd be nothing unusual in it combining with a cobalt salt, creating a further cobalt compound – but an inactive one this time.'

'So B12 supplement could render the cobalt salt harmless. The cobalt salt would no longer be able to grab the oxygen needed by the haemoglobin.'

'Exactly. The B12 effectively denies oxygen to the bacteria. That's how Nicholson got the disease under control. He's still lethal if he's carrying cobalt nodules, because, as we saw in the lab, the bacteria revert to spores. And Nicholson already had B12 in his system. The B12 might well not work unless you already had its protection at the time of infection.'

'B12 vaccinations?'

'Could be the only way. We've seen how the bacteria spread. Let's hope Nicholson doesn't make it to land.'

'What about us?'

'We probably won't make it either.'

'There's always the cargo ships. We might float into their path.'

'I hope not. Judging by what's just happened, they'll kill us.'

'There's not much food, I'm afraid,' Kathy said.

'The water won't last long either.' Saul saw the extra two containers which Nicholson had taken for his lifeboat escape were still tied to the bathysphere. 'Those containers could be infected,' he said.

'Well let's at least bail out the water from inside. Clear up a little. Done any survival training?'

'No. But I can see I'm going to have to start learning. First thing is a hook to fish with. I could use strands of rope for the line. Then we want something to catch rainwater.' Saul looked up at the bright blue sky.

Kathy grinned and put an arm round his waist. 'We'll make it. We've come this far. And someone has to raise the alarm.'

'Have you thought, really thought, what will happen if Nicholson gets ashore with plague spores. It will spread and it'll spread fast. Like a forest fire. Can you imagine trying to put whole continents on to weekly B12 injections? It simply wouldn't work. Can you really see the Coordinator, or the State Department, or the CIA shouldering responsibility?' Saul gazed around the ocean. Nicholson was a speck in the distance and growing fainter.

Two days later, it still hadn't rained and Saul had enjoyed no success as a fisherman. He clambered out on to the flotation ring soon after waking to check his line, hardly bothering to search the panorama he had scanned the previous day until his eyes had grown sore. But as he turned back to join Kathy inside for the last of the stale bread and chocolate, he almost fell off the flotation ring in surprise.

There, looming a few hundred yards away, was the hull of a deep-sea trawler. There was no mistake. It wasn't one of the American cargo ships. The name, *Fujiyama*, was painted boldly on the side. Never in his life had Saul thought he would be pleased at the prospect of meeting Japanese fishermen.

'Hey,' he shouted. 'Over here.' He waved madly.

'What's happening?' Kathy called from within the bathysphere. A moment later, she appeared through the open hatch.

Saul was still waving. He had no further need to do so. He could see a Japanese sailor in the bow of the trawler waving back. Another sailor appeared with a line ready to throw.

'Why bother with fish if you can catch a fishing boat?' he said to Kathy who had climbed out and joined him on the flotation ring and was hugging him hard.

Two weeks later, a little girl shook the shoulder of a woman lying on a beach under the shade of a colourful, striped parasol.

'Hey, mom, wake up,' she said.

The woman mumbled in irritation.

'Mom, quickly,' the girl insisted. 'I want to show you something.'

The crowd on the beach had thinned. It was the middle of the day and too hot for most of the holiday crowd. The woman stretched and yawned. 'What do you want, honey?'

'I've found a funny boat.'

'Huh?' The woman grunted and closed her eyes again.

The little girl shook her mother's shoulder again. 'Look, over here.'

The woman opened one eye to see where her daughter was pointing. As she tilted her head, she caught the glint of the sun on a plane bringing in yet more tourists. Against the glare on the sea, she could make out the shape of a boat.

'It looks empty,' the girl said. 'Can I play in it?'

The woman stood and shielded her eyes to get a better view. 'Honey, go to the front desk,' the woman said. 'Tell the man there's a raft drifting. You got that?'

The girl nodded and ran off.

The woman walked to the water's edge, keeping her eye on the inflatable which was still some fifty yards from

206

shore. The sand burned the soles of her feet. The water felt cold by comparison then warm and welcoming. She swam an accomplished breaststroke, reached the black, rubber inflatable and pulled herself up to look inside. The inflatable tipped towards her a little.

'Oh, Jesus,' she said softly.

A man lay on the slatted floor, his face and arms burnt brown except in patches where the skin was strangely pink and shiny.

She turned to the shore. Her daughter had arrived with the hotel bellboy. A small crowd had begun to gather.

The woman splashed a little water on the man's forehead. His face was burnt and scarred. The man groaned. There was a canvas bag at his feet and another bag which he gripped by his side. The woman splashed a little more water on his face. His eyes flickered and then opened.

'Hey, fella,' she said softly. 'You made it. Welcome to Hawaii.'

ACKNOWLEDGMENTS

Thanks first and foremost to Andrew Bailey with whom I began work on this story in 1979. It was one of a number of film treatments we prepared together – and he shares in any success that the novel enjoys. I am grateful to my brother, Dr Nicholas Finer, for assistance with the grim medical material at the heart of the story – although in time-honoured fashion I acquit him of responsibility for any subsequent errors of my own invention. I offer equally traditional thanks, but nonetheless heartfelt, to my wife Linda for her enthusiastic support as well as for typing the final manuscript.

The technological information about deep-sea mining and seabed exploration was garnered from many sources. I owe a particular debt to the Woods Hole Oceanographic Institution in Massachusetts and to the US National Oceanic and Atmospheric Administration.

The book would probably have remained unwritten without the personal encouragement from Hilary Rubinstein, my literary agent, and Paul Sidey, my editor at Hutchinson. I am grateful to them for guiding me to publication.